BATHED IN MOONLIGHT

The wind-stirred palm grove, moonlight and shadow made moving patterns on the earth. Footsteps came from behind. Fiona turned. It was Brian. "You're not fair," she cried. "Leave me alone."

"You don't want me to do that," he said, his hand forcing her face toward his. "Don't talk to me about fair. Not after I've waited all this time."

RIPE FOR SURRENDER

She pushed against his hard shoulders, trying to wrench her lips free. But even as she fought she was aware that his kiss, and his arm holding her, had set up a wild clamor in her blood. With a soft, triumphant laugh, he bent and lifted her into his arms.

She made no effort at all to stop him.

THE SILVER DOLPHIN

Velda Johnston

GOLDEN APPLE PUBLISHERS

THE SILVER DOLPHIN

A Golden Apple Publication / published by arrangement with
Dodd, Mead & Company, Inc.

Golden Apple edition / January 1984

Golden Apple is a trademark of Golden Apple Publishers

ISBN 0-553-19759-2

Published simultaneously in the United States and Canada

PRINTED IN THE UNITED STATES OF AMERICA

For Brian O'Brien, author and adventurer,
with appreciation

THE SILVER DOLPHIN

Chapter 1

Outdoors a frigid January wind swept the village streets. But in this narrow upstairs meeting hall, packed with people avid to know whether I, or anyone, had killed my aged husband, the air seemed stiflingly hot.

All my life I had known most of the people in this room, including the jurymen who sat at a long pine table facing the audience. The jury was not the collection of craftsmen and small tradesmen who had deliberated upon the town's last violent death, that of a whaleboat steersman killed in a brawl in Josie Carpenter's place down near the waterfront. Instead, some of the village's most prominent men, including a grizzled whaleship owner who thirty-odd years before had served heroically in the War of 1812, had been chosen for this particular inquest. That was not surprising. My husband, Torrance Ravencroft, had been one of their own sort, a man even richer and shrewder than any of the other Ravencrofts.

Minutes before, I had given my own testimony. Seated at a small table at right angles to the jury table, I had answered the questions put to me by the coroner, Job Law, a man with a body and flushed face as round as the barrels turned out by his cooper's shop on lower Main Street. As I described finding Torrance on the flagstone kitchen floor at the foot of the steep stairs, with his head lying at an odd angle and the wreckage of his wheelchair, which he himself had designed, scattered all around him, I had been aware of the unnerving scrutiny of more than a hundred pairs of eyes. It was, at best, a neutral scrutiny. Even the most charitable-minded must have believed—in part correctly—that when I married Torrance two years

1

earlier it had been for his money. Why else, they must have thought, should a young woman not yet twenty marry a man almost four times her age? And now, surely, they were open to the conviction that I had killed for that same money. Even if I had let my grief for Torrance show in my face and voice, some of these people would have believed I was acting.

Most keenly of all, of course, I was aware of the Ravencrofts sitting on the third bench from the front. There was grim-faced John Ravencroft, a tall beaver hat perched on his knees. Even as a small child I had found something awesomely biblical in his face, with the deeply carved lines bracketing his mouth and the dark eyes sunk deep beneath prominent brows. Now, at sixty-odd, he had the look of one of the harsher Old Testament prophets. Next to him sat his wife, Aurelia. Her face, with its high-bridged nose and prominent dark eyes, was pale, but not more so than usual. With fleeting irrelevancy, I thought of how she must feel uncomfortably warm in her heavy brown woolen cape and matching bonnet, both trimmed with otter fur. But, if so, her appearance did not betray it. Perhaps in her case a chilliness of temperament kept her quite literally cool in this crowded room, with its windows sealed against the winter. Beside her sat Dora, the elder of the Ravencrofts' two living children. Past thirty now, Dora remained good-looking enough so that strangers, upon first meeting her, must have wondered why she was a spinster. Later on, of course, after they had become aware of what my maid Dilsey called Dora's "spooky ways," they would no longer wonder. One of her spooky ways was to keep her head lowered while regarding others from eyes rolled up under their lids. Even though I did not turn my head to make sure, I knew that she must be staring at me from rolled-up eyes as I sat in the witness chair.

No need to wonder what she and her parents were thinking. They hoped that the jury would demand my indictment for murder and that I would be convicted. Then, and only then, would they rather than I inherit Torrance's money.

Brian Ravencroft, Dora's one-year-younger brother, did not attend the inquest. If he had been there, forcing upon me the memory of my past folly and of my past humiliation at his hands, I surely could not have maintained my composure. As it was, I got through my testimony rather well, I think, telling of the crashing sound that had awakened me in the early morning hours and of finding Torrance at the foot of the stone steps leading down to the cellar kitchen. I testified, too, that before I hurried down those steps I had heard the dwindling-away sound of a horse moving at a gallop down Madison Street. A stir in the audience—bodies shifting weight, voices whispering—gave me the impression that my words had evoked skepticism. *She's afraid the verdict will be murder*, I could imagine them thinking, *and so she wants to plant the idea that someone beside herself and that quadroon maid of hers could have been in the house that night.*

But, despite that murmuring, I managed to finish my testimony and walk, with head held high, back to my place beside Dilsey, on the end of a bench in the center of the room. After that, though, I found myself trembling. Perhaps it was Dr. Dillworth's testimony. He was on the stand now, a big-bellied, white-haired man, whose manner conveyed both pomposity and kindliness. Even though he chose to use medical terms—cervical vertebrae for the aged neck broken in the fall, and tympanum for the ruptured eardrum, which had leaked blood down the side of Torrance's still face—his account summoned up for me, even more vividly than my own testimony had, the memory of my husband on the kitchen flagstones. I began to feel dizzy. Something—perhaps memories, or the Ravencrofts' hostility, or the suspicion of the other spectators, or all three—seemed to be pressing close around me, so that I found it hard to breathe. I said, in a low voice, "Dilsey."

Her white-turbaned head turned toward me. "I feel faint," I said. "I'm going outside for a while. You stay here."

As I had expected, protest and alarm leaped into her brown-skinned face. "You feel bad, you need me with you."

"No, I don't. Stay here. You may be called upon to testify." I did not think she would be. Constable Howard Simon had already read into the record her statement that she had been asleep in her room at the top of that big house on Madison Street at the time of Torrance's death. Still, she might be called to the stand.

Despite her soft protest and the anxiety in her dark eyes—eyes that could flash with rage or contempt but that had always looked upon me with affection—I rose and walked toward the door at the rear of the room. Again I heard that rustling sound as people turned to watch me leave. But no one tried to stop me. I had already given my testimony. And I had not even been indicted for murder—at least not yet!—let alone convicted of it.

I went down the steeply pitched stairs, passed the door to the constable's office, and opened one half of the double doors that led to the street. Wind snatched the door-knob from my hand and flattened the door against the building wall. Standing out on the sidewalk, I pulled and then pushed the door until it was closed. Turning, I looked down the slope of Main Street. The clock in the steeple of the Presbyterian church, its voice made faint by the eastward-blowing wind, began to strike the hour. I counted twelve strokes.

On this cloudless day the sun was bright, but seemingly without warmth. Across the wide street, thick icicles hanging from the eaves of Hewlitt's Merchandise and Food Store shot colored fire like so many prisms. On my side of the street the horse trough, which stood in front of the constable's office, was covered with a layer of ice, although already more than one driver that day must have broken the icy coating to allow his horse to drink. Farther down Main Street only a few figures, shoulders hunched, moved along the sidewalks or in and out of the shops and taverns. On a day like this, most of those who had not attended the inquest preferred to stay indoors.

At the foot of Main Street, Long Wharf stretched out into a bay that was brilliantly blue and flecked with white-caps. And tied up alongside the wharf were ships. I could not be sure of how many—from this angle their riggings seemed to merge into a confused tangle of masts and spars—but I knew that nearly all of them must be whalers. Now-adays, only a few ships carried on Sag Harbor's once-flour-ishing trade in West Indian rum and molasses; and as far as I knew, none of those few was in port. Apprehensive as I was about what those leading citizens upstairs might de-cide, I still had room for an emotion that the sight of whale-ships had evoked in me ever since I was a little girl. It was a longing to be aboard one of those ships as it left Long Island behind and moved through ever-warming seas to quite different islands, where graceful, bronze-skinned people swam out to meet the ships, and the air was fragrant with flowers I'd never seen, and palm trees swayed like giant feather dusters against the sky.

The Ravencroft ship, the *Silver Dolphin*, was moored down there along the wharf. She had been for three months while her master, Brian Ravencroft, tried to raise money to replace that lost on his last disastrous voyage—a voyage which, even though it took him to the south of Tierra del Fuego, that frigid tip of South America, and almost as far north as the Arctic Circle, had gained him only a few barrels of whale oil. And even those had been swept away by the same typhoon that, off the Japan coast, had badly damaged his ship.

Brian. The *Silver Dolphin*. I smiled to myself grimly as I thought of the lordly Ravencrofts' son and heir going hat in hand to bankers here on eastern Long Island and in New York. At the same time, I felt a twist of pain. It was not too long ago that I had been confident that soon, as the captain's bride, I would sail aboard the *Dolphin* to those islands of laughing people and frangipani-scented air. But that dream had been shattered beyond hope of mending one night in a tawdry room above a tavern a few miles north of New York City.

That sense of vertigo and breathlessness had passed. Now I felt chilled by the wind whipping the skirts of my gray woolen cloak and the green woolen dress beneath it. I began to walk down the sidewalk, past the mercer's shop with the office of Lawyer Gerald Winship on the second floor, past the bank owned by my across-the-street neighbors, the Stacewoods. When I reached the next corner I turned back. Respectable women might drive along lower Main Street, especially if escorted, but they did not venture there on foot. Lower Main Street belonged to the whaling crews—those motley groups made up of Sagaponack Indians, South Sea Islanders, and white men of every nationality—and to the merchants who supplied them with cooked food and clothing and rum, and to the women from establishments like Josie Carpenter's.

As I slowly retraced my steps, I told myself that I

really had no cause for anxiety. Surely those jurymen would decide, as Dr. Dillworth already had decided, that it had been an accident. An old man, who of late had suffered from head noises, had thought he heard something or someone in the cellar kitchen. In that self-designed wheelchair of his, he had moved out into the ground-floor hall and back along it to the door leading to the kitchen stairs. Somehow, probably because he had lost his balance while he opened the door, he had plunged down the steps to his death.

Surely they would decide that that had been the case. And surely it would not take them long to do so. Constable Simon had testified even before I had. And after Dr. Dillworth there would be no one else to testify, not unless they chose to call Dilsey to the stand. Once the testimony was complete, they should not have to deliberate for long in that small room behind the hearing hall.

But what if the verdict was not accidental death? What if, even if they did not name me as responsible for my husband's death, they decided that someone had indeed wheeled the old man, perhaps already unconscious from a blow on the head, back to that kitchen door and then pushed him down the steep stairs to his death on the flagstones? But I must not think like that, especially not when Dilsey and I were now spending our nights alone in that big house. Just as terrifying as the thought of my standing trial for murder was the thought that someone else—perhaps someone seated up there in the hearing hall—had entered the darkened house that night and flung an aged man to his death.

Trying to shove the thought aside, I paused in front of Mrs. Bennet's shop where, in the window, a display board held sketches of the latest fashions in gowns and millinery. A wooden sign with the painted word "closed" hung from the knob of the shop's door. I did not need to wonder why Mrs. Bennet had chosen to forego any business that might come her way on this frigid morning. I had seen her among the spectators in the hearing hall.

Because of the bright sunlight the glass of the shop window reflected my face almost as distinctly as a mirror would have. I could even see that, in my unusually pale face, my eyes looked greener than ever. A few tendrils of red hair had escaped the confines of my gray bonnet to curl along my cheeks and forehead. My hair, like that of the father I dimly remembered, was fiery red, not the carroty red of my mother's. As I tucked the stray curls back inside my bonnet, a memory stirred.

My mother crossing the kitchen, her thin, pretty face contorted with the effort of carrying the heavy soup kettle she had just taken from its fireplace hook. "Fiona! How many times must I tell you? Don't get underfoot when I have something hot in my hands."

I had waited until she had placed the kettle on the big iron trivet that rested on an oak table. Then I asked, "Why did you call me Fiona?" No little girl I'd ever heard of, and no little girl in *Moral Tales for Young Minds*, the book my mother sometimes read to me when she was not too tired at night, had been named Fiona.

She smiled down at me. Her voice, with its burr of her native Scotland, grew soft. "It's an Irish name, but even so we gave it to you because we wanted you to have a name that no one in either my family or your father's had, and that no one here in Sag Harbor had. You seemed to us such a—such a very special child. We had waited and prayed for you for so long. More than five years. It was as if God felt your father should work off his bond before—"

She broke off, but I knew what she meant by his bond. My mother and father, both offspring of impoverished Scottish crofters, had been able to come to America after their marriage only because he was willing to sign an indenture. A man who, in my mother's phrase, had always been "clever with numbers," he had obtained passage money for himself and his young bride by pledging his services as a clerk for five years to John Ravencroft.

"Anyway," she said, "we wanted you to have a special name. Perhaps it would have been more fitting if we had named you Prudence, or Charity, or even Martha, after me."

"No, Mama. I like my name."

And I had continued to like it. I had never felt any of that dissatisfaction with my given name that so many children feel. Others might consider it odd, even outlandish, but for me it was a reminder, all through my childhood and growing-up years, of how much my parents had wanted me and had been proud of me. Footsteps slow now, I moved on up the street.

Before I reached the building that housed the constable's office and the hearing hall, its door opened and Dilsey hurried toward me, her face alight. "It's all right, child, it's all right! They went into the back room for about ten minutes, and then they came out, and then the old captain"—I knew she must mean Captain Larrabee, our hero of the 1812 war—"he said it was death by mis-some-thing-or-other."

"Misadventure." I felt a flood of relief. Almost immediately it was followed by an emotion less pleasant. What if the verdict was mistaken? True, I knew that I was innocent of Torrance's death. But what if someone else had entered that house while I lay asleep? Again I thrust the thought aside.

Others were coming out of the building now. Most of them looked at me with tentative smiles. A kind of adventuress I might be—I'm sure that nearly all of them thought that of me—but at least they had less reason to fear now that they had harbored a murderess in their midst.

I did not see John and Aurelia Ravencroft or their daughter. Obviously they had chosen to remain upstairs.

Nodding in response to those smiles, those subdued murmurs—"Such an ordeal for you, Mrs. Ravencroft" and "Let us know if there's anything we can do for you, Fiona"—I moved with Dilsey up the sidewalk to the point where Madison Street branched off Main. She and I would walk back to that big white house where long ago my mother had worked in the same flagstoned kitchen where only days ago my husband had met his death. We would go back to that imposing house which, through a twist of fate, had now fallen to the sole ownership of myself, Fiona MacWain Ravencroft.

Chapter 2

I cannot remember a time when I did not hate the Raven-crofts.

No, that is not quite true. During those very early years of my childhood, while mother worked as cook in that Madison Street house, I did not know that I had any reason to hate the Ravencrofts. And I seldom even saw them. In the daytime, if the weather was inclement, I stayed in the kitchen with my mother. Otherwise I played with my toys—a wooden doll my father had carved for me and some tin doll dishes my mother somehow had managed to buy me for my fourth birthday—on the grassy area behind the kitchen. That way, my mother, looking at intervals through the windows set high in the wall, could make sure that I was safe. At night I climbed with her, first to the ground-floor hall, then back along it a little way to the foot of the servants' stairs, and then up two flights to a small room with a slanted ceiling.

That was my whole world, the big kitchen and the little room under the eaves. The Ravencrofts were shadowy figures who occupied the two floors between. Since they were grown-ups—even Dora, twelve years old when I first came there, seemed to me an adult—they were less inter-esting to me than the big orange tomcat who lived in the carriage house and sometimes allowed me to hold him. And certainly they seemed to me less real than the three other servants, a coachman and two maids, employed by the Ravencrofts.

Brian did not figure in my earliest memories of that house. By the time my mother and I came there, he was already attending a boys' boarding school near Boston and

9

spending his Sundays with his Boston uncle. I cannot recall just when it was that I gathered, from the servants' mealtime talk around the table at one end of the big kitchen, that the uncle's name was Torrance Ravencroft and that he was very rich, even richer than his younger brother John, whom I had somehow assumed to be not only the richest man in the village but in the whole world.

It must have been in late June, a little more than two months before my fifth birthday, that I first saw Brian. At least I recall that the big catalpa tree between the house and the carriage house was covered with its orchidlike clusters of blooms. And I remember the blossoming tree because the orange cat, which for some reason I called Tiger, had climbed the tree and then found himself unable to descend. He clung to a branch yowling; I stood on the ground wailing; and my poor mother, who had left her work to run up the outside steps from the kitchen, tried to comfort me.

A boy came around the corner of the house. His eyes, dark blue under curling black hair, seemed to take in the situation at a glance. He went into the carriage house, came back with a short wooden ladder, and set it against the catalpa trunk. He climbed, detached the frightened, spitting cat from the limb in which its claws were embedded, and brought it to me. "Here," he said, holding out the still-struggling animal. But Tiger leaped to the ground before I could grasp him and streaked toward the carriage house. I did not care. All my attention now was centered worshipfully on this boy, this hero. Somehow, even though he was only a year younger than his sister Dora, I thought of him as a boy, not a grown-up.

My mother said, "Now thank the young gentleman."

I stared up at him, tongue-tied.

"That's all right," he said. "What's your name, little girl?"

"Fiona."

"Mine's Brian. I'm home for the summer, so I'll probably see you now and then." He nodded to my mother and then walked around the corner of the house.

He certainly did see me, and not just now and then. I soon discovered that nearly every afternoon he walked down to the bay to go fishing with some other boys of about his age. Despite my mother's injunction to stay where she could watch me through the kitchen windows, I would steal out along the driveway to the street and wait until Brian returned, sometimes alone, sometimes with a companion or two. Like any twelve-year-old boy who finds himself worshiped by a girl not yet five, he reacted at first with amused tolerance and then with growing irritation. He tried ignoring me, and frowning at me, and ordering me to "go back to your mother." Nothing worked. I would stand there looking after him until the front door of the Ravencroft house—a beautifully carved and fanlighted door, like those of all the fine Sag Harbor houses—shut him from my sight.

He went back to that Boston school in the fall. The next summer, and the summer after that, he did not return to Sag Harbor. Instead, he accompanied his uncle, who among other things was an importer of fine wines and spirits, on his business trips to France and the British Isles. After my first disappointment when he did not return, I ceased to think of him. By that time I had another hero or, rather, heroine.

Her name was Dilsey Turman, and she was not only grown up but one year older than my mother. She was also mostly black and the most recently hired of the Ravencroft servants. Mrs. Ravencroft had wanted her, so Dilsey explained to me, because she had "a real light hand with sewing and fixing ladies' hair and ironing their dresses. And she needs me not just for herself but for that daughter of hers that's growing up."

I liked Dilsey, first of all, because she liked me. But what fascinated me was her fund of stories about whaleships, Caribbean islands, and something she called "witching." All these stories were legacies from her parents. Her father had been a slave named Ben Turman. His owner, a Connecticut man, had placed him on various Sag Harbor whalers, pocketing at the end of each voyage whatever money was due to Ben for his "lay," or share of the voyage's profits. On one of those voyages Ben's ship had put in at the island of Jamaica. There he had met a handsome mulatto girl. She stayed in his mind after he returned to Sag Harbor.

A year later Ben's owner died. Perhaps his conscience had begun to trouble him over forcing a man to risk his life again and again in a fragile whaleboat, with no recompense to Ben himself except rations of salt pork and weevily bread.

Anyway, by the terms of the will Ben received not only his freedom, but several hundred dollars. He returned to Jamaica, bought the girl's freedom, married her, and brought her back to Sag Harbor. She was the one who had schooled Dilsey in West Indian voodoo practices.

My mother did not mind my listening to whaling yarns, but she put a stop to the "witching" stories as soon as she became aware of them. That happened one morning when, returning to the kitchen from her weekly menu consultation with Mrs. Ravencroft, she found Dilsey at the ironing board, pressing the pleated flounce of a blue pelisse and instructing me in the various ways of warding off the "evil eye." Standing beside her, I was drinking in every word.

"Dilsey!"

She turned to my mother. "Yessum?"

"I'd rather you didn't tell Fiona such stories."

"Young'uns like to hear about juju and such, ma'am."

"No doubt. But superstition is against my religious principles."

Dilsey's voice was mild. "Some folks' superstition is other folks' religion, and the other way 'round."

From the startled look on my mother's face I knew that such a thought had never occurred to her. After a moment, she said, "That may be. But I still don't want her to hear such stories."

Dilsey said, "It'll be like you say, ma'am," and I knew with gloomy certainty that it would be.

A few minutes later Dilsey went upstairs with the pelisse over her arm. I said, "Why does Dilsey call you ma'am? She's as much a grown-up as you are."

"Yes, but I'm white and Dilsey isn't."

I turned that over in my mind. "Is that why Dilsey eats alone, instead of with you and me and Jim and Mary and Ellen?" Jim was the coachman. Mary and Ellen were maids. All five of us took our meals together at the big kitchen table. Half an hour after my mother had cleared away, Dilsey would come into the kitchen and carry over to the table the food that had been saved for her.

"Yes, Fiona. She doesn't eat with us because she isn't white."

I pondered that, thinking how much livelier mealtimes

would be if Dilsey was with us, instead of just Jim, with his boring talk of how Andy Jackson was going to save this country, and Mary and Ellen, with their whispering and giggling over the handsome young coachman recently hired by the Stacewood family across the street.

I said, "I don't think that's a very good reason for her not eating with us."

Sighing, my mother moved over to the hearth and stirred up the coals beneath a goose browning on the spit. "You may be right, Fiona. But that's the way the world is, and it's apt to stay that way for a long, long time."

Perhaps my mother did not trust Dilsey's promise to stop telling me voodoo stories. Whatever the reason, she began to take me with her whenever she went upstairs to go over the next week's menus with Mrs. Ravencroft. The first time my mother led me into the library, she said, "I hope you won't mind my bringing Fiona with me, ma'am."

Mrs. Ravencroft looked at me from those prominent brown eyes. "It is all right, Martha. Perhaps it would be well for the child to learn something about meal planning. It may help her when she herself goes into service. Now sit down, Martha. I am in rather a hurry today."

How could she be so sure, I wondered, that I would go into service? I might become a great actress, like the one I had heard Mary and Ellen talking about, a New York actress who had appeared at Sag Harbor's Assembly Building in a play called *The Belle of London*. Some foreign prince might sail his ship into Sag Harbor and fall in love with me and take me back to his own country to meet the king and queen. Or I might marry at sixteen, the way I'd heard that lots of girls did.

The table at which my mother and Mrs. Ravencroft sat was of black lacquer, ornamented with writhing red dragons. I knew it must have come from China. Talk at the servants' table often turned to the Ravencroft possessions, and to which of them had been brought from China in Sag Harbor ships. Bored with the two women's talk of mutton and tallow and wheat flour, I looked at the walls, lined on three sides with shelves of leather-bound volumes, and then wandered to the doorway. Across the wide hall the double doors to the front parlor stood open. I could see a rich, Turkey-red carpet, and draperies of a darker red, and many small tables covered with ornaments of ivory and porcelain, and a marble fireplace with a full-length portrait of a man in knee breeches and a tricorne hat hanging above it. Probably, I decided, the man was Samuel Ravencroft, Mr. Ravencroft's father.

Only a few days before at dinner Jim had talked of him. "You know how the Ravencrofts got their money, don't you? From old Sam Ravencroft. And you know how *he* got his money, don't you? He was a privateer during the Revolution." Jim snorted. "Privateer! Same thing as a pirate, except Congress gave him the license to rob. He looted half a dozen British ships and sent them to the bottom, and kept most of the loot for himself. And from what I've heard of John Ravencroft's business dealings—yes, and those of that Boston brother of his—they take a lot after their daddy."

Ellen, the elder of the housemaids, had said then that he ought to be ashamed of himself talking of his employer that way—biting the hand that fed him, so to speak. Jim answered, "Feeds me, hell. I work damned hard for the little bit of wages he pays me." To which Ellen answered that she didn't hold with radical talk, or with cursing, either.

I was aware of my mother's footsteps crossing the library. She touched my shoulder. "Come, Fiona."

Over a narrow strip of brown carpet we moved down the wide hall toward the entrance to that cellar kitchen and the foot of the servants' stairs beyond. On the white-paneled walls oil lamps in brass brackets alternated with gilt-framed portraits. My eye was caught by one that I hadn't noticed as we walked toward the library about half an hour earlier. It was the painting of a slender, dark-haired boy, with his hand resting on the head of a brown-and-white setter. For a moment I thought the boy was my hero of two summers before. Then I saw that he was thinner than Brian, with sharper features and with a certain haughtiness in the dark eyes and a petulant droop at the corners of his mouth. Even though I, of course, did not formulate the thought to myself, his face impressed me as both self-willed and weak.

I said, "Who is that?"

"Henry Ravencroft. Come on, Fiona."

"The one who died?" I had overheard Mary and Ellen talking about an older Ravencroft son, who had been thrown from a horse and killed at the age of twenty. Mrs. Ravencroft, Ellen said, had never recovered from the blow of her son's death.

My mother said in a low, vehement voice, "Yes, he's dead."

I looked up at her and felt profound shock. She was staring at the portrait with both hatred and bitter triumph.

Numb and bewildered, I moved with her down the hall. How could it be that my firm but kindly mother, my God-fearing mother, could feel glad—and I was sure she felt glad—that the boy in the portrait was dead? After a moment I remembered that he had been a grown-up by the time he died. That made me feel a little better, but not much.

Then I heard voices coming from an open doorway just ahead, a doorway that I knew led to the sewing room, and for the moment I forgot about Henry Ravencroft. One voice, soft and slurred, was Dilsey's. Although I had seldom heard the other voice, I recognized it as Dora Ravencroft's.

"—must sew your mama's dress first, Miss Dora."

"Tell her you have to send away for another kind of thread. Tell her anything, but make my dress first. If you don't, do you know what I'll do? I'll put a hex on you. All your teeth and your hair will fall out, and you'll go blind."

We had reached the doorway now. I saw Dora slumped in a chair. Her legs beneath her green muslin dress slanted down to her extended heels in what struck me as an unladylike, even masculine, way. Dilsey stood before her, a length of yellow satin in her hand and on her brown-skinned face an expression that managed to blend respect with stubbornness.

Dora turned her head and looked at us in that chilling way of hers, her chin tucked down and her brown eyes rolled up beneath half-lowered lids. But before she could say anything, my mother seized my shoulder with one hand and with the other opened the door to the kitchen stairs.

Later that day, Dilsey came down to heat pressing irons on the fireplace trivet. Since my mother was kneading bread dough at the long table at the other end of the room, I was able to move close to Dilsey and whisper my anxious question: "Oh, Dilsey! Will she put a hex on you?"

"No." Dilsey's voice held contempt. She gave my head a brief pat. "Don't worry yourself about that, child. Hexing is a white folks' word for something they can't even do. They learn about other things, going to school the way they do, but witching is something only us can do."

I said, much relieved, "Oh, I'm so glad." Then I began to think of what she had said about school. I didn't go to school. Pamela Stacewood, the banker's daughter across the street, had started school that year, even though she was no older than I. On several mornings I had stood at the corner of the Ravencroft house and watched Pamela, pale blond hair shining in the sun, strapped books dangling from her hand, move down the sidewalk toward the school on Latham Street. Why didn't my mother send me to school? Poor as we were, surely she could afford the dollar a term the school charged.

That night, after I'd gotten into my cot in our third-floor room, I looked over at my mother. She sat in her gray-flannel nightgown on the edge of the larger bed, plaiting her reddish hair into braids. I said, "Mama, why don't I go to school?"

Her busy fingers paused for a moment. "Why, because I teach you."

Certainly she had taught me to read. I could read not only *Moral Tales for Young Minds* all by myself now, but I could read the hymns we sang on Sunday morning at the Presbyterian church, that draughty frame structure, which Sag Harbor people called God's Old Barn. My mother did not allow me to browse freely through the Bible. Perhaps she feared I might ask awkward questions about Tamar or Noah and his daughters. But I had read all the Gospels and sometimes, while she worked in the kitchen, she asked me to read aloud to her from the Psalms. What was more, even though she was not "clever with numbers," as my father had been, she had taught me simple addition and subtraction and the multiplication table.

I said, "But other children learn in *school*."

She looked at me through the lampglow. I saw dread in her eyes and something like despair, as if she had little hope of averting whatever it was she feared. "All right," she said, "you'll go to school some day, but not just yet."

She rose, blew out the lamp. I heard the bed creak

as she stretched out her body, a body that must have been tired indeed, after fourteen hours of work in that flagstone kitchen.

My thoughts turned to that moment in the portrait-hung hall. I said into the darkness, "Mama?"

"Yes?"

"Did you know Henry Ravencroft, the one who got killed?"

After a moment she said, "Yes, your father and I—" She broke off. "Yes, I knew him. Now please, Fiona! Go to sleep."

I didn't bother her again, but neither did I go to sleep immediately. I felt sure that, in some inexplicable fashion, my mother's hatred of Henry Ravencroft was connected with her reluctance to send me to school. And my father, that father I barely remembered, was also a part of it. But the sharpness of my mother's last words to me had made it clear that it would be no use to keep questioning her. My thoughts fumbled with the problem for a few more minutes and then I slid into sleep.

My mother's refusal to send me to school darkened my young world only a little. After all, I had her and Dilsey and Tiger. And I found some aspects of life pleasant indeed. Sundays for instance. I liked church—the singing, and the light slanting through tall windows, and the worshipers in their best clothes. And I loved Sunday afternoons. As soon as my mother had cooked the Ravencrofts' three-o'clock Sunday dinner and set out cold food in the pantry to be served by Ellen for their supper, she had all the rest of the day off. Always, the first thing we did during those precious hours of her freedom was to walk about a half mile down sloping streets to the woods south of Otter Pond. There, in the spring and summer, we would collect ladies' slippers or marigolds or butterfly bush and, in the winter, evergreen branches or wild holly. Retracing our steps to the burying ground, only about a hundred yards from the Ravencroft house, we would place our bouquet on my father's grave. "Duncan MacWain," the headstone read, "beloved husband of Martha and father of Fiona. Born Ross County, Scotland, 1797. Died in this place, 1825." Sometimes, after that, we would go down to the bay and walk along the sand, looking out over the water to Shelter Island. A few times we paid

Sunday visits to the house at the foot of Rector Street where my mother and father had lived for five years before my birth and for more than three years afterward, until the time of his death. It was a tiny brown sparrow of a house, a saltbox with two small rooms in front and a kitchen extending across the back. There was a lilac bush in the rear yard and a bed of wild purple flags, which still bloomed each spring, although it had been more than ten years since my mother had dug them up from a boggy spot in the woods. The little house was empty—in fact, it had stood empty ever since our tenancy of it had ended—but we could not go inside. Its owners, East Hampton people, kept it locked. We could look in through the uncurtained windows, though, at the little rooms with their plain pine walls and their floors of random-width pine boards.

Our infrequent visits to that house awoke in me conflicting emotions. Of course I felt drawn to a house that held for me two fragmentary memories from the first three years of my life—one of my mother, mixing bread in that kitchen on a sunlit morning, and one of my father, his laughing young face and bright red hair shining in the light from the hearth as he tossed me, squealing rapturously, into the air and then caught me. At the same time, the sight of the little house brought me a vague depression, a sense of warmth and safety and happiness, once known but now forever lost.

My seventh year ended, and my eighth. I was a week short of my ninth birthday that early September afternoon when, with my mother, I paid the last of those Sunday visits to the little house. I'm not sure why I found that last time particularly painful. Perhaps it was because I had become old enough by then to imagine the feelings of others, rather than just experiencing my own. I thought of what it must have meant to my mother to leave this little house, where she had been a cherished young wife and mother, and go to work as a servant in that big house on Madison Street. As we stood there on the little porch, I had a sense of tightness in my chest and of tears pressing against the back of my eyes. I said, "Mama, let's not stay here."

She threw me a quick glance and then said, "All right, my darling." Much as she loved me, she was a Scotswoman, and therefore not given to easy endearments. That highly unusual "my darling" made me think that she had somehow guessed what I was feeling.

As we moved up Division Street, through the reddening light of near sunset, I found myself wishing that I were a grown-up, with money in my pocket, and able to say, "You don't have to go back to work in the Ravencrofts' kitchen tomorrow or any other day, ever again." But I was not a grown-up. And even when I did grow up, I would not have much money in my pocket, not unless I was able to use that "cleverness" that Dilsey and the other servants, and even my mother had mentioned from time to time. And even clever people needed book learning.

"Mama, will I go to school this year?"

It took her a long time to answer. Finally she said, in a weary voice, "When school opens, you can go."

Later I was to understand the reason for her decision. She had faced the fact that she could not hope to protect me much longer against knowledge and against the cruelty of children. Right then, though, all I realized was that I was to get my fondest wish.

Chapter 3

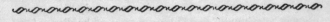

I had been attending the school on Latham Street a full week before I learned why my mother had feared to send me there.

Until then, that week had been a delight. True, on the first day Mrs. Bowen, the widow lady who ran the school, had not believed my assertion that I could read. Accordingly, she placed me in the front of the room with the six- and seven-year-olds and put an alphabet book in my hand. Very soon, though, she discovered that I could not only read, I could read as well as most of the big boys and girls, the twelve-year-olds who would go to work next year or, if their parents were well off, would go to New York for further education, or cross Long Island Sound to schools in Connecticut. Pleased and surprised, she had me illustrate my proficiency to the whole class by reading aloud from *Pilgrim's Progress*.

I was elated, of course. How marvelous to see that beaming approval in Mrs. Bowen's face. Isolated from other children until then, I had not even heard the term "teacher's pet," and I had no way of knowing that I courted both unpopularity and reprisals.

On Saturday I found out.

The school was in session only a half day on Saturdays. At Mrs. Bowen's request, I stayed for a few minutes after the others had left. She had decided, she said, to allow me to take home with me one of her own books, Milton's *Paradise Lost*. Proudly clutching the book to my chest, I walked outdoors.

They were waiting for me just inside the picket fence,

20

Pamela Stacewood, two other girls of about my age, and an older girl and boy. The boy said softly, "Jailbird's brat!"

As I looked at him, startled and uncomprehending, Pamela said, "Your father stole two thousand dollars from Mr. Ravencroft."

Speechless, I stared at her face, pretty and smiling in its frame of pale yellow hair. Then I found my voice. "That's not true!"

Someone snickered, and Pamela said, "Yes, it is. They locked him up in Auburn Prison, and he died there."

I screamed with rage then, and dropped the book, and launched myself at her. She dodged behind the big boy and girl.

"Fiona!" Mrs. Bowen called from the schoolhouse doorway. "What is it?"

The other children moved hastily through the gate and down the sidewalk. Sobbing now, I turned and saw Mrs. Bowen moving toward me, her stout figure blurred by my tears. I picked up the book and called out, "It's all right now, ma'am," and went out the gate. Much as I liked her, I did not want to wait for her to comfort me. All I wanted was to reach my mother and hear her deny the monstrous things Pamela had said.

Only minutes later I ran down the outdoor steps to the kitchen. My mother turned a startled face as I burst into the room. I said thickly, "My father wasn't a thief, was he? He didn't die in prison, did he?"

Her face went white. After a moment she said, "Go up to our room. I'll be there as soon as I can. I'll have to find Dilsey and ask her to watch the soup for me."

I obeyed. In that cramped top-floor room, hot from the September sun, I sat on the cot, hands gripped together in my lap, too sick and frightened now even to cry. Why hadn't she just said, "Why, of course it isn't true!"

My mother came into the room and sat on her own bed, facing me. I said, "Is it true?"

She said, "Oh, my baby! I see now I should have told you before I let you go to school. But I was hoping that no one would say anything. I was hoping that for just a little while longer—"

"Then it is true." My throat was so tight it was hard to get the words out.

"Part of it. Your father did die in prison. They—they sent his body back to me, and I buried him here." Her voice gathered speed. "It was lung fever. No wonder he fell sick in that terrible place. They say the cells are only seven feet long and a little more than three feet wide, and the food is—" She broke off and then added, "He'd served only six months of his sentence when he died."

"But why?" I whispered. "Why did they lock him up in that awful place? Did he—did he—"

"No!" My mother came over and sat beside me. Gripping my shoulders, she turned me toward her. "Duncan MacWain never stole anything in his life! But you must not let the Ravencrofts know I told you he was innocent. Promise me that, Fiona, promise me!"

Bewildered, but with a little of the heaviness gone from my heart, I said, "I promise." Then I added, "But if he didn't steal, why did they put him in prison?"

Her hands dropped from my shoulders. She did not reply directly. Instead, she said, "You know that your father indentured himself to Mr. Ravencroft in return for our passage money from Scotland, don't you?"

I nodded.

"Under terms of the indenture, Mr. Ravencroft paid him a little money, enough for the rent on that little house where we lived and food for himself and me. After the indenture was up, he went on working for Mr. Ravencroft, only at regular wages. Each day he'd come to this house and work on ledgers in that little room off the library. There was a strongbox in there. Your father, as well as Mr. Ravencroft, had a key to it."

She stopped speaking for a moment and then went on hurriedly, "One night Mr. Ravencroft found two thousand dollars missing from the strongbox. He and the constable came to our house and searched and found the money in a sealed package up in the attic."

Everything inside me seemed to knot up. "But you told me my father didn't take the money!"

"He didn't."

"But then how—"

"Henry Ravencroft stole that money." Her voice was

thick with an old bitterness. "We didn't even know what was in the package he had left with us."

I thought of that portrait in the ground-floor hall. That young-boy face, with its blend of hauteur and petulant self-indulgence. "You mean he stole from his own father?"

"Yes. Mr. Ravencroft had always been tightfisted. And even though he was only eighteen, Henry was already spending every cent he could get hold of on drink and gambling and the girls at—" Again she broke off and then said, "He must have learned that his father kept the strong-box key hidden in a little cloth sling nailed to the underside of his desk. Anyway, Henry came to our house one night and asked your father if he could leave a sealed packet up in our attic for a day or two. Naturally, Duncan had to say yes. Henry was his employer's son."

"But didn't you even ask—"

"What was in the package? Of course your father asked. Henry winked and said, 'Letters from a certain lady. A gentleman couldn't be expected to tell you more than that, now could he, MacWain?'

"I still don't know why he didn't run away with the money right then," my mother said, "instead of leaving it with us. But Mr. Ravencroft was sick in bed with the quinsy at the time. I suppose Henry thought he could get out of town before his father was able to discover the theft. But it didn't work out that way. Even though he was still sick, Mr. Ravencroft went down to his strongbox for something or other the next night and found the money gone. When he brought the constable to our house, your father and I had just gone to bed and you—you were about three and a half then—you were asleep in the trundle bed. The pounding on the door woke you up, and you began to scream—"

Her face was white now, and her voice had a hushed quality, as if she was reliving the shock of that night. "The house is so small that the constable was able to find the packet within a few minutes. He broke it open. Then he took your father away with him."

I imagined my bewildered and terrified parents and my own small, screaming self. I said, again with that knot-ted-up feeling in my stomach, "But didn't you tell them about Henry?"

"Of course we did. And Mr. Ravencroft, at least,

believed us. I could tell by the look that came into his eyes for a moment that he knew exactly what his son was capable of. But of course he said it was nonsense. And later on at the trial both Mr. and Mrs. Ravencroft testified that their son had no need to steal because they had always given him as much money as he had asked for. That was a lie, of course, but Duncan couldn't prove it. They sentenced him to ten years in Auburn. But of course within six months—"

She broke off. I cried fiercely, "But Mama, if Mr. and Mrs. Ravencroft knew my father was innocent—Oh, Mama, what are we doing here with terrible people like that?"

"Sh-h-h!" she said, as if she feared my wild young voice might carry to the floors below. "We're here because they asked us. And they asked us, I'm sure, out of a guilty conscience. The day after your father's trial, Mrs. Ravencroft came to our house and said that it wasn't fair that you and I should suffer for my husband's crime. She said that out of Christian feeling she would offer me employment at fair wages for as long as I—

"Don't look at me like that, Fiona!" she burst out. "What else could I do? The little bit of money we'd saved went to the lawyer who defended your father. I couldn't have gone to work as a servant for anyone else, not and kept you with me. People don't like to hire a servant with a young child. The only other way I could have kept you with me would have been for us both to go to the workhouse. And so you and I came here. And they do pay me fairly good wages. I get a dollar a week, plus my own room and board and yours too, of course. That's as much as they pay Jim. In the almost six years we've been here I've managed to save a hundred and four dollars, and it would have been even more if I hadn't bought that headstone for your father's grave.

"And it's not as if the Ravencrofts haven't suffered too," she went on, with a certain bitter satisfaction in her voice. "Henry Ravencroft broke his neck in a fall from a horse only a few months after your father died. Worthless as he was, he was the eldest son, and it must have been a real blow to John Ravencroft. And it almost killed Mrs. Ravencroft."

"You mean she loved him that much?" I found it hard

to believe. Mrs. Ravencroft seemed to me too cold, too complete-in-herself, to love anyone.

"Yes. Whatever love she has in her belonged to Henry. Now listen to me, Fiona." Again she grasped my shoulders. "I've told you this only because I can't bear the thought of your believing your father was a thief. I just can't bear it! But you mustn't let the Ravencrofts know that I've told you that their son stole that money. And so you must promise me again."

For several seconds, battling my sorrow and my rage, I was silent. Then I said, "I promise."

She drew me close to her. "That's my good girl," she said, stroking my hair.

After a moment I said dully, "I don't think there's much more I can learn at that school. If you ask Mrs. Bowen, I think she'd give you your dollar back." I looked at *Paradise Lost,* resting where I had placed it beside the white basin on the washstand. "And you could give her book back to her."

My mother's arm tightened around me almost painfully. After a while she said, "All right. Tomorrow's Sunday. I'll go to see Mrs. Bowen in the afternoon."

I meant to keep my promise to my mother. And yet I broke it less than forty-eight hours later.

On Monday morning my mother took me with her to her weekly conference with Mrs. Ravencroft. As we entered the library, my mother's employer, seated at the lacquer table, turned her pale, handsome face toward us. She said, in a tone of mild surprise, "Dilsey told me that the child had started school."

My mother said, "She didn't like it, and so I told her that she wouldn't have to go."

Mrs. Ravencroft nodded. "It's just as well. She does not need much education. It would only serve to make her discontented later on. Now sit down, Martha."

When my mother was seated in the other chair drawn up to the table, Mrs. Ravencroft went on, "Martha, I'm sorry to have to tell you that Sunday's joint of mutton was overcooked. It was quite, quite dry. I had to apologize to Reverend Percy." Lowell Percy, the Presbyterian minister, took Sunday dinner with the Ravencrofts once a month.

"I'm sorry. I can't imagine what went wrong. I cooked it just as I always have."

"Now, Martha. You couldn't have. You must have made a mistake. And fibbing about it won't help the situation any. Face up to it, Martha. We pay you a generous wage. For you not to deliver satisfactory service in return is the same as stealing. You can see that, can't you?"

My mother's face was pale. "Yes, Mrs. Ravencroft."

Often before I had witnessed my mother endure her employer's bullying. And although I had felt resentment and a shrinking humiliation, it had never occurred to me to do anything but remain silent. Now, though, a wild fury seized me.

"You shut up!" I screamed. I rushed to the table and brought my fist down. "Don't you dare call my mother a thief, you awful old woman!"

My mother was on her feet, trying to draw me away. I grabbed the table's edge and hung on. "You killed my father! You sent him to prison and he died. My father didn't steal that money. Your son stole it, your son stole it!"

Mrs. Ravencroft had stood up, so abruptly that her chair had crashed to the floor. Her face went scarlet. Then the color drained away, leaving her paler than ever. Behind me a door opened. Twisting from my mother's grasp, I whirled around. Mr. Ravencroft stood, grim-faced, in the doorway of the little room that served as his office. Over his shoulder peered the round face of James Claybuck, the young man who had been his clerk for the past three years. John Ravencroft demanded, "What is all this?"

His wife said, "This child, this monstrous child—" She turned to my mother. "What wild tales have you been telling her?"

My mother said, in a shaking voice, "I tried as long as I could to keep her from hearing how her father died. The children at that school told her. It is bad enough that she had to learn that her father died in prison. I don't want her to think that he was a thief."

"And so you told her that my son, *my* son, stole from his own father. You had better take that lie back, Martha, right this moment."

"Yes, you'd better, young woman." Mr. Ravencroft

had moved farther into the room. "Whatever gave you the notion you could slander your employers?"

Even my mother's lips were white now, but her voice had stopped shaking. "I am slandering no one, and I have told no lie."

"Are you out of your senses?" he asked sternly. "Now tell the child the truth. I know it is hard for her to learn that her father was a criminal, but she would have had to know sooner or later. Now tell her the truth." He smiled. As nearly as I could remember, I never before had seen him smile. To me, a smile on that thin, harsh face seemed almost as grotesque as a false nose. "And make her understand that she must not repeat to others that absurd lie about my son. If you do that, there will be no need to talk of your dismissal."

"I did not lie to Fiona," my mother said. "And you need not bother to dismiss me. I have decided to leave. Come, Fiona."

We were about halfway across the room when Mr. Ravencroft said, "I have great influence in this town! If you leave this house, you may have to wait a long time for other employment."

My mother, with my hand in hers, kept on walking. "I know that," she said.

Neither of us spoke again until we had climbed to that little top-floor room. Then she said, opening a drawer of the rickety pine bureau that served us both, "Reach under my bed, Fiona, and bring out the hand trunk."

I placed the trunk on the bed. I said, frightened and miserable, "Oh, Mama! I'm so sorry."

"You couldn't help it." She turned to me. Even though her eyes were clouded with worry, her lips smiled. "Anyway, I was proud of you."

"What are we going to do?"

"Pack our things, and then go to Mrs. Markley's on Rector Street." Mrs. Markley's boarding house, unlike the waterfront establishments, offered meals and shelter only to the respectable—elderly widows, bachelors with regular employment in Main Street stores and offices, and visiting couples from across Long Island Sound or from New York.

I thought of asking my mother to wait, so that I could

find Dilsey and say good-bye to her and ask her to be sure that poor old Tiger was fed. But I didn't. Sag Harbor was small enough so that I was sure to see Dilsey before long.

In less than half an hour mother and I had packed our worldly possessions. When we left that hot little room, I turned toward the service stairs. "No," my mother said, her chin raised, "not this time." We walked to the front staircase and descended through the silent house to that beautiful front door. I don't know to this day whether or not any of the Ravencrofts, watching from windows, saw our proud exit down the walk and through the gate in the picket fence.

In a rambling old structure on Rector Street, a few minutes later, plump Mrs. Markley, puffing after the first few steps, led us up two flights to her only vacant room, a corner one with green, flocked wallpaper, a floral carpet, a handsome walnut four-poster bed, and a small fireplace with a white marble mantel. What luxury, after that stifling little cell we had left! But while I was looking around me with dazzled eyes, I heard Mrs. Markley say, "Board and room will be seventy-five cents a day for you, Mrs. MacWain, and fifty cents for your little girl. Well, I'll leave you now. Supper is at seven."

A dollar and a quarter a day! At that rate how long would my mother's one hundred and four dollars last? While my mother and I placed the contents of our hand trunk in the handsome walnut highboy, I worked out the sum in my head. Even if my mother spent no other money at all, we would be able to go on paying Mrs. Markley only about eleven weeks.

At last I said, "What will we do when the money is gone?"

She answered, after a moment, "Oh, I will have found work before that."

But I remembered Mr. Ravencroft's threat to keep others from hiring her. And I could tell, from the worry in her eyes, that she too remembered the threat and believed it.

In the big ground-floor dining room that night, my mother and I ate, not at the big table that stretched down the center of the room, but at a small one set before the unlighted fireplace. Also seated at the smaller table were two middle-aged couples from Connecticut; Mr. Winkler, the old-maidish teller of the Seaman's Bank; and Mrs. Hewlitt, whose late husband had owned the Main Street establishment that still bore his name, Hewlitt's Merchandise and Food Store. The supper fare was both good and plentiful—poached fish and roast beef and boiled onions and two kinds of pie. But I was too oppressed by anxiety over what would happen to us to really enjoy the food, and I could tell that my mother felt the same way.

When we left the dining room and went out into the center hall, I looked through a doorway into the parlor. A tall, glass-doored case, its shelves crowded with books, stood beside the fireplace. "Mama, do you think we could take a book up to our room?"

"You go on upstairs. I'll find Mrs. Markley and ask her."

A few minutes later she came into our room with a book called *Pride and Prejudice* in her hand. While she sat mending the loose hem of her best dress, a brown merino, I read aloud. The book was very good, but all the time I was reading about Elizabeth Bennet and her sisters I was conscious of worry at the back of my mind.

Up the stairwell came the muffled boom of the tall clock in the ground-floor hall. "Heavens!" my mother said, and crossed to the wardrobe with the merino in her hand. "Nine o'clock. We had best get to bed."

We had started to undress when someone knocked. My mother rebuttoned her bodice, smoothed her hair with both hands, and opened the door.

A stout woman with black hair and improbably red cheeks stood out in the hall. She wore a dark purple dress, a black velvet bonnet with purple plumes, and a black velvet cloak, its edges flung back over her shoulders on this warm night.

She said, "Good evening, Mrs. MacWain. I'm Josie Carpenter."

Even I knew that name. More than a year ago, one summer day when I had accompanied my mother to Hewlitt's store to order the next week's food, I had looked out through the store window and seen a large woman, resplendent in a violet-colored silk dress and bonnet, pass by on the sidewalk. Behind me, one of the woman customers at the grocery counter said, "That's Josie Carpenter."

Her woman companion, evidently a newcomer, asked who Josie Carpenter was, and the first woman said, "She runs a red-light place on the waterfront. Wouldn't you think she'd have the decency to stay away from upper Main Street?"

I turned. The two women noticed me then, and stopped talking.

Now, as my mother stood there with her hand on the doorknob, her face was what people sometimes call a study. At last she said, "I'm afraid I don't understand." She did not ask how it was that her visitor had been able to walk into this highly respectable boarding house. I suppose that Mrs. Markley's front door, like that of almost every inhabited dwelling in Sag Harbor, was left unlocked at night.

"It's simple," the woman said. "I've come to see you. May I come in?" Then, as my mother didn't move, "I think you'll find it to your interest, Mrs. MacWain."

Hesitantly, my mother stepped back so that the woman could enter and waved a tentative hand toward one of the two small armchairs flanking the fireplace. Josie settled her ample body into one, and my mother sat facing her. I stood over beside the highboy, admiring the plumes in our visitor's bonnet and the brightness of her complexion.

She said, "I hear you lost your employment today."

My mother stiffened. "How did you hear it?"

"Mrs. MacWain, in my business I hear everything that happens around here sooner or later, and usually sooner. But what I'm here about is this: How would you like to work for me?"

My mother made a strangled sound, as if someone had thrown ice water into her face. She stood up. "Please leave."

"Wait! That's not what I mean." At the time, I didn't understand the amusement in Josie's voice, but I understand it now. My mother, slender and gray eyed and not much past thirty, was still attractive. But with her work-reddened hands and her carroty hair strained back from her face and her almost prim manner, she was scarcely the sort to appeal to a woman-hungry man just off a whaleship.

"Please, Mrs. MacWain. Please sit down. I wouldn't expect anyone like you to even come near my place here in Sag Harbor."

After a moment, my mother sat. "Then what did you mean?"

"As you may have heard, I live across the cove in North Haven, in the old Carruthers place. I bought it five years ago. I've never invited any of my girls there. My life in North Haven is very quiet, and completely separate from my business.

"Now I've got a housekeeper," she went on, "but the cook I've had for the last twenty years is no longer up to the work. I want to pension her off and hire you."

When my mother did not answer, Josie went on, "I'll pay you a lot more than that skinflint Ravencroft did. And there are three nice rooms off my kitchen, a kind of annex. Those rooms will be yours. You can have complete privacy there. What's more, pick out an assistant if you want to. I'll hire her, too."

My mother said, in a bewildered voice, "But why do you want me to work for you?"

"Because I hear you're a good cook and, as you might guess from the look of me, I like good food. And I hear you're honest. You never arranged to have the Ravencrofts billed for more than they owed, so that you and the merchants could split the difference. I just can't stand any kind of crook.

"But it's more than that," she went on. "I heard that John Ravencroft told you he'd keep you from getting another position. He can do it, too. I don't want to see you victimized by the Ravencrofts, not again."

My mother said uncertainly, "Again?"

"A lot of people in this town suspected that your husband didn't take that money. I *know* he didn't. Henry Ravencroft used to come to my place. The useless young fool was crazy about one of my girls. Her name was Daisy. Daisy was as much of a fool as he was. She told me Henry was going to get some money out of his father's strongbox so she and him could run off for a fling in New York. They weren't able to run away as soon as he'd stolen the money. Daisy had gotten word from Connecticut that her sister was sick and she'd better go over there right away. That's why Henry left the money with your husband, along with some sort of cock-and-bull story. Something about the package holding love letters, wasn't it?"

My mother nodded.

"I thought that was what your husband testified to at his trial."

My mother's voice shook. "If you knew Henry Ravencroft stole that money, why didn't you come forward to testify at my husband's trial?"

"Mrs. MacWain, I certainly wish I could have. Maybe feeling guilty over not helping your husband then is one of the reasons that makes me want to help you now. But do you really think my testimony would have done much good, even if I could have gotten that little slut Daisy to back me up, which I never could have? And by testifying I might have done myself a lot of harm. The respectable people in this town put up with places like mine because they have to. After all, this is a seaport. But they are not too happy about it. And I'm sure they'd manage to make things hard for me if I started poking my nose into the affairs of people like the Ravencrofts.

"Now think about it, Mrs. MacWain. What are you going to do if you don't take up my offer?"

My mother remained silent.

"But if you do take it, you'll have better wages than you could get anywhere else, and a nice place to live. And you'll be able to do a lot of things for your kid. Look at her, Mrs. MacWain! Red hair and green eyes and that face. And I hear she's smart as a whip. You could send her to a girls' boarding school in Brooklyn or someplace, where she'd learn things like French and piano playing and fine manners. A few years of that, and she's sure to find the sort of well-off young husband you'd like for her to have. But if she grows up here, without much schooling, and with people remembering about her father—"

She threw me a swift look and then said, "Excuse me, Mrs. MacWain. Maybe I shouldn't have talked like this, especially in front of your little girl."

"It's all right," my mother said slowly. "And Mrs.—Miss—"

"It's Mrs. Carpenter, if we're going to be formal, and I guess that's best. I really was married once."

"Mrs. Carpenter, I accept your offer."

Chapter 4

Now, as I moved up the street beside Dilsey on this January day, toward the house where my old husband had met his violent death, I found myself thinking of that long-ago conversation between my mother and Josie Carpenter. When Mrs. Carpenter spoke of my finding a well-off young husband, she must have been visualizing the sort of man that Brian became. I'm sure it would never have entered her mind, any more than it did mine, that I would marry a man who, although in actuality Brian's uncle, was old enough to be his grandfather.

Not that I gave much thought, even after I was enrolled at Miss Frawley's Academy in Brooklyn Heights, to the possible husband for whom I was being groomed. The present seemed too enjoyable for me to speculate about the future.

I loved everything about that school. I loved all my classes, from eight o'clock Calisthenics to four o'clock Social Decorum. Calisthenics consisted of our stretching our arms high and swaying from the waist, "like graceful young trees in the wind," while the music mistress played a waltz on the piano. Social Decorum was really not a class at all but afternoon tea, with a different girl presiding at the tea urn each day, and all of us chatting about the weather, or the school's last trip en masse aboard the ferryboat to see *The Fair Penitent* at New York's most magnificent theater, the Park. Why, I even loved the view from the fourth-floor dormitory, a big room I shared with about a dozen seven- to ten-year-olds. From that height I could see clear across the densely clustered buildings at the foot of

Manhattan Island to the green New Jersey shore beyond the Hudson River.

No one at the academy tried to conceal the fact that the school's purpose was to produce, not learned young women, but ornaments of the parlor and ballroom. Nevertheless, we did study such subjects as French and history, and sometimes took trips to such historic spots as Fraunces Tavern in Manhattan, where General Washington had bade farewell to his troops. And for those pupils who really liked books, there were shelves in Miss Frawley's office filled with volumes of eighteenth-century poetry and with expurgated editions of Shakespeare and Gibbon.

Miss Frawley was about forty, with calm blue eyes and blond hair so light that you could scarcely see the gray in it. She was far too wise to play favorites among her charges. Except that she was especially gentle with the newly arrived and homesick, she treated all the girls with the same pleasant firmness. Nevertheless, I received the impression that she was pleased whenever any of the pupils showed an inclination to acquire a little knowledge as well as the ability to paint china, embroider, and pour tea without spilling any. From the first, she brought out all my capacity for hero worship. I quite literally adored her. Had I been baptized as a Catholic rather than a Presbyterian, I think I might have assumed that Miss Frawley, shortly after her death, would be beatified by the Vatican.

In early June, chaperoned by one of the elderly housemaids who worked at the academy, I made the three-day journey by stage to Sag Harbor, where my mother met me at the station. In those days the Sag Harbor–North Haven bridge had not been built. People often rowed across the narrow stretch of water, sometimes with their horses swimming behind them. But those in wheeled vehicles had to go the long way around, circling the cove. When our hired carriage reached North Haven, we drove about two miles down the main road and then turned down a tree-bordered side road to Josie Carpenter's red brick house. The carriage took us down the drive, past a grape arbor where two benches faced each other across a vine-shadowed table, and deposited us at the entrance to the comfortable three-room kitchen annex. I knew it was comfortable because I had stayed there more than a week the previous fall before enrolling at the academy. I was pleased but not surprised to see Dilsey hurrying out to meet us. My mother had already written me that, taking advantage of Josie Carpenter's offer to hire an assistant for her, she had asked Dilsey to come to work in the North Haven house.

I enjoyed that summer. In fact, I enjoyed nearly all of my Sag Harbor summers while I was going to Miss Frawley's. In a light skiff, which Hiram, Josie Carpenter's aged black coachman, kept tied up down at the cove, I sometimes rowed out from shore and tried my luck with a bamboo fishing pole. As is the case with many anglers, I suspect, the possibility of catching a fish was less important to me than enjoying the smell of salt water, and the warmth of the sun on my face and hands, and the gentle rocking of the boat. Sometimes I would row across the cove at its narrowest point, leave the grocery order my mother had given me with a clerk at Hewlitt's Store, and then wander south along Main Street to that stretch of houses, built with whale-oil money, which people had begun to call Captains' Row. Here some of the big frame residences, set well back from the street, were even more impressive than John and Aurelia Ravencroft's house. And with riches pouring into Sag Harbor in greater volume than ever, more mansions were being built. Almost every day I went there the sound of saws and hammers was loud on the summer air.

During those walks, as well as at church on Sundays, I of course met people I had known for as long as I could remember. One morning I saw, moving toward me along the sidewalk in front of Captains' Row, two girls who had been part of the group who had lain in wait for me that bitter afternoon in the yard of Mrs. Bowen's school. As they drew nearer, the quality of the smiles on their supposedly innocent young faces made me feel that they knew that my mother's present employer was a "bad woman." But they did not attempt to stop me, and they said nothing more than, "Hello, Fiona." Perhaps there was a dangerous glint in my eye.

As for the grown-up acquaintances I met, I sometimes saw concern as well as curiosity, in their faces, but none of them tried to question me. I realize now how unusual that was. In most villages at least a few people would have made it their business to see that I was removed from Josie

Carpenter's house. But then, Sag Harbor was an unusual town, far more tolerant and sophisticated than most places of its size. It had to be, to live with its own contradictions. And it had many contradictions. It had lower Main Street, where whaleship crewmen of every sort, including Fiji Islanders with bones thrust through their noses, staggered in and out of taverns; and it had an upper Main Street, where people dined on pheasant and the finest of wines, under crystal chandeliers. It had bawdy houses, and more grog shops than any community on eastern Long Island, but it also had a literary society whose meetings attracted the serious minded from all over the Hamptons. And although its housewives gossiped over back fences like small-town housewives everywhere, those who were married to ships' officers often did much of their shopping in Hong Kong.

As it happened, I was in no moral danger whatsoever in Josie Carpenter's house. Sometimes I saw her moving away down the drive in her carriage, or sitting out under the grape arbor on warm afternoons, but that was all. She respected my mother's privacy completely, never entering the kitchen annex. Any request of hers was relayed to my mother through the housekeeper, a large, stately looking woman of mingled African and Shinnecock Indian blood. What was more, Josie had told the truth when she said she lived quietly in North Haven. She had no visitors at all.

And yet, one June day in my fifth year at the academy, I thought for a terrible half hour that I might be expelled because of Josie Carpenter.

With other members of my class, I had just returned to the school from a matinee performance of *Così fan tutte* at an opera house in New York. In the ground-floor hall I started past the open doorway to Miss Frawley's reception room and then halted. Inside the room, near the closed door of Miss Frawley's office, sat Pamela Stacewood and her mother.

Mrs. Stacewood stared at me, first with astonishment and then with growing indignation. She was a large, pale-faced woman who could never have been half as good-looking as her daughter. She said, in a taut voice, "Fiona, will you come here, please?"

I stepped into the room. Although I was already weighted with dread, I was still able to observe that

Pamela's oval face, in its frame of lemon-colored hair, was now even more exquisite than it had been the last time I saw her, almost a year before.

Mrs. Stacewood said, "Are you enrolled at this school, Fiona?"

"Yes, ma'am."

"I heard you were attending some school in Brooklyn, but I never dreamed—" As if she felt she had been deliberately deceived, she threw an outraged look at the door of Miss Frawley's office. Pamela, no longer a teasing nine-year-old but a demure fourteen, sat with eyes modestly cast down.

I managed to say, "You never dreamed what, Mrs. Stacewood?"

"Never mind. Don't let me keep you, Fiona."

I went upstairs. Even in my distress, even with tears stinging my eyes, I remembered not to run. Miss Frawley's young ladies did not run on stairs. In my empty dormitory room I stood at the window and looked out over Manhattan to the New Jersey shore, hazed with the tender green of spring. Mrs. Stacewood would tell Miss Frawley that my mother cooked for Josie Carpenter, and that I lived with my mother in Josie's house each summer. And Miss Frawley would have to tell me not to come back in the fall. She would tell me ever so nicely, but she would tell me. I went on standing there, aware of each passing moment, aware that soon I would have to go down to the first-floor parlor for tea. Thank heaven it was not my afternoon to pour.

From the doorway a high young voice said, "So here you are. I've been looking all over." I turned and saw little Janey Reed, who, as a first-term girl, was one of those who carried messages for the mistresses. "Miss Frawley wants you in her office."

On feet that felt weighted, I went down to Miss Frawley's office, tapped on the door, and then, at her "come in," went inside. She said, "Hello, Fiona. I—" She broke off. "Child! Don't look like that!" She came from behind her desk and put her arm around my shoulders. "It's all right. Now sit down."

I sat on the straight chair drawn up to the desk, and she went back to her own chair. "Now, as you know," she said, "there was a Mrs. Stacewood here. She had thought she might enroll her daughter with us next fall."

I said wretchedly, "And then she saw me."

"Yes, and told me that your mother's employer was a—a woman of notorious reputation."

"Oh, Miss Frawley! I'm sorry, so sorry!"

"Stop that, Fiona. There's nothing to be sorry for. And what she told me was not news to me. I've known for several years."

As I looked at her, speechless, she said, "I had heard—a rumor, and so I asked a friend of mine to find out about it. He has built a house in East Hampton, less than ten miles from your village, and he spends each summer there. He managed to strike up a conversation with the old coachman of—of your mother's employer. The coachman said that Mrs.— Is it Carson?"

"No, Carpenter."

"He said that Mrs. Carpenter lives very quietly, and that your mother, in effect, maintains an entirely separate establishment. My friend said that he felt the old man was telling the truth. He also said that he had learned that your mother attends church each Sunday. In short, I gathered that she is just the sort of woman she impressed me as being when she brought you here five years ago. Naturally, I saw no reason to ask you to leave."

I said, still anxious, "But now, after Mrs. Stacewood—"

"I told Mrs. Stacewood that I was sorry indeed that her daughter would not be with us next fall, but that we could not dream of giving up Fiona MacWain, one of our best pupils."

Suddenly she smiled. "Oh, Fiona! Do you think that none of the other girls enrolled in schools like mine has anything dubious in her background? This is still a new, raw country. It doesn't have a large, well-established upper class from which we can draw our pupils. If we limited ourselves to such pupils, we would not survive. I'll tell you a little secret. When I first opened this school I had as a pupil the small daughter of one of the most notorious women in New Orleans. After the girl was graduated, she went to Paris to visit a cousin. A French duke fell in love with her and married her."

Then, as I began to cry from sheer relief, "Now, Fiona! You don't want to look all red and splotchy at tea, do you? Dry your eyes and run along."

That same year, a few weeks after the academy closed, I saw Brian Ravencroft again, for the first time since my mother and I had marched proudly out of his parents' house.

During that summer of my fourteenth year, old Hiram allowed me, for the first time, to drive the lightweight two-wheeled cart that the former owners of Josie Carpenter's property had left in the carriage house. Until then he'd said that I was not strong enough to drive a horse, even a small one. But this summer, with the cart hitched to a piebald pony rented by the month from the Sag Harbor Livery Stable, I drove all over North Haven's leafy lanes. Sometimes alone, sometimes with my mother or Dilsey, I drove across the newly constructed bridge to Sag Harbor and visited the cemetery where my father was buried.

On this particular day in early July, I drove alone across the bridge and then along upper Main Street, past the big houses rising white and stately behind their summer-green lawns. About a mile farther on, I followed a meandering route to Old Sagg Road and then drove, past farmhouses and open fields, through woodland fully leafed out and melodious with bird calls, to the village of Sagaponack. There I struck out over a rutted road that ran through blossoming potato fields to the long line of dunes and the Atlantic beyond. Leaving the pony tethered to a fence post, I walked between two dunes and then, a few yards from the water's edge, spread out an old blanket and sat down. The day was bright, with floating, fair-weather clouds that seemed to make the blue sky even vaster and the horizon more distant. Close inshore the sea was almost millpond calm except for its edging of breakers, but farther out I could see whitecaps and a three-masted schooner scudding before a brisk wind.

The hooves of Brian's mount were soundless in the deep sand. It was not until I heard the jingle of a bridle that I knew someone had joined me. I twisted around and saw a dark-haired young man astride a bay horse. Reining in, he smiled down at me.

"Red hair and green eyes. It can't be anyone but Fiona MacWain."

I felt an odd breathlessness. "That's right."

He dismounted and stood there with the reins in his hand. He said, dark blue eyes looking down at me, "I'm Brian Ravencroft. Do you remember me at all?"

"Yes, of course." But the truth was that I had almost forgotten him these past five years. I thought of him only when I read in Sag Harbor's weekly newspaper that he had entered Yale College, or that he was spending his vacation as a supercargo aboard a ship in the coastwise trade, or that, having been graduated from Yale, he planned to serve as third mate aboard one of the whaleships in which the Ravencroft family held an interest.

Now, looking at him as he stood there, a young man of more than average height, with broad shoulders, a tanned strong-featured face, and a well-cut mouth with a full lower lip, I wondered how I could have forgotten him for five minutes.

He said, still smiling, "Tell me, Fiona, what have you been doing all these years?"

So he didn't know. Well, there was no reason why he, so seldom even in Sag Harbor, should know anything about the daughter of his family's ex-cook. I said, "I'm going to a girls' school in Brooklyn, Miss Frawley's Academy."

He answered, after a moment, "Why, that's splendid." But I had seen the puzzlement in his eyes. How was it that the Ravencrofts' ex-cook could send her daughter to a boarding school in Brooklyn? Better to answer that question myself, I thought swiftly, than have him ask it of someone else.

"My mother has a very good position. She's cooking for Josie Carpenter."

Astonishment in his face now. I knew he must be remembering my mother, with her severely dressed hair, her almost austere manner. But he recovered swiftly. "Oh, she is? And you spend your vacations with her?"

I nodded.

"I'll bet you like coming back here, after your winters in Brooklyn. Say, do you ever go fishing in the cove?"

We went on talking of inconsequential matters. How

kind he was, how tactful. And how devastatingly attractive. I was finding out that falling in love at fourteen is a far more complicated business than falling in love at four. When I was four, I not only wore my heart on my sleeve but held it out to him with both hands. At fourteen, I found myself hoping that he did not notice the color I could feel in my cheeks.

And for me, of course, love at fourteen was complicated by the inescapable thought that Brian was not just Brian. He was the son of John and Aurelia Ravencroft, and the brother of Henry.

At last he said, "Well, I'd better get back to the Harbor. I'm sailing on the *Westerly* tomorrow morning, and I have things to see to."

The *Westerly!* On her last whaling voyage she had been gone two and a half years. And Brian was leaving aboard her tomorrow. As I sat here, I had been hoping that for at least a few weeks this summer—

He swung into the saddle. "Fiona."

"Yes?"

"How old are you?"

"Fourteen."

He smiled down at me. "Grow up as fast as you can, won't you?"

My heart seemed to swell. I wanted to say, "I will, if you'll promise to wait for me." But of course I couldn't say that. I gave him the only proper answer, a demure smile.

"Good-bye," he said, and turned his mount toward the dunes.

He did sail on the *Westerly* the next day, and in the fall I went back to Miss Frawley's. But this time, for me at least, it was not a case of out of sight, out of mind. All through that year, and through all the additional years of my schooling, I thought of Brian frequently, even though, from the age of fifteen onward, I began to meet other young men. Some of them were the brothers of classmates who lived in Brooklyn and who, with Miss Frawley's permission, invited me to their houses for dinner. Others were carefully selected young men asked to Sunday afternoon receptions at the school, with only the sixteen- to eighteen-year-old girls present, and Miss Frawley herself presiding at the tea table. If any of these young men had interested me, I might have forgotten Brian, but none of them did.

In my sixteenth summer, though, I met an old man who interested me.

Although the time was early June, the day was almost as muggy as late August, the sort of day when at Josie Carpenter's request, relayed through the housekeeper, my mother prepared no hot dishes. I had asked her if she wanted to drive into Sag Harbor with me to order next week's groceries. Seated in a rocker in her living room, a book in her lap, my mother smiled up at me. Her face was fuller and far less weary than in the days when, without assistance, she had cooked each day for at least nine people. No, she told me, she preferred to sit in this nice cool room.

Thus I was alone in the pony cart when, around four o'clock, I turned into Josie Carpenter's drive. A moment later I realized that she was sitting out under the grape arbor, wearing lavender muslin. And, for once, there was someone with her, a man. About a hundred feet beyond them, near the coach house, a liveried driver sat on the box of a graceful landau.

As I neared the grape arbor, I was surprised to see Josie heave her lavender-clad bulk off the bench and thrust out a lavender parasol, signaling me to stop. When I drew rein, she said, "Fiona, I want you to meet Torrance Ravencroft."

Why, I thought, this must be Brian's Boston uncle. I murmured something, and he smiled at me. "Forgive me for not getting up, my dear," he said, "but I am afflicted with a particularly painful form of rheumatism."

Josie said, "Would you mind getting down and sitting with us for a few minutes, Fiona?"

Wondering, I left the cart, tied the pony's reins to one of the grape arbor's supports, and sat down beside Josie. Gray light filtering through the vine leaves overhead showed me that her visitor was a man of seventy-odd. Because of his beaked nose and prominent brow ridges, he bore a resemblance to his younger brother. The hazel eyes under the bushy brows, though, were not somber like John Ravencroft's, but alive with shrewd humor.

He said, "So you're Fiona." He studied my face. "Josie says that you are smart, too, which is hard to believe. Nevertheless, I do believe it because I've never known Josie to lie. And I've known her ever since before she came to Sag Harbor, which was over thirty years ago, back in the days when Josie and I were young."

"*I* was young. You were just younger than you are now. Don't pretend we're the same age."

He smiled. "Yes, you were young, and very lovely." He turned to me. "Did you know that Josie was once the prettiest dancer appearing on the New York stage?"

I shook my head. Had this old man and this middle-aged woman, I wondered, been lovers in those days? Later I was to learn that they had. What was more, when Josie first came to Sag Harbor, some years after the end of their love affair, Torrance, for the sake of auld lang syne, had loaned her enough money to buy her waterfront establishment on the other side of the cove. But on this sultry afternoon I did not know all that. I knew only that there seemed to be a humorous liking between them, touched with a kind of late-autumnal flirtatiousness.

He said to me, "A few minutes ago I gave myself the privilege of going back to pay my respects to your mother. And I use the term advisedly. I have nothing but respect for anyone with spirit enough to stand up to my brother John."

So Josie must have told him about how my mother and I had stalked out of that Madison Street house nearly seven years before. I said, feeling a little embarrassed, "You live in Boston, don't you?"

"I've lived there for twenty-two years. But I'll be there only a few months more. You see, I've bought the old Ravencroft house on Madison Street."

I said, bewildered, "Your brother's house?"

"Yes. My father built it, and both John and I were born there. But twenty-two years ago I sold John my share of the house and went to Boston. Part of my reason was that I had a chance to buy a partnership in an importing firm owned by a Yale classmate. But also, I was glad to leave because I couldn't stand John and Aurelia. Couldn't stand my nephew Henry, either, even though he was only ten then. He was a liar, and a whiner, and sly as they come."

If Torrance Ravencroft had ever heard that injunction

to never speak ill of the dead, apparently it had not impressed him. But then, I reflected, remembering with a stir of old grief and rage what Henry had done to my parents, it could be that no one but Henry's mother had ever been able to think well of him.

I asked in a constrained tone, "Didn't you like Henry's sister and brother, either?"

"Dora and Brian? They were just toddlers when I left Sag Harbor. About three and two years old, I guess. I neither liked them nor disliked them." The shrewd glance he threw me made me feel that I must have betrayed self-consciousness as I spoke of Brian and his sister.

"Later on," he said, "when John and Aurelia sent Brian to that school near Boston, I was surprised at how well the boy was turning out. In fact, I was so pleased with him that I liked having him to Sunday dinner each week. I even took him to Europe for a couple of summers."

I nodded, remembering.

Josie said, "It's a pity that Dora had turned out more like Henry than Brian. I heard that last week she lost her temper with a maid who was doing her hair and tried to hold a hot curling iron against the woman's arm."

"A strange young woman, from all I hear," Torrance said. "She's handsome enough, and yet it seems she makes everybody's flesh crawl."

His tone was quite cheerful, as if the people he spoke of had no relation to himself. What a wicked old man, to feel no vestige of family loyalty! And yet, even as I thought that, I found myself liking him. I said, "Are you living in the Madison Street house now?"

"Good Lord, no. I'll stay at Mrs. Markley's boarding house until my brother and his family move out."

"But where will they move to?"

"I guess you haven't heard, being home for only two days," Josie said. "But John Ravencroft is building himself a big, fancy mansion on Captains' Row, in what they call the Italian style."

"Italianate, Josie, Italianate," Torrance Ravencroft said. "John has been getting very rich lately. Most of the ships he has an interest in have made excellent voyages. In fact, he's going to build a whaler as well as a new house. The ship's under construction in Philadelphia right now—

I hear they'll name her the *Silver Dolphin*—and Brian will be the master."

For the two days I had been home from school, I had wondered where Brian was. I had not asked my mother. I hadn't wanted her to know I had that much interest in Henry Ravencroft's brother. But now I asked, "Is Brian in Sag Harbor?"

I had thought my tone casual enough, but again Torrance Ravencroft shot me a shrewd look from under those heavy brows. "No, the *Westerly*'s still at sea, with Brian aboard her. But she may be dropping anchor at Long Wharf any day now. Josie, will you signal my coachman?"

Josie extended her arm in front of me and waved the lavender umbrella. With one hand grasping a cane and the other pressing down on the table, Torrance Ravencroft hoisted himself to his feet. He said, through the sound of approaching wheels, "Well, Miss Fiona, if you're going to be here all summer I imagine we'll see each other again."

We did. Several times, returning from the beach at Sagaponack, or from doing errands for my mother or Dilsey, I found Torrance seated with Josie in the grape arbor. I would sit with them for a few minutes, enjoying his accounts of his European travels and his sometimes salty comments on townspeople whose aquaintance he had renewed after his twenty-two-year absence.

But the *Westerly* did not return. Five times that summer the flag went up on Beebee's Mill on its hill in Sag Harbor, a hill high enough so that the flag was visible from North Haven. Each time I knew that the small boys must be running through the streets shouting, "Flag on the mill, ship in the bay!" I knew, too, that a whaler must be sailing past Cedar Point toward Long Wharf now, and that the frock-coated shipowners, eager to hear how much whale oil she carried, must be putting out in rowboats to meet her.

All that summer, whenever I saw the flag on the mill, I made some excuse to drive my pony cart across the bridge. But each time I found that the newly moored ship, with what looked like half the town swarming up her gangplank or standing on the wharf to shout to crewmen on her decks, was not the *Westerly*.

In September I returned to school. In March a letter from my mother casually mentioned that "the Ravencrofts' son" was back in town. By the time I returned to Sag Harbor for the summer, the *Westerly* had sailed again, with Brian aboard her, this time as captain.

It went on like that for another year. The *Westerly* returned, but weeks before the spring term at the academy was over, Brian had sailed again, this time as master of the Ravencrofts' own ship, the *Silver Dolphin*.

And then, two-thirds of the way through my eighteenth year, I had to face the fact that the day of my graduation, which had always seemed so comfortably far in the future, would soon be here.

What would I do after that? At the moment I had no prospects of the sort of marriage my mother and Josie Carpenter had hoped I would make. Perhaps, if I had encouraged some of the young men I had met here in Brooklyn—but I had not. As for the young men in Sag Harbor, few of them that I would consider marrying would have the courage to defy their families and marry me, the daughter of a convict and of Josie Carpenter's cook.

And Brian? It was unlikely that his ship would return for at least six months. Probably it would be away much longer. And anyway it was absurd of me to attach any sort of hopes to Brian. After all, what was there between us? Just my own fourteen-year-old infatuation with him, and his laughing admonition to grow up as fast as I could. He must be twenty-five by now, I realized. For all I knew he was engaged to be married. Anyway, it was almost certain that he had forgotten all about his conversation four years ago with a young girl on the beach at Sagaponack.

And so, then, what was I to do? Go back to Sag Harbor and open the sort of school that I myself had attended for one week, long ago? Tolerant as my fellow townsmen were in some ways, I doubted that they would want to send their children to a school conducted by Duncan and Martha MacWain's daughter. Take a clerk's position in a Sag Harbor store, or work as a servant? Certainly there would be no disgrace in that, but it would make my years at the academy seem a waste, and therefore would disappoint my mother bitterly.

Night after night in late May of that year I lay awake in the dormitory long after the quiet breathing—and sometimes snores—of the other girls told me that they slept. I would stare into the dark and wonder what I was to do.

A little more than a week before graduation day, Miss Frawley called me into her office. "Fiona, have you made any plans about what you will do once you leave us?"

"No, Miss Frawley."

"Then why leave us? Why not return in September and become a member of my staff?"

As I looked at her, too overcome for speech, she went on, "Miss Arledge is leaving us to live with her sister in Maryland." Miss Arledge taught history, music, and china painting. "Now you are fully qualified to take over her history and music classes. As for china painting, I have decided that, instead, I will offer classes in watercoloring. I hear that is what fashionable schools in England and on the Continent are doing.

"I know," she went on quickly. "You know nothing about watercolors. But I am sure that after about a year's instruction you will have the necessary skill to teach such a class. I know a Madame Bayar, a Frenchwoman who lives in Manhattan and gives lessons in both oil painting and watercolors. In addition to teaching your history and music classes, you could go to Madame Bayar once or twice a week."

She paused. "Well, Fiona?"

"Oh, Miss Frawley!" Her right hand lay on the desk. I picked it up and held it against my cheek.

She said severely, withdrawing her hand, "How emotional you are, Fiona!" But I could tell she was pleased. "Now I take it that you do want to join the faculty here? Good!"

On a winter day about seven months after that afternoon, Brian came back into my life.

The intervening months had been pleasant enough. Sure now of my immediate future, I was able to enjoy my summer in North Haven. Several afternoons, returning from one sort of excursion or another in the cart, I found Josie Carpenter and Torrance Ravencroft in the grape arbor and sat with them for a few minutes. Now that John Ravencroft's new mansion—a brownstone structure that looked as if it had strayed from New York City out to eastern Long Island—had been built on Main Street, Torrance had moved into the old Ravencroft house on Madison Street. A family named Todd were his servants. Joseph Todd was gardener-coachman, his wife was cook, and their two daughters, Clara and Irene, were housemaids. Each night, after dinner was served, the Todds went home to their own small house on Garden Street.

I asked, "But don't you mind being alone at night?"

"You mean, when I'm all crippled up? I'm able to undress myself and get to bed. And if I need anything during the night—well, I can get to any place I want on the ground floor, now that I've got my chair. It sure beats hobbling around with a cane."

"Your chair?"

"My wheelchair. I designed it myself. Made a sketch of it and sent it to these furniture makers in New York."

In the fall, a member of the faculty now, I returned to Miss Frawley's school. I enjoyed teaching my classes. And I enjoyed even more my twice-weekly journeys to Manhattan, where Madame Bayar, a plump, blondish woman, whose English was excellent except for its French accent, lived in a tall old brownstone south of Washington Square. Oh, not that I proved to have any talent. ("You will never be a painter," Madame Bayar told me. "But I can teach you how to impart a certain amount of technique to the little ones.") However, I enjoyed the lessons in her big second-floor studio. And I enjoyed the trips by hansom cab from the ferry to her house and back again. How exciting to travel through a city of two hundred thousand people, with horse-drawn cars clanging up and down the avenues, and expensively dressed men and women moving along the sidewalks past the fine houses, some in the Dutch style—red brick with white trim—prevalent more than a century ago, others of modern brownstone.

On an afternoon in late February I descended the stairs of Madame Bayar's house to the sidewalk. It had begun to snow, but I didn't mind. It was what I had heard Madame call the blue hour, that lovely time when gas lamps bloom through the early dark. As I stood there, waiting for an empty cab to stop beside me at the curb, a horsecar moved down the center of the street, its lighted windows golden in the blue twilight. I would have loved to ride in a horsecar.

But Miss Frawley felt that a young female in her care, whether pupil or faculty member, should not ride alone in a crowded public conveyance.

Several hansom cabs whirled past, affording me a brief glimpse of their passengers. Despite the beauty of the evening, I was beginning to feel both anxious and a bit chilled when a cab moved past and then, abruptly, angled in to the curb. The passenger got out and moved toward me. "Fiona? Fiona MacWain?"

For a moment I could not speak. Then I said, "Yes."

He was close to me now, his hat in his hand. Light from the gas lamp shone on his smiling, square-chinned face and on his curly dark hair, now rapidly whitening with snowflakes. "I was sure it was you." He added, "I'm Brian Ravencroft."

"I know. Please, Brian. Please don't stand there with snow falling on your head."

He laughed and put on his hat. "Where are you going?"

"To the Brooklyn Ferry terminal."

"Let me take you there."

Madame, if she were watching from an upstairs window, would not approve. Miss Frawley, if she heard about it, would not approve. "Thank you," I said, and walked with him to the waiting cab. As we moved away down the street, I had the absurd feeling that the cab horse was really Pegasus, and that Brian and I were being carried high in the air through the snowy twilight.

The *Silver Dolphin*, he told me, had returned to Sag Harbor ten days ago from her maiden voyage, holds filled with barrels of whale oil. "It was a good voyage, but it showed me that there were several things wrong with the *Dolphin*. She's back at the shipyard in Philadelphia right now, and I've been ordering a new sextant and new gimbals for the lamps in the owner's cabin and a few other items at ship chandlers' shops in Manhattan. She ought to be fine when she sets out for her second voyage a few months from now."

Have been ordering. "Then you've finished your business here in Manhattan?"

"Yes. I'll take the stage to Sag Harbor tomorrow morning."

I had been hoping that this time I would see him again, and soon. Why did he have to keep appearing in my life—and then just as abruptly disappearing? My illusion that we were drawn through the air in a magic chariot was gone now. The horse was just a tired old cab horse, drawing a vehicle that smelled of some recent passenger's cigar.

He said, "Surely this is your last year at the academy."

"I have already graduated. I teach there now. I teach history and music. And I'm taking lessons from a Madame Bayar here in Manhattan twice a week, so that next year I can teach watercoloring."

"You do?" he said vaguely. He was looking at me in a way that quickened the beat of the pulse in the hollow of my throat. "Do you know that you have turned out even lovelier than I thought you would?"

I managed to speak quite evenly. "Thank you."

"Surely you don't have to catch this next ferry. You're a teacher now, not a pupil. Let's go to that place next to the Park Theater on Park Row. We can have tea or coffee there. Then I'll put you aboard the next ferry."

The temptation was almost irresistible. But what was the point in remaining in his company for an additional hour when, after tonight, I might not see him again for another two or three years, if ever? I would only be courting unhappiness.

"I'm sorry, but Miss Frawley would be both worried and displeased if I did not return on time. And I must not risk dismissal." It was not that I thought she would dismiss me, not for one offense. But I wanted to prevent his trying to persuade me.

We were nearing the Battery now. Instead of residences, chandlers' shops and warehouses lined both sides of the street. He said, "When is your next art lesson?"

"Thursday afternoon, from two-thirty to four-thirty."

"Do you think you could cut that time in half? Then you could meet me at that coffeehouse next to the Park Theater, and we could have an hour together before you catch the ferry."

"But you won't be here! Tomorrow you're taking the stage to—"

"No, I'm not. It has just occurred to me that in the long run it might pay me to extend my stay here, so that

I can familiarize myself with the chandlers' establishments in Manhattan and with the facilities for ship repair here. They might prove more satisfactory than those in Philadelphia."

As a pretext it was gauze thin, but I felt no desire to challenge it. He said, his face very serious now, "Well? Will you meet me at that coffeehouse? About three-forty-five, say?"

"Yes," I said. "I'll manage it somehow."

On Thursday, so as not to lose my courage, I broached the matter as soon as I entered Madame Bayar's studio. She heard me out and then said, "Is he the young man whose cab stopped here last Tuesday afternoon?"

So she had been watching from the window. "Yes. Oh, please let me leave an hour early, Madame. It's so important."

"Don't you realize that you are asking me to betray Miss Frawley's trust in me?"

"Please! Ordinarily I would never ask a thing like this. But I have to be with him as much as I can now. He will sail in a few weeks. And it may be as long as three years before I see him again."

She asked softly, "Are you in love with this young ship's captain?"

I gave a shaky laugh. "I have been in love with him since before I was five."

She herself did not laugh. Instead she said, "*Ma pauvre enfant!* Perhaps it is because I am a Frenchwoman, but—yes, you can leave at three-thirty."

For half an hour I worked silently over a still life of straw flowers in a blue bowl. At last, with an impatient exclamation, Madame took the brush from my hand. "You are not even looking! There are no blue flowers in that bowl. You might as well go to your young man right now."

When I entered the coffeehouse about twenty minutes later, Brian was already there. He hurried over to meet me and then led me back to his corner table. He had a glass of port and I had tea, and we talked of our separate lives these past few years, during which he had circled the earth and I had traveled back and forth between one end of Long Island and the other. But the really important things we said with our eyes, not our tongues.

In a hansom cab later on we rode in almost complete silence. Then, just before we reached the ferry building, he drew me close to him and brought his lips down on my own. For a moment, but only a moment, I resisted. Then my arms went around his neck and I was kissing him with shameless ardor.

On the ferry ride over to Brooklyn I stood at the rail, not really seeing the dark water or the lanterns of ships anchored in the bay, not really aware of anything except my own happiness. I did not even think of the future.

But I did think of it often during the weeks that followed, and with increasing confidence. Madame continued to allow me to leave early so that I could meet Brian, and after each meeting I was more sure than before that he loved me. Oh, there would be difficult times ahead. His parents would oppose our marriage as strenuously as they could. My mother would be dismayed at the thought of my marrying Henry Ravencroft's brother, John Ravencroft's son. But when she realized how deeply in love I was she would give me her blessing. As for John and Aurelia Ravencroft— well, what could they do to stop us? We were not children. I was nineteen, and earning my own living. And Brian was a whaling master, with three successful voyages to his credit.

On Tuesday and Thursday afternoons, after we met at the coffeehouse, we usually stayed at our corner table. Sometimes, though, we drove or walked through the city streets until it was time to catch the ferry. To me those minutes we spent together came to seem cruelly brief, and I could tell that they did to Brian, too. At last he said, a few minutes after we met at the coffeehouse one Tuesday afternoon, "Don't you think your Miss Frawley would permit you to stay overnight with Madame Bayar?"

I said, "But why?"

"So that, for once, you won't have to rush off to that damned ferry! Forgive me, Fiona, but you don't know how much I want to spend several hours with you, take you to supper some nice place—"

"But I don't see how—"

He pulled a watch from his waistcoat pocket. "There's enough time for us to go back to Madame Bayar's house right now. You can ask her to invite you to stay with her next Thursday night."

As I hesitated, he said quietly, "Please try, Fiona. If either Madame Bayar or Miss Frawley refuse—well, there's no harm done. But at least try."

"I'll try."

A few minutes later, while Brian waited in a cab parked at the curb, I talked to Madame Bayar in her ground-floor parlor, a pleasant room where light from the coal fire in the grate flickered over furnishings she had brought from France and over the paintings, many of them her own, that lined the walls. When I had made my plea she said softly, "I think I understand. You believe your young man wants to propose. But he also wants the proper ambience. Not a coffeehouse or a hansom cab, but a romantic place, with flowers on the table, and wine cooling in a silver bucket. Is that it, *ma petite?*"

I said, from a tight throat, "Yes, Madame. That is exactly it."

After a moment she sighed. "What is it you Anglo-Saxons say, that one might as well be hung for a sheep as a lamb? You may tell Miss Frawley that I have invited you to stay with me Thursday night so that—so that—"

"So that I might meet some of your friends at a little party you plan to give?"

She said, somewhat drily, "I see that you have already thought out what I am to say. Very well. Tell her that."

I felt my face grow warm. I did not like involving Madame Bayar in a lie. I did not like deceiving my adored Miss Frawley. Once I was engaged, I would tell her of the deception, and ask her forgiveness. But right now I felt justified in any amount of deception, as long as it would help make certain that by the time Brian sailed again I would be his fiancée or—even more to be desired—his wife.

"Thank you, Madame, thank you!"

She took my face between her hands, tilted it downward, and kissed my forehead. "Now run along. Don't miss that ferry."

On Thursday afternoon, heartbeats fast, I entered the coffeehouse on Park Row. Smiling, Brian rose from the corner table and hurried toward me. "I've already paid the waiter." He took my arm. "And there's a cab waiting at the curb to take us to supper and then bring us back to Manhattan."

"Take us where?"

"You'll see."

As we went out the door, I said, "Apparently you were quite sure that I would get Miss Frawley's permission."

"Well, she gave it, didn't she?"

Yes, she had given it, so promptly and trustingly that I had felt ashamed of myself. But I wouldn't think about that tonight.

It was March now, and the days were longer. As we drove north along wide cobblestone avenues to Washington Square and beyond, the light lingered. By the time that we had driven through Union Square with its quadrangle of fine new houses and into the open countryside beyond, dusk was falling. I said, "Won't you please tell me where we are going?"

He smiled. "Well, all right. I've already ordered our supper at a tavern about four miles from where we are now. It's famous for its food. Lots of New York people drive up there, and the Albany stage stops there for meals."

"You ordered our supper? How?"

"I sent a note by the Albany stage that left Manhattan this morning. As you say, I was quite sure that you would get Miss Frawley's permission."

"How could you be so sure?"

He took my hand in his square, warm one. "I suppose it was because I don't see how anyone could resist you."

We said little after that. I was happy just to ride, holding hands with Brian, through darkness rich with the smell of newly turned earth, and loud now and then with the shrill voices of spring peepers in some brook or pond.

At last we turned into a graveled area before a two-story structure of white frame. Light poured from its long windows onto at least a dozen hansom cabs and private carriages, most of them with a driver waiting on the box. We left our cab and crossed to the door. Only seconds after Brian lifted the brass knocker and let it fall, the door opened.

A thin man of middle age, with dark hair and a clean-shaven face, bowed to us and said, "Good evening."

"I'm Brian Ravencroft."

"Oh, yes, Mr. Ravencroft. We have reserved the up-stairs dining room for you, just as your note requested. Come in, please."

We stepped into a wide hall filled with the sound of many voices. Through an archway at my right I could see a dining room, where men and women, some in evening dress, sat around white-clothed tables. "This way, please." The thin man led us up the stairs, opened a door, and stepped aside, bowing.

Aware that Brian followed, I moved into the room. Behind me the tavern's host said, "We have already placed the wine there beside the table, sir, just as you ordered. The bell rope is to the right of the fireplace. Ring whenever you want the waiter to start serving supper." I heard the door close.

I stood frozen. Oh, here were the flowers Madame Bayar had visualized, purple and yellow crocuses in a crys-tal bowl on the stiffly starched tablecloth. Here, too, was the silver wine bucket on its stand beside the table. But there was also an archway across the room, its curtains of dark green velvet pushed back. And beyond the archway was a wide couch, covered with some fabric of lighter green and strewn with multicolored pillows. Chilled and sick, I stared at it.

I felt his hands on my upper arms, turning me toward him. "Fiona—"

I pulled away and stood with my back pressed against the table's edge. "How could you?" I said, in a voice I wouldn't have recognized as my own. "Oh, God! I thought you loved me."

Again his hands grasped my arms, trying to draw me into his embrace. "What are you talking about? You know I'm crazy about you. I have been for weeks."

I shook myself free of his grasp. "Crazy about me!" I said thickly. "I was the one who was crazy. Crazy to think I could expect any kind of decent treatment from a Raven-croft."

I saw first a disconcerted look and then a growing

anger in his face. "Now listen here, Fiona! I thought you would guess what I had in mind for—for tonight. After all, you've been meeting me alone for weeks now, something that a conventional girl just doesn't do. Besides—well, you and your mother *have* been staying for years in Josie Carpenter's house."

Pain and rage had sped my heartbeats, so that it was hard to breathe. "Oh, yes! My mother went to work for Josie Carpenter—after the Ravencrofts turned her out. But she would not have been working for them or anyone if you Ravencrofts hadn't murdered my father."

"Murdered your— What on earth are you talking about?"

"He went to prison for something your brother did, and he died there! You know that, you know that!"

His face was quite cold now. "I know some people say that. But if that is how you feel about my family, I wonder that you ever had anything to do with me."

"I wonder, too!" My voice broke. "But I couldn't help it. I was in love with you, and I thought that you loved me too, and respected me—"

His face softened a little. He reached out his hand. "Fiona—"

"Don't touch me. I don't love you now. I loathe you. I think I hate you even more than I hate your parents, and that foul brother of yours who broke his neck. Oh, how glad I am he broke it! It shows that perhaps there is a little justice in the universe, after all."

His face was very white now, and his pupils were so expanded that his eyes looked almost black rather than dark blue. He said coldly, "I take it that you would like to return to Madame Bayar's house right away."

I inclined my head.

"And I imagine you would prefer to go there alone."

"Definitely."

"Very well. I can stay here tonight and return to New York by stage tomorrow." His voice was colder still now, and perfectly even. "I'll take you to the cab."

We descended the stairs. Our footsteps crunched over the gravel. By the light from the tavern windows I could see that the face our cab driver turned to us held surprise. Brian opened the hansom's door and, hand under my elbow, helped me inside. I thought fleetingly, "This is the last time he'll ever touch me." He closed the door and walked toward the box. I heard him say something to the driver. Evidently he also handed him money, because I heard the driver say, "Thank you, sir." The cab started up. From the corner of my eye I saw Brian, white faced, bow to me as the cab rolled past him.

About two hours later I knocked at the front door of that handsome brownstone house south of Washington Square. Madame Bayar herself, not her elderly parlormaid, opened the door. I realized that the Frenchwoman had waited up for me. In hope of hearing the romantic details of my engagement supper? Or had she, somewhere at the back of her mind, feared that a marriage proposal was not what Brian intended?

She said, "So you are back." Then, "Fiona! What is it?"

Unable to answer, I stepped past her into the hall. She stood stock-still for a moment. I think she must have sensed, all in a flash, much of what had happened. "Come in by the fire," she said.

We went into the parlor. Still in my cloak, I sat down in one of the two armchairs flanking the small fireplace and held my cold hands out to the warmth. She said, sitting opposite me, "Are you all right?"

"Yes." And I was, in the sense she meant. I was still a maiden. It was my spirit that had been ravaged and humiliated, so brutally that perhaps I would never again be able to trust any man completely.

She asked, "What happened?"

I told her of the private dining room, and that alcove where many couples must have bedded down for an hour or so. For the first time I wondered if Brian had been to that place before, with some woman more complaisant than myself. True, the proprietor had not seemed to recognize him, but then, discretion would have impelled him to pretend that it was Brian's first visit.

Madame Bayar's face had a stricken look. "I am so ashamed, Fiona. I should never have aided you to keep seeing that man. You were young and in love. You could not be expected to realize what might happen. But I, at my age—oh, what would Miss Frawley think of me, if she knew?"

"She won't know," I said with an effort. "I have said nothing to her about him in the past, and I certainly will not do so now." Nor would I tell my mother. "And don't blame yourself, Madame. If you hadn't helped me to keep seeing him, I would have contrived some other way. That is just how much of a fool I was."

I got to my feet. "If you will tell me which room is mine for tonight, I will go to bed now."

Chapter 5

During the weeks that followed I was thankful indeed for the distraction of work. In order to face my pupils each day, I had to maintain at least a surface composure. Beneath that surface the humiliated pain gradually burned itself out. By the time I returned to North Haven for the summer only hatred remained, a cold hatred for the man who had caused me to love him and then treated me like a trollop. And I felt quite sure that not even the hatred showed.

On the stage to Sag Harbor I had heard a passenger mention to his companion that the "Ravencrofts' big new whaler" was off on another voyage. But even though I knew that I would not encounter Brian on Sag Harbor's streets, I stayed on the North Haven side of the bridge as much as possible. Just the sight of ships tied up at Long Wharf would remind me of that absurd dream of mine about sailing aboard the *Silver Dolphin* as Brian's wife. And then, feeling my throat grow so tight that I could scarcely breathe, I would know that I had not quite conquered the pain, after all.

As well as they knew me, neither my mother nor Dilsey seemed to notice any alteration in me. It was a comparative newcomer in my life, Torrance Ravencroft, who became aware that I had changed.

I found that out one afternoon when my mother asked me to deliver a cake to the Presbyterian church. It was her contribution to the "bake sale" with which the women of the parish raised money twice a year. Unable to think of any excuse to refuse, I harnessed the pony to the old cart and drove to the church and back, looking straight ahead as the cart rattled past the foot of Long Wharf.

When I turned into Josie Carpenter's drive, I saw Torrance Ravencroft's landau back beside the carriage house, with Joseph Todd on the box. Then I saw Torrance himself, sitting alone under the grape arbor, a tall glass of what looked like lemonade in his hand. He called out, "Come keep an old man company for a few minutes."

I reined in, descended from the cart, and tethered the pony to the grape-arbor post. "Where is Mrs. Carpenter?"

"In the house. Her housekeeper had just brought this out"—he gestured toward a tray holding a glass pitcher of pale yellow liquid—"when Josie said she felt one of her dizzy spells coming on and had better lie down." As I slid onto the bench opposite him, he reached for the empty glass sitting beside the pitcher. "Have some lemonade?"

"Thank you."

For a while we sipped our drinks in silence. Then he asked abruptly, "What happened to you?" When I raised an eyebrow inquiringly, he said, "You look older than when I last saw you."

"By a strange coincidence, I am older than I was at this time last summer, a year older."

"Don't be flip with me, young woman. You know what I mean. You look—harder. It's as if you've been wounded in some way, and now the scar tissue is showing. So I want you to tell me what happened."

I looked at him, this man who, no matter what he thought of his other relatives, had seemed fond of his nephew. Why shouldn't I tell him? After all, he too was a Ravencroft, and why should I spare the feelings of any Ravencroft?

I said, "Your nephew happened to me."

In short, swift sentences I told him the story. When I had finished he sat in silence for a moment and then said, "The fool, the damned young fool. You're beautiful and intelligent and you've got spirit. How many women like that can he hope to meet?"

When I didn't answer, he asked, "Are you still in love with him?"

"No!"

His deep-set eyes studied me. "I think you are. But

you'll get over it. And there are plenty of young men who will have sense enough to appreciate you."

"Are there? I'm afraid that almost any young man who learns that my father died in prison and that my mother works for Mrs. Carpenter may feel that in my case there is no need to propose marriage."

After a moment he said sadly, "Perhaps you are right."

I set down my glass and stood up. "Well, I'll leave you now."

For a moment I thought that he was going to tell me that he had something more to say. Then he nodded. "Goodbye, Fiona."

I was with my mother and Dilsey in the big kitchen the next morning, helping them put up strawberry jam, when someone knocked on the outside door. My mother said, "See who that is, will you, Fiona?"

Wiping my hands on my apron, I went to the door. Joseph Todd, Torrance Ravencroft's coachman, stood there, gaunt and lantern-jawed. He held a small white envelope. "Good morning, Miss MacWain. I have a note from Mr. Ravencroft."

I thanked him and closed the door. A moment later my mother asked, "Well, what is it?"

I looked up from the note in my hand. "Mr. Ravencroft sends us both his compliments. And he wonders if I will go for a drive with him at two o'clock this afternoon."

"I don't see why not," my mother said slowly. "I imagine he's lonely, poor man."

Dilsey said, with a sniff, "At least he's human, not like that John Ravencroft and his wife and that spooky Dora."

My mother said, faint reproof in her tone, "Life can't be too easy for Dora, a woman of twenty-seven still living at home."

"That's where she wants to be, ma'am, just so long as that brother of hers comes home every once in a while. She's always been way too fond of him, even when they was both real young."

My mother said, in a shocked voice, "Dilsey, I hope you don't mean that the way it sounds."

"But I do, ma'am, I do! Other folks talk about how she carries on whenever he's here, walking down the street clinging to his arm, and glaring at any girl he stops to talk to."

I remembered how, in that Park Row coffeehouse one afternoon, Brian had spoken of his sister with considerable irritation. She kept insisting, he said, that he take her on a voyage with him.

The coffeehouse. Brian. That private dining room with the curtained alcove. I said, turning to leave the kitchen, "I think I'll see if my green muslin looks all right to wear this afternoon."

Promptly at two, Torrance arrived. While Joseph Todd was still getting down from the box, I walked out to the carriage. When I was seated beside Torrance, he said, "It's nice of you to give an old man the pleasure of your company, Fiona. Now where would you like to drive? Around North Haven and then maybe down to the beach at Noyac?"

"That sounds lovely."

It was almost July then. As we drove along a winding road, between two walls of pines and deciduous trees, I noticed that the maple and oak leaves had lost their spring paleness and taken on the deep, rich green of full summer. For a while we talked of the warmth of the day, and the beauty of the pink-flowered mountain laurel sometimes visible in among the trees. Then he said abruptly, "I had a slight stroke last winter."

"Oh, I'm sorry." I really was sorry, and that made me realize how much, even though he was a Ravencroft, I had come to like this man with the cynical and yet humorous eyes and the salty tongue.

"It wasn't serious, not this time. But a thing like that sets a man to thinking. Specifically, I got to thinking about my will. I don't want my relatives to get my money. No, not even Brian. And that's not just because of what you told me yesterday. I've always felt it was bad for a man still in his twenties to inherit a lot of money. Takes away his incentive to make money on his own.

"Now I could leave all I've got to some charity," he went on, "but John and his wife would try to break a will like that, and they'd have a good chance to do it."

He paused for a moment. I just sat there, puzzled and silent.

"Ever since yesterday, I've been thinking of what you said about how young men, once they learned about your father, and about Josie Carpenter—" He broke off, and then went on swiftly, "Fact is, Fiona, I'd like for you to have my money, you and that fine brave mother of yours. But there'd be no point in leaving it to you. The Ravencrofts would break such a will in nothing flat. True, if you were my adopted daughter— But there's a law against the adoption of adults. And so that leaves only one thing. Marriage."

My face swiveled toward him. He laughed. "If only you could see your expression! Now, Fiona, I really shouldn't have to assure you that what I propose is marriage only in the legal sense. Women have not interested me for some time now. This marriage would be only a way to insure that a few years from now you will be a rich woman, so rich that no man would dream of treating you as my nephew did. You'll find that when you're rich people will be willing to overlook where your father died and where your mother worked after that."

I sat motionless, thinking of what it would be like to be insulated by wealth against the humiliation and pain that had been my lot, and my mother's, more than once in the past.

"Of course, I'm not being entirely philanthropic. Even though my romantic days are over, it would be pleasant to have you ornamenting that big old house on Madison Street. And it would be pleasant to have your company. Tell me, do you play chess?"

I shook my head.

"If you decide to accept my proposal, I'll teach you." Again he laughed. "I suppose it would seem at least a shade less inappropriate if I proposed to your mother rather than you. But to judge by my impression of that lady, she would never accept."

He was right about that. Mother would regard such a marriage as a wicked mockery of one of God's sacraments.

"But I would like your mother, too, to live in the Madison Street house. Let Josie find herself another cook. Your mother has worked long enough." He paused. "Well, Fiona?"

"I don't know." But I think I did know, even then, that I was going to accept.

"Then think about it. Talk it over with your mother. I'll take you home now, so that you can do just that."

Several hours passed before I talked to my mother. Around nine that night, I tapped on the door that connected my small bedroom with her larger one. When I walked in, I found her seated at her dressing table in her high-necked white muslin nightgown, brushing her light-red hair, which still showed no touch of gray. She smiled at me in the mirror and then turned to face me. "What is it, dear?"

I sat down a few feet from her in a small pine rocker. "Now please don't say anything, Mother, until I've finished." I told her of my conversation with Torrance. As I spoke, I saw growing horror in her face.

At last she said, "Fiona, you just cannot marry that old man, no matter how rich he is, and no matter how kindly disposed he is to you and me. You're a lovely girl, Fiona. You must marry a nice man of your own age."

I wanted to say, "Like Brian Ravencroft, for example?" But of course I didn't. I couldn't let my mother, who loved me and was so proud of me, gain the slightest hint of what had happened in that sordid private dining room north of New York City.

Bitterness must have shown in my face, though, because she said, "It's not just Torrance Ravencroft's money, is it?" There was sorrow in her voice now. "For you the main consideration is getting even with John and Aurelia Ravencroft."

Yes, I thought. And perhaps, in one way or another, with Brian Ravencroft.

"Oh, Fiona, Fiona! Don't you know that it is wicked to feel the things I see in your face right now? Remember, daughter. The Lord said, 'Vengeance is mine.'"

My voice was dry. "Perhaps sometimes He needs a little help."

My mother, at that moment, looked every one of her forty-four years, and more. At last she said, "I pray that you will not do this. But you are of age now, and I cannot stop you. And you are my daughter, so I will not turn against you."

I said, "And if I do marry him, will you come to the Madison Street house to live? Torrance would like you to." She was silent for several seconds. I wondered what she was thinking. Just of me? Or also of the years when she had toiled fourteen hours a day in the cellar kitchen of that house?

"Yes," she said, "I'll live there with you."

Chapter 6

O ne afternoon, almost a month later, in the parsonage of the Sag Harbor Presbyterian church, Torrance and I were married. Our only attendants—in fact, the only other persons present beside the minister—were my mother and Gerald Winship, who lived halfway between Sag Harbor and the nearby village of Bridgehampton. A dark, slender man in his late thirties, Winship was Torrance's lawyer and chief business advisor. After the ceremony, the four of us drove ten miles to East Hampton for a wedding dinner at the Governor Bradford House, a stately structure on the village's wide and tree-bordered Main Street.

Except for my mother—and even she tried to keep smiling—it was a cheerful outing. Torrance was in fine fettle, recounting exploits of his father, the privateer, and speaking, even boasting a little, of his own sharp business practices in Sag Harbor, Boston, and Europe during his younger days. Gerald Winship, his thin face filled with sardonic humor, urged the old man on. As for me, I of course felt none of the tremulous happiness a young woman is supposed to feel on her wedding day. Where that emotion should have been there was only emptiness. But I did feel a kind of grim elation. I had seen the will that Gerald Winship had drawn up for Torrance, a will that cut off his brother, nephew, and niece with the customary dollar, left certain sums to his servants, and bequeathed the rest of his estate to "my wife, Fiona MacWain Ravencroft." We were safe now, my mother and I. Never again would we be at the mercy of the selfish, the powerful, the brutal.

Near the end of our dinner at the Governor Bradford House, when all of us except my mother had partaken freely of the wine, Torrance clapped a heavily veined hand to his forehead and said, "Good lord! I'm supposed to give the bride a present, and I forgot all about it."

I felt amused. He had willed me his entire fortune, and yet he felt chagrined at not giving me a present. "Any time will do," I said lightly.

"What sort of present shall it be?"

Gerald said, "I have a suggestion. Why not give her a gold-plated high chair?"

Torrance looked taken aback for a moment, and then burst into laughter. "Winship, you young dog, you're a man after my own heart."

As we drove back through the red-gold sunset light, the two men kept up their good-natured chaffing. Just before we reached the lawyer's house on Bridgehampton Turnpike, we passed a long stretch of uncleared land filled with oaks and maples and a few cedars. From the conversation of the two men, I gathered that Gerald Winship had been trying to buy these acres adjoining his own land. "What do you want with more acreage?" Torrance said. "You're no farmer."

"Neither are you. Why do you want to hold onto it?"

"Why not? I'm in no need of raising money."

Gerald shook his head. "Torrance, you are a self-centered old reprobate. How do you expect to ever get past Saint Peter?"

Torrance appeared to consider the question for a moment. "I'll bribe him," he said finally.

We dropped Gerald at his house, a modest yellow clapboard, and then drove on to Sag Harbor. It was dark by the time the carriage stopped in the drive of the big house on Madison Street. With Torrance leaning heavily on Joseph Todd's arm, we moved toward that beautifully fanlighted door. Before we reached it, it opened. Dilsey stood silhouetted in the warm lamplight. My mother and I had asked her to join us in the Madison Street house, and she had been helping me prepare the second-floor suite— a sitting room and two bedrooms—which was to be my mother's and mine.

She smiled a welcome, her teeth very white in her brown face. She and Joseph Todd helped Torrance back along the wide hall to his specially made chair in the library, that room where, long ago, I had flung my childish rage into Aurelia Ravencroft's cold, pale face. When the two servants had left us—Joseph Todd to join his family in their Garden Street house, Dilsey to turn down my mother's bed and mine before going to her own room—Torrance wheeled his chair to a rosewood liquor cabinet and opened its door. "Would either of you ladies care for something? Madeira, perhaps?"

My mother and I declined. He said, reaching for the brandy decanter, "Well, I shall have a spot and then wheel myself back to my bed. I had not dreamed that getting married would be such an exhausting business."

My mother and I said good night then, and left him. At the foot of the wide front stairs my mother, hand on the newel post, looked back along the hall. I said, "It's not there." When she looked at me inquiringly, I added, "Henry Ravencroft's portrait isn't there. It was when Dilsey and I first started preparing the sitting room and bedrooms upstairs. Torrance told me his brother and sister-in-law had asked to leave the portrait and several other articles here until they were entirely settled in their new house. But Torrance must have taken it to them anyway, because the next time Dilsey and I came here the picture was gone. I guess he realized that you and I would not like to live with it for even a little while."

"In many ways," my mother said slowly, "Torrance Ravencroft is a good man."

Together she and I climbed the stairs.

Chapter 7

Although there could be no doubt that Torrance Raven-croft's wildly unsuitable marriage was being talked about over every dinner table and at every social gathering in Sag Harbor, the townspeople for a while managed to restrain their curiosity about us. Our only visitor was Gerald Winship. Not even the Stacewoods across the street called upon us, although often, when I went in or out of the house, I saw a feminine hand—Pamela's or her mother's or one of the maids'—draw a lace curtain aside for a moment or two. From the John Ravencrofts in their new Main Street mansion—how strange to think they were now my in-laws—there was nothing but thunderous silence. Not even a congratulatory note arrived.

But the drive beside our house did not stand empty. Almost every day, and sometimes several times a day, wagons lumbered up from Long Wharf to deliver goods Torrance had ordered before our marriage. Most of the articles came from his own importing house in Boston, although a few were supplied by a New York firm. There were two enormous Ming Dynasty vases to flank the foot of the stairs, rosewood chairs and chests made more than a hundred years before for a ducal family in England, blue Meissen china banded with gold, a huge Aubusson carpet for the parlor, and for the other rooms Oriental rugs so silky that I felt they should be hung on the walls rather than walked upon.

When the first of that flood of expensive articles arrived, I said to Torrance, "But why? The furnishings of this house are still good."

"I'm just having fun," he said blandly. "Imagine how

John and Aurelia must feel. They hear of furniture and art objects finer than anything they can possibly have arriving here by the wagonload, and yet unless they knuckle under and call on us they are not going to get to see them."

They did not knuckle under—not right away—but others began to. The Stacewoods were the first to call upon the newlyweds, just as Torrance had predicted they would be. ("When I came back here three years ago, I deposited a lot of money in Tom Stacewood's bank. If I should take a sudden notion to withdraw it—") All three of them came—Mr. Stacewood, a stout, totally bald man, whom I rather liked; Mrs. Stacewood, fatter and paler than ever now, so that in her ecru muslin summer frock she reminded me of a large loaf of unbaked bread; and Pamela, so beautiful that it was hard to believe that she was her parents' daughter. They sat on rosewood chairs, which once had supported the derrières of English nobility, Mrs. Stacewood and Pamela sipping the tea I had poured into Meissen cups and Mr. Stacewood drinking sherry from one of the soap-bubble-thin Venetian glasses, which had been delivered only the day before.

I thought of Mrs. Stacewood that afternoon at the academy, sitting with her demure daughter beside her and staring with dismay at fourteen-year-old Fiona MacWain. Surely it must cost them a lot now, less than six years later, to sit smiling pleasantly at that same Fiona. The thought brought me a certain amount of satisfaction, but not as much as I had expected to feel when I saw them crossing the street toward our door.

After that, there was scarcely an afternoon when I did not serve tea to one or more members of the gentry. Sometimes my mother was there in the front parlor and sometimes not, but Torrance was always present. When he and I were alone he called me Fiona, or "my girl" or "my dear." But in front of guests he delighted in calling me "sweetheart" or "my little rosebud." Blandly, he would pretend not to notice the embarrassment on our visitors' faces.

We had been married about three months when, early one afternoon, someone who was a stranger to me came to the house. At the time, Torrance was in his ground-floor bedroom, taking a nap. I was in the library, moving ivory chessmen about on the board in an attempt to solve the chess problem Torrance had set for me the night before. I heard the knocker strike, and then the footsteps of Clara Todd, the elder of the two Todd daughters, coming down the hall. She appeared in the doorway, almost as gaunt and lantern-jawed as her father. All the Todds looked like that, even Mrs. Todd, who was her husband's second cousin.

Clara said, "A gentleman to see Mr. Ravencroft, ma'am. I put him in the parlor."

I said, rising, "Thank you, Clara."

When I entered the parlor a young man, who had been looking at the portrait of Privateer Samuel Ravencroft above the fireplace, turned around and then stood stock-still. He was in his early or middle twenties, with fair, slightly curling hair and a sun-browned face. And in his gray eyes was a look of such startled admiration that I felt my face grow warm.

I said, "Good afternoon. I'm Mrs. Ravencroft."

He bowed. "My name is Steven Slater, Captain Slater."

A whaling captain? Probably. Commanding a whale-ship was such a dangerous and physically arduous job that most whaling masters were under thirty.

He went on, "I wondered if I might see Mr. Raven-croft."

"He's asleep now, but he should be awake in another ten minutes or so. In the meantime, would you like a glass of sherry?"

"That would be pleasant indeed, ma'am."

I opened the liquor cabinet and poured a glass of sherry for him and some blueberry cordial for myself. As we sat facing each other, he in an armchair and I on a tapestry sofa, which had arrived from England via New York the preceding week, I asked, "Do you live on eastern Long Island?"

"No, I was born in Boston and my parents still live there. But for the past two years I've commanded one of Mr. Ravencroft's whalers, which sails out of New Bed-ford." He paused. "That is what I am here to see him about. I would like to buy an interest in the whaleship I now command."

"Well, I wish you success. But I have no idea what he will say. I know little about his business affairs."

"That doesn't surprise me. Why should a beautiful young—" He broke off, looking embarrassed, and then asked, "Were you born in Sag Harbor?"

"Yes."

"It's a handsome town, and the surrounding countryside is beautiful, so I hear."

"It is." I spoke for a few moments about the many freshwater ponds, the level farmlands, and the broad beaches, with their fine white sand and their dunes covered with silver-green eel grass.

"I may stay here a few days," he said. "Perhaps you and Mr. Ravencroft would be kind enough to show me some of the countryside."

I said, a bit uncertainly, "Why, yes. I think that might be managed."

"Forgive me, but I've been wondering. You seem too young to be Mr. Ravencroft's daughter. You're his granddaughter, perhaps?"

I said, after a moment, "No, Mr. Ravencroft is my husband."

He looked stunned. "Your husband!"

"Didn't you hear me introduce myself as Mrs. Ravencroft?"

Faint resentment mingled with the embarrassment in his face, almost as if he felt I had deliberately made a fool of him. "I thought you said Miss Ravencroft. But then, I guess I wasn't listening closely. I was too busy—"

He broke off. As we sat in awkward silence, I heard the sound of wood-rimmed wheels moving over the hall carpet. Torrance, seated in his chair, appeared in the parlor doorway. The visitor and I both got to our feet but, before either of us could speak, Torrance exclaimed, "Slater, my boy! What brings you to Sag Harbor?"

"I came to see you, sir."

"Did you now? I assume you and my wife introduced yourselves?"

"Mrs. Ravencroft paid me that honor."

Torrance's deep-set eyes, which never seemed to miss anything, went from Steven Slater's stiff face to mine and then back again. He said, with a chuckle, "Shocking, isn't it, an old hulk like me married to a young girl. Infuriating, too. But if you young fellows will just be patient—well, I won't be around forever."

I said, appalled, "Torrance!"

He laughed. "Perhaps you'd better leave us, Fiona. I suspect that Captain Slater has come here upon a matter of business."

I turned to the blond young man. "If you do stay here in Sag Harbor for a few days, perhaps we can take you on that tour of the countryside."

He bowed. "I am afraid I must forego that pleasure, ma'am. I have just remembered that I have business engagements in New Bedford next week."

So he was still angry with himself and with me. "I'm sorry," I said. "Good-bye, Captain Slater."

At dinner that night I asked, "Are you going to sell Captain Slater an interest in that ship?"

From the other end of the damask-covered table Torrance said, "So he told you that's why he had come here, did he? No, I want to keep complete ownership of that particular vessel. But Gerald Winship is negotiating my purchase of a Sag Harbor whaler, and I might let young Slater have an interest in that one, as well as the command of her." His eyes twinkled at me. "When he thinks it over, I imagine he won't mind sailing out of Sag Harbor. He was really smitten with you, Fiona. And, come to think of it, when the time comes for you to shop around for a second husband, you might do worse than young Slater. He comes of good stock, and he's the best captain I've got."

From the corner of my eye I saw that my mother, seated between us, had become rigid. What a wicked mockery of a marriage, I could imagine her thinking, in which a husband advises a wife whom to choose as his successor! She said nothing, though.

But then, my mother was mostly silent these days. She seldom helped me preside over the tea table when we had afternoon callers. Except on Sundays, when she accompanied us to church, she spent most of her time in her room, sewing or reading. I was not surprised when, in the tenth month of my marriage to Torrance, she told me that she wanted to go back to Scotland to visit my grandparents.

"I might stay quite a while." As she spoke she sat in

the rocking chair that she had used at Josie Carpenter's, and that had been Josie's parting gift to her. Her gaze was directed at a branch of the big maple outside, its swelling buds rosy against the tender April sky. "It would seem a pity to go all that way just to visit them for a few weeks."

I said, feeling guilty, and already missing her, "You haven't been happy here, have you?"

She turned to face me. "No. But don't think it is just because I don't approve of your marriage. I just wasn't meant to be rich, Fiona. I find it hard to be idle, and yet there is nothing I can do here."

She was right about that. She would not have dared to appear in that kitchen where she had worked for six years. In fact, Mrs. Todd was so insistent upon reigning belowstairs that, the few times I'd had reason to go down to the kitchen, I had sent Dilsey ahead with a message, warning of my visit.

I asked miserably, "Just how long do you think you'll be away?"

"At least a year. You see, Fiona, your grandparents are old. For a while, at least, I'd like to help them around the croft and with the sheep."

Two weeks later she sailed on a cargo-passenger ship bound for Bristol. I missed her even more than I had thought I would, but a memory of the afternoon she sailed sustained me. As the ship moved slowly away from Long Wharf my mother had stood at the rail, waving her handkerchief. She was crying, just as I, on the dock, was crying. But she looked happy, too. Happy at the thought of embracing the parents she had not seen for a quarter of a century, and the thought of wandering over the moors, springy underfoot with heather, and climbing up through those wild glens she had told me about. I knew I shouldn't begrudge her such happiness.

My mother had been gone only two weeks when I again saw Brian.

Dilsey and I, both laden with paper-wrapped packages of lawn and muslin, to be made into summer frocks, emerged from Hewlitt's Store that bright May morning. Brian was moving rapidly up the sloping Main Street sidewalk. At sight of each other, both he and I stopped short.

I was not surprised to see him. I knew from half a

...en sources that the *Silver Dolphin* had returned the day before, after more than a year's voyage. I also knew that this, the *Dolphin*'s second voyage, had been an abysmal failure. She had returned with not enough whale oil in her hold to pay for the flour, butter, rum, dried beef, and other supplies with which she had set sail.

Brian's face flushed and then went white under its sun-browned surface, giving him a muddy look. "Good morning, Mrs. Ravencroft."

There had been sardonic emphasis on the last two words. I kept my voice as even as I could. "Good morning."

"Is this your carriage?"

I nodded.

He opened the carriage door, took the packages from my arms and Dilsey's, and placed them on one of the seats. Then he handed us both inside. I said, looking out at him as he stood on the sidewalk, "Thank you."

"Not at all, Mrs. Ravencroft. Or am I being too formal? After all, we are related now. Perhaps I should call you Aunt Fiona."

"As you like," I said coldly.

His gaze locked with mine for a moment. Then he burst out, "I didn't know about it until yesterday. God, Fiona! How could you have done it?"

Angry color burned my face. "What right do you, of all people, have to censor my conduct?" I leaned farther out the window. "Joseph! Take us home now."

Cold faced and narrow eyed, Brian stood there as the carriage moved past him.

Perhaps two minutes later, as the carriage rolled along Madison Street, Dilsey asked, "How long have you been in love with that young man?"

I glared at her as she sat on the seat facing me. "In love! What kind of crazy notion is that? You couldn't know it, but I have every reason to hate him."

"Two things are the same, sometimes. A man we love hurts us, we hate him, but we still love him. We just don't know it, that's all."

"And you," I said furiously, "don't know what you're talking about. So just keep your mouth shut."

Never in all the years we had known each other had I spoken to Dilsey in that manner. She looked as if I had

struck her. Appalled, I leaned over and covered her ⸱
with mine. "Forgive me, Dilsey. It was him I was angry
with, not you. But you're wrong about my feelings. If the
hurt's bad enough, love can turn completely to hate, with
no chance of reversing itself."

Chapter 8

By mid-June Brian had outfitted the *Silver Dolphin* for her next voyage, signed on a crew, and sailed. I was glad. Now I could walk or drive through the village streets without fear of meeting him.

As for Steven Slater, he was in Sag Harbor most of that summer, outfitting the *Capricorn*, the whaleship in which Torrance had sold him an interest, and which he would command on her first voyage under her new ownership. Often he came to dinner at the Madison Street house. Although instinct told me that he was still attracted to me, his manner could not have been more gravely respectful if I had been Torrance's age. On the last of those evenings, though, as we sat at the dinner table, I looked up and saw his reflection in a wall mirror. Evidently he had no idea that he was observed, because he was looking at me with such ardor that I felt an instinctive stir of response.

The next morning Torrance and I rode down to Long Wharf and, from the carriage windows, watched Steven Slater's ship sail down the bay and disappear around Cedar Point.

Summer gave way to autumn, with maples along Main Street so brilliantly red and gold that they seemed to flame like torches. The first long spell of freezing weather brought out the skaters on Otter Pond. In the early winter dusk, reluctant to leave, they built bonfires along the shore and skated over ice that shimmered with rosy reflections. Neither happy nor unhappy, just reasonably content, I spent my days making out menus, playing chess with Torrance, and exchanging afternoon calls with almost a score of families. When the weather again grew warm, I often rode out

on the sure-footed bay mare, which Torrance had given me
for my birthday, and which I had named Satin. Often I rode
through the woods where my mother and I, back in the days
when she worked in John and Aurelia Ravencroft's kitchen,
used to gather flowers for my father's grave. Sometimes
I crossed the bridge to guide Satin along North Haven's
winding lanes. On a sunny afternoon in June, I rode to Josie
Carpenter's house and sat with her for half an hour under
the grape arbor.

She said, eyeing me narrowly, "Weren't you afraid
someone would see you turn in here?"

"Why should I be afraid? Everyone knows that I
stayed each summer in this house while I was growing up."

"Yes, but that was before you were pouring tea nearly
every afternoon for all those high-toned people. Now you've
got something to lose."

"My position, you mean?" I asked coolly. "I won't
lose it, not when at least a third of those high-toned people
owe Torrance money, or do business with him in one way
or another. That's one thing I've learned. If you're rich and
powerful you can break the rules that the poor and weak
had darned well better keep."

Josie laughed, but there was ruefulness in the sound.
"You're right, of course. But it seems sad you should have
learned that so young."

A few minutes later I prepared to leave. Perched on
the sidesaddle, I looked down at her and said, "Come to
see us soon."

She looked up at me. Her hair was still improbably
black, and she still wore dresses in the lavender-to-purple
range—that day she wore violet-colored lawn—but she was
even stouter than she once had been, and lines had etched
themselves deeply around her mouth. She smiled. "No,
Fiona. I don't think even Torrance would want the Stacewoods across the street to see me entering your house. But
thanks for asking. And you come see me any time. Any
time within the next month, that is. I'll be gone after that.
I've already sold this house and my place in Sag Harbor."

"You'll be gone! Gone where?"

"Rhode Island. I never told you I was born there, did
I? Well, I was. My people had a farm near Providence. I'm

going back there and buy it, or one like it, if it isn't for sale, and live out my days where I spent my childhood."

"I'll miss you," I said, and meant it.

We said good-bye then. As I wheeled Satin and started down the drive, Josie called after me, "Remember me to your mother when next you write to her."

As it happened, there was a letter from my mother waiting for me when I reached home. Seated with Torrance in the library, I read her account of my grandfather's rheumatism, and of the spring lambing, and of a gathering of the MacWains at Kyle Lochalsh, with more than a hundred people dancing reels and listening to the pipes. When I had finished her letter, I asked, "Did you get any mail?"

"Yes, a letter from young Slater. He met the *Minerva* just south of the Solomons, and sent over his and the crew's letters by longboat." The *Minerva*, a three-hundred-ton Sag Harbor whaler, had moored at Long Wharf that morning. "Slater's doing fine. Four sperm whales and six finbacks. He thinks he should be bringing the *Capricorn* home with holds filled by early winter."

Torrance gazed across the hall into the parlor. "You know, when Slater comes back, maybe we should give a party to celebrate a successful voyage. We've never given a big party. We'll invite everyone, including your in-laws. Which reminds me. Slater's letter also said he'd crossed paths with the *Silver Dolphin* some weeks back, near Hawaii. Brian's luck is still bad. His holds are practically empty. He and my brother seem to be having a rough time of it."

I knew what he meant. John and Aurelia Ravencroft's plight had become tea-table gossip. Their new house on Captains' Row had cost them far more than they had expected. To make up the difference, John Ravencroft had sold his interest in several whalers and invested in a mining company. The company had failed.

I said, "If your brother turns to you for financial help, will you give it to him?"

"Perhaps." His tone was so curt that I looked at him in surprise. After a moment, he went on, "Once, a long time ago, after I'd left Sag Harbor for Boston, I found myself in grave financial straits. I turned to John. He told me that my trouble was no doubt a divine punishment for my profligate ways, and that he would have to think and pray for a long time before deciding whether or not to interfere with the workings of the Almighty. While he was still playing cat-and-mouse with me, I managed to raise the money elsewhere. Now maybe it will be my turn to keep him on tenterhooks."

For a moment his face was harsh. Then, to my relief, the twinkle came back into his eyes. "But it would be no use for me to try to tell John that the Almighty made that mining company fail just to punish him. I'd bust out laughing."

As it happened, Brian Ravencroft returned to Long Wharf before Steven Slater did. And the news of the *Silver Dolphin*'s disastrous voyage, passed from ship to ship, reached Sag Harbor even earlier. For a while, off the coast of Japan, he had seemed to be having a run of good fortune—three enormous sperm whales pursued, killed, and brought alongside in as many days. But before he could get all the whales stripped of their blubber, the advance winds of a typhoon struck the *Dolphin* like a gigantic paw and almost capsized her. Not only the two valuable whales floating alongside the ship were lost. The tryworks—big cooking vats in which blubber was rendered into oil—were swept away, and so was the whale oil already in barrels, and part of the mainmast. Somehow, the badly mauled ship had managed to get through the gales at the tip of South America and limp home.

That was in early December. Now and then I caught a distant glimpse of Brian on the village streets, but we did not meet face to face. Much of the time, I heard, he was in New York, trying to raise money to repair his ship and outfit her for another voyage. When he was in Sag Harbor he apparently stayed close to his parents' house. At least Torrance and I did not encounter him at any of the parties or "at homes" we attended that holiday season.

Steven Slater's *Capricorn* dropped anchor at Long Wharf a week before Christmas, its holds filled to capacity. The next night, formally polite as ever, and with his fair skin still deeply tanned from the tropic sun, he took dinner with us. Midway through the meal Torrance said, "I suppose you are going home to Boston for Christmas."

"I am, sir."

"Well, I hope you'll be back in Sag Harbor by New Year's Eve. Mrs. Ravencroft and I will be giving a party. We hope you'll attend."

"I will, sir, and with pleasure."

I always feel sad when I think of Torrance planning that party for New Year's Eve, the last New Year's he would ever see. Just as when he had filled the house with costly treasures, he brought all the gusto of a boy to the task of planning that party. He wrote to New York and arranged for a three-piece orchestra to play for dancing in the dining room, which would be cleared of furniture for the occasion. In the back parlor, hard liquor as well as punch and wine would be served, and there would be a buffet table. Far from leaving the matter of food to Mrs. Todd and me, Torrance insisted that we should serve turkey as well as pheasant, shrimp as well as oysters, and far more condiments than Mrs. Todd and I thought necessary. As for decorating the house, he decreed that we should use hothouse flowers from New York, as well as holly and mistletoe and pine boughs from our Long Island woods. About ten days before the party, he decided that it wouldn't do to have one of the Todd girls open the door to our guests. Accordingly, he sent a message by the stage to a Brooklyn employment agency, asking that they supply us with a butler.

On New Year's Eve, supporting himself with a cane, he stood beside me in the hall. He wore formal black, with a ruffled shirtfront. I was in emerald-green velvet and wore the emerald earrings Torrance had bought for me because, he said, they matched my eyes. As if he could not restrain his impatience any longer, Captain Steven Slater arrived on the stroke of nine, the hour set for the party to begin. "Good evening, ma'am," he said, as he bent over my hand. Only his eyes told me what he thought of the green velvet and the emeralds.

Gerald Winship was the next to arrive. He looked at me and then said, "Torrance, as your lawyer, I advise you to move to the Middle East, where you could keep her shut away in purdah. Don't you realize that to display a treasure is to tempt thieves?"

Torrance looked vastly pleased. "Cool off with some fruit punch," he advised. "You'll find it in the back parlor."

People arrived in a flood after that. The Stacewoods, with Mrs. Stacewood majestic in oyster-colored velvet and Pamela almost ethereally lovely in ice-blue satin. Then our War of 1812 hero and his wife, and after that, in an almost continuous stream, occupants of other houses on Division Street, Madison, and Captains' Row. The air was filled with a babble of voices and laughter and the strains of waltzes and polkas from the dining room.

Around nine-thirty, Torrance said, "Fiona." I looked at him. His face was tired, with a white look around the mouth. "I think I'll rest for a while."

With him leaning on my arm, we walked back along the hall to the library. I settled him into his wheelchair, kissed his cheek, and then went out, closing the door behind me.

More guests arrived, and still more. Then, around ten, the hired-for-the-night butler opened the door to John and Aurelia Ravencroft. With them was Dora, in dark-red velvet that seemed to lend a little color to her handsome but too-pale face. The fourth member of the party was Brian. Above his white shirtfront, his face had been burned by the southern sun, not to the light golden-brown of Steven Slater's face, but to a deep mahogany. The sight of him was a shock. True, I had addressed the invitation to Mr. and Mrs. John Ravencroft "and family," but I had not expected Brian to come.

Trying to keep my smile in place, I extended my hand to the elder Ravencrofts, and then to Dora, and then to Brian. Face expressionless, he bowed and took my hand. Brief as the contact was, it brought me a flood of memories. Brian on the beach at Sagaponack, no doubt amused by the infatuation in my fourteen-year-old face. Brian standing bareheaded in the falling snow in front of Madame Bayar's house. Brian trying to pull me into his arms in that private dining room above the tavern.

Something drew my gaze to Dora Ravencroft. For a moment, before the look was veiled, I saw cold hostility in the prominent brown eyes, which were so like her mother's. Was it, I wondered, just the hostility that all the Ravencrofts must feel because I, not they, stood to inherit

Torrance's money? Or was it more than that? I remembered Dilsey saying that Dora Ravencroft had always been "way too fond of her brother."

I said, "There's a buffet in the small parlor and dancing in the dining room."

About fifteen minutes later, I realized that no more guests would arrive. I left the hallway to mingle with those in the main parlor, where Dilsey and Clara Todd moved about with trays laden with glasses of wine. After a while I went through an archway to the small parlor, where Mrs. Todd and her younger daughter stood behind a buffet table. Finally I moved on to the dining room. There an orchestra played in one corner. From the crystal chandelier a dozen swags of interwoven holly and evergreen boughs radiated to the walls. And over the polished floor at least twenty couples swirled and dipped. I saw Gerald Winship dancing with Dora Ravencroft, and Steven Slater with Mrs. Wren, the pretty young wife of Sag Harbor's newest doctor. And I saw Brian dancing with Pamela Stacewood. They made a dramatically handsome couple, he with his dark curly hair and deeply sun-browned face, she with her pale hair and wide-set blue eyes and delicate features. I felt a stab of unpleasant emotion, and after a moment realized with dismay that it was jealousy.

Dr. Wren's gray-haired mother, seated beside me on one of the gilded chairs that lined the walls, looked up at me and said, "It is a festive scene, Mrs. Ravencroft." She daubed at her upper lip with a lace handkerchief. "But I should think it is rather warm in here for the dancers."

"I'll attend to that." Glad of the excuse to be alone for a moment, I circled the edges of the room to a door leading to a glassed-in side porch, where Torrance and I often took our meals in warm weather. Leaving the door open behind me, I crossed the darkened porch and opened one of the several glass panes, which had been equipped with hinges. The temperature that night was well above freezing, and so the air that came through the opening felt only pleasantly cool to my flushed face.

Why, I thought bitterly, had he come here? I had looked forward to this party. Why did he have to spoil it for me? But then, a party was a trivial matter compared to everything else that he had spoiled for me.

In the room behind me the orchestra finished playing a waltz. After a moment it struck up a polka. I went on standing there, looking out at a stretch of side lawn and bare-branched trees, bathed in the diffused light of a full moon shining through a thin overcast.

"Fiona."

I whirled around.

"May I have the honor of this dance?"

"No!" In my angry suprise, I did not even think of using one of the polite formulas for refusing such a request.

Brian said, after a long moment, "You are afraid to dance with me, aren't you?"

With dismay, I realized that he was right about that. I was afraid to feel one of his square hands clasping mine, and the other warm against my back. I said, keeping my voice low, lest it be heard through the music, "What utter nonsense. I don't want to dance with you because I loathe you. How else could you expect me to feel?"

Again he was silent for several seconds. Then he said, "I apologized for what I did."

"Apologized! Oh no, you didn't. Instead you *explained*. You explained that you had assumed it would be all right to treat me like a slut. After all, didn't my mother work for Josie Carpenter?" My voice thickened. "You snob. You stupid, insensitive, boorish snob."

Anger thickened his voice, too. "At least I didn't try to buy you, the way my uncle has. Maybe I should have tried that approach. But then, at that time I didn't know you were for sale."

Without my volition, my open hand caught him across the cheek. "Get—" I wanted to say, "Get out of my house," but I couldn't force the words through my rage-tightened throat.

With the blood pounding in my temples I walked past him. In the doorway to the dining room, even more crowded now with dancers, I paused for a moment, forcing my lips into a smile. Then I circled the wall toward the opposite door, the one leading into the hall. I had almost reached it when I became aware that Steven Slater was beside me. "Mrs. Ravencroft, may I have the honor of—Mrs. Ravencroft! What is it?"

I forced my lips into a wider smile. "Nothing. Just

a touch of faintness. Please excuse me, Captain. I'll be back in a few minutes."

Up in my room, I opened a window and stood there, breathing deeply of the moist night air, until the enraged pounding of my blood slowed somewhat. After closing the window I moved to my dressing table. My cheeks were still flushed. At the washstand I bathed my face and wrists in cool water. Back at the dressing table I tucked a stray ringlet of hair into place. Then, aware that I must not stay away from my guests any longer, I descended the back stairs and moved along the hallway toward the entrance to the parlor.

I was passing the library's closed door when I heard Torrance's voice through the heavy panels. To judge by his tone, he, too, was in a rage. "The damnable impertinence of you!" I heard him say. As I hesitated there in the hall, I heard a second voice, equally enraged, but speaking in such a low tone that I could not tell whether it was a man's voice or a woman's. Then I heard my husband say, "Never mind our relationship! Nobody talks to me like this, not without paying for it."

Relationship. There were three of Torrance's blood relations here tonight, and one relative by marriage. Did that mean that Brian was in the library, goading my husband to fury just as he had goaded me? Or perhaps Brian's father, or even his sister? Then I realized that Torrance might not have meant blood relationship at all, but another sort. Financial, for instance.

Should I go in? No, Torrance would not like that. Probably the argument did concern business matters, and although he sometimes volunteered to me a bit of information about his financial affairs, he always resisted any attempt of mine to learn more. Nor was there any point in my speculating about who was in there with him. Probably Torrance had business dealings of one sort or another with at least a score of our male guests.

I walked on down the hall and through the archway into the main parlor. Aurelia Ravencroft was still there, I saw, now talking with Dr. Wren. Did that mean that both her husband and son were still here also? Surely not. Surely Brian had had the decency to leave. Nevertheless, my nerves were taut with the fear of seeing him as I drifted back, stopping to chat with one group of guests after another, toward the dining room. When I reached it, I saw with relief that Brian was not on the dance floor. The door to the glass-enclosed side porch still stood open. Just to make sure that he was gone I circled the room to that open doorway and looked out into the semidarkness of the porch. No sign of him.

I turned to find myself face-to-face with Captain Slater. "May I have the honor—"

"Of course," I said.

I danced a polka with Steven Slater and then a waltz with Gerald Winship and then another polka with Steven. After that, aware that some of the guests might be leaving soon, even though midnight was still almost half an hour away, I moved slowly back through the crowded back parlor, where I saw Torrance, now in his wheelchair, talking to men gathered around him with glasses in hand. No matter how angry he had been during that exchange in the library, he looked unruffled now. I moved on to the main parlor, where Dilsey was handing around glasses of champagne on a silver tray. I beckoned her to me and said in a low voice, "Dilsey, did you happen to notice when young Mr. Ravencroft left?"

"I did. Must have been almost an hour ago. And he looked plenty mad."

"Good!"

She looked at me with sorrowful sternness. "You're going to want that man real bad some day. Acting the way you do, he might not be around when that day comes."

Much as I loved Dilsey, I often found her an exasperating woman. In some ways she felt it important—far more important than I did—that she "keep her place." For instance, here in this big house she had insisted upon occupying a third-floor room, even though the second floor, with myself as its only occupant now, had five empty bedrooms. On the other hand, she could lecture me more sternly than my mother ever had.

I looked around to be sure that there was no one close enough to overhear us and then said, "Dilsey, I won't have you talking like that. It's absurd. Why, it's even indecent! After all, I am a married woman."

She nodded. "And that grieves me something terrible. It's young Mr. Ravencroft you ought to be married to, and you know it. Maybe you still could be someday, if you'd just—"

"Dilsey! I won't let you—"

The grandfather's clock in the hall began to strike. A cheer went up. Even before the clock finished sounding midnight, people were singing "Auld Lang Syne." I took a glass of champagne from the tray and said, "Don't let's quarrel. You're my old and dear friend. Happy New Year, Dilsey! Happy eighteen-forty-five!"

She smiled at me, teeth brilliant in her brown face. "Happy New Year, child."

By two-thirty the orchestra and our imported butler had long since left for Mrs. Markley's boarding house, where they were to spend the night at Torrance's expense before taking the stage back to New York. The last of our guests, too, had said good night and stepped out into the diffused moonlight.

In the front parlor I looked down at Torrance, sitting in his chair, and saw that he looked very tired indeed. I said, "I think our party was a success."

"Yes. We showed 'em how to bring in the New Year," he said, but his tone lacked its usual jauntiness.

I said hesitantly, "Torrance, didn't you have an argument with someone in the library tonight? I was going past in the hall and I heard—"

"Fiona, I don't want to talk about it! I don't want to get all riled up again." Then, less sharply, "I don't want to talk about it tonight, anyway. I'm awfully tired. Would you mind pushing me back to my room?"

Grasping the handlebar at the back of his chair, I propelled him down the hall to his bedroom. During my childhood in this house it had been the gun room, its walls hung with pistols and rifles and ancient fowling pieces. It was next door to what was still the sewing room, that room where once I had heard Dora Ravencroft, sprawled in a chair, threatening to "put a hex" on Dilsey.

The corners of his sheets and blankets had been turned down by one of the Todd girls, and his nightshirt placed across the foot of the bed. I said, "Since you're so tired tonight, couldn't I help you?"

"No, Fiona. Anyway, I plan to stay up and read for a while. Go to bed."

"Torrance, you really should have some man as a body servant."

"My dear, when I grow so helpless that I have to be undressed like a baby and put to bed, I shall choose not to be around at all." Usually his references to his physical state were cheerful, even humorous. Now he sounded somber. "Good night, Fiona."

I went to my room and undressed. Tired by the long evening, I fell asleep almost as soon as I had stretched out in bed.

A noise awakened me and brought me sitting bolt upright in the darkness. Somewhere below, some object had crashed with a sound of splintering wood. But even as I got out of bed and lit a lamp and thrust my arms into the sleeves of a dressing gown I was aware that before the crash there had been another sound, like that of wooden wheels bumping over stone stairs. With the lamp in my hand throwing my grotesquely elongated shadow on the walls, I left my room. Because the sound had seemed to come from the rear of the house, I moved as quickly as I could down the back stairs to the ground floor.

The door to the cellar kitchen stood wide open. As I moved toward it with the lamp held high, I was aware of another sound beside the alarmed pounding of my heart. The sound of hooves, moving at a gallop, was dwindling away down the street.

I looked down the stairs. Yellow lamplight fell on my old husband, his body sprawled amid the wreckage of his chair. He had not undressed. I could see the gleam of his ruffled white evening shirt.

I don't remember screaming, although Dilsey said later that it was my scream that had awakened her. I don't even remember going down those stairs. I do remember the chill of the flagstones penetrating through my nightgown and robe as I knelt there, the lamp on the floor beside me, and my hand thrusting beneath that ruffled shirt to rest over a heart that seemed to be no longer beating.

A sound. I looked up to see Dilsey, in a gray flannel gown and a ruffled white nightcap, standing halfway down the steps. Her dark face looked frightened and appalled in the upward-striking light.

"Dilsey, get dressed as fast as you can and go fetch

Dr. Dillworth." Thank God, I thought, that he was only four doors away. "And while you're there," I added, as she started to turn, "ask him to send someone to wake up the constable."

Dilsey turned back toward me. "The constable?"

"Yes. I think someone may have—go on, Dilsey. Hurry!"

Chapter 9

∞∞∞∞∞∞∞∞∞∞∞∞∞∞∞∞∞∞∞∞∞∞∞∞∞∞

A few minutes later I heard the distant sound of the front door closing, and knew that Dilsey was on her way to the doctor's house. I stayed on my knees beside Torrance. I felt all but sure that he was dead. And I felt almost equally sure that what had happened to him was not an accident, felt it so strongly that I wanted the constable there. I'm not sure why I felt it. Was it because I had heard Torrance quarreling with someone earlier that evening? In itself that should not have been sufficient to make me suspect that he had been attacked. As a successful and sometimes overly sharp business man, he must have had many an altercation during his long life without enraging anyone to the point of attempting murder. Was it because I had heard someone on horseback moving away down the street? That certainly was not much of a reason. In the early hours of New Year's Day, it was not at all strange that a few people, returning home from parties, should be abroad in the streets. No, I think the main reason I thought of an assailant was that I could see no reason why Torrance should have opened the door to the kitchen stairs, let alone plunged down them.

Footsteps along the ground-floor hall. I stood up, lifted the lamp from the floor to place it on the table, and turned around to see plump Dr. Dillworth descending the stone steps. "Hello, Fiona." He dropped to one knee beside Torrance. "What happened here?"

I told him of being awakened by the sound of a crash, and then finding Torrance on the flagstones. After that I stood silent while Dr. Dillworth thrust his hand under Torrance's shirt and then felt for his pulse.

At last I asked, "Is he—"

"Yes, he's gone."

Even though I had been almost sure of that, my heart seemed to twist with a sense of loss. So he was dead, that high-handed and—to my mother and me, at least—generous old man who had lived by his own rules.

I said, "How is it that he— Do you think that someone—" I could not go on.

Dr. Dillworth raised an incredulous face. "So that's why you wanted me to send someone for the constable! You think someone pushed him down these stairs. Why, that's nonsense." Laboriously he got to his feet and began to dust off the left knee of his black broadcloth trousers. "I'd say that he heard something, or thought he did, down here in the kitchen and wheeled his chair back along the hall to investigate. When he opened the door to the stairs he became overbalanced, and his chair plunged down the steps."

I looked around me. The kitchen, bathed in lamplight, seemed in perfect order. "But what could he have heard? There are no rats in this house. We don't keep a dog or cat or any sort of animal. True, we don't lock our doors, any more than anyone in town does. But if a thief did come in, I don't see why he'd come in through the kitchen. It would be simpler to use the rear entrance to the ground floor."

"You weren't listening to me. I said he might have *thought* he heard a sound. The last time he came to me he said that he was bothered by head noises."

How very like him, I thought, not to complain about that to anyone but his doctor.

"Now why don't you go upstairs?" he said. "I'll wait down here until the constable comes."

Constable Howard Simon, a dark-haired, barrel-chested man of about forty, arrived a few minutes later, and at my direction walked back along the hall to the kitchen stairs. By that time I had sent Dilsey back to bed, and so I waited alone in the parlor until I heard shuffling footsteps on the kitchen stairs. The two men, I realized, were carrying Torrance's body up from the kitchen. I heard a door being opened and knew it must be the door to Torrance's room. After an interval it closed.

Dr. Dillworth and Howard Simon came into the parlor. From the annoyance in the doctor's face, and the stubborn set of the constable's jaw, I knew they'd had a disagreement.

The constable said, "I'll be back after daylight, Mrs. Ravencroft, to remove your husband's body." I realized that he meant to take Torrance to the mortuary, a small structure behind the building that housed the constable's office. "You see," he went on, "I'm going to order an inquest."

I said, "An inquest! But Dr. Dillworth says Torrance's death was an accident."

"I certainly do! Inquest!" Dr. Dillworth snorted. "Just a waste of time."

"I don't think that most people in this village would agree with you. And I have to listen to people. I'm not as lucky as you, Doc. I have to stand for reelection every two years."

He turned to me. "Sometime tomorrow afternoon I'll be by to get a statement from both you and your maid. Well, good night, Mrs. Ravencroft."

The two men left. Knowing that I must try to sleep, despite an awareness of Torrance lying there in that ground-floor room, I climbed the stairs and went back to bed. Sometime after the windows became rectangles of dawn gray, I did fall asleep, only to awaken with a start from an evil dream—something about being lost in a dark place—which vanished before I could recall any of its details. From the angle at which sunlight fell through the windows, I knew that it must be at least ten o'clock. For a moment I wondered why I had slept so late. Then, with a stab of sorrow, I remembered.

I dressed. As I started down the stairs, I saw Dilsey climbing toward me. She said, "I was going to look in to see if you'd waked up." Then, after a moment, "He's not here. They came for him, the constable and another man. I wanted you to rest, so I didn't wake you. I hope that was all right."

"Yes," I said.

"If you want, I'll bring breakfast to your room."

"No, thank you. I'll have it in the dining room."

The constable came early in the afternoon and took statements from Dilsey and me. After he left, she and I searched through drawers and desk cubbyholes in the library until we found a bunch of keys. We tested them and learned that one fitted the front door, another the rear entrance to the ground-floor hall, and still another the outside door to the cellar kitchen. "From now on," I said, "the doors are to be locked at night." Even though Dr. Dillworth had all but convinced me that Torrance's death had been an accident, I still felt that from now on I would sleep better behind locked doors.

At ten o'clock that evening I went up to bed. Tired as I was, I could not sleep. By eleven I had finished a novel I had been reading, Jane Austen's *Persuasion*, and extinguished the lamp. Still I could not sleep. I lay there in darkness, hearing the muffled boom of the grandfather clock downstairs sound eleven-thirty, twelve, half-past twelve. Finally, I decided that, if I were to lie awake, I might as well go down to the library and get another book. I lit the lamp on the bedside stand, got out of bed, and put on a robe.

I had just emerged from the library, the lamp in one hand and a volume of *Pickwick Papers* in the other, when I heard a distant sound—a kind of clang, as if some metallic object had fallen onto stone. The sound had come from the rear of the house, probably from that cellar kitchen.

I froze. Even though Dilsey and I had locked all the doors four hours earlier, someone had gotten in. Someone, down there in the kitchen, had brushed against a pot hanging on the plaster wall or the stone face of the fireplace, or perhaps knocked something metallic onto the flagstone floor.

No, not someone, I told myself sharply. Something. Some creature, such as a cat or a squirrel, which had gotten into the house last night, and made a sound that had caused poor Torrance to open the door at the head of the steep stairs. Obviously, the creature was still here.

But I had to make absolutely sure that no human was prowling around the kitchen. Otherwise I would not sleep at all tonight. I laid the book on the hall table. Slippered feet soundless over the hall carpet I walked back, past the former gun room, which had been Torrance's bedroom, past the sewing room. I stood motionless for a moment and then flung open the door to the kitchen stairs.

An instant later, as I stood there, feeling a current of cold air eddy around my bare ankles, I turned rigid with fear. Oh, not that I saw anything. Light from the lamp I held showed me only the steep stone stairs and a stretch of flagstone floor, with the fireplace, its banked fire faintly glowing, beyond. But someone was down there. I knew it. I could smell a still-smoking wick, as if someone, hearing me turn the doorknob, had hastily extinguished the large lamp that stood on the kitchen table.

And I could *feel* someone down there, someone lurking in a corner unreached by the light from the lamp I held. I could feel someone's fear and hatred. And I knew, as surely as I knew anything, that if I went down into that cellar kitchen I, too, would meet death.

I stepped backward, closed the door. It had a thumb latch. I pushed the little bolt into place and then stood with my back to the door, considering. Whoever was down there might decide that I, seeing nothing, had gone back to bed. In that case, he might linger long enough for me to catch him. And I wanted to catch him, I thought, my anger stronger now than my fear. Whoever was down there had killed a helpless old man, and I wanted him to suffer for it.

As rapidly and quietly as I could, I moved up the back stairs to the second floor, the third, and knocked softly on Dilsey's door before I entered her room.

She sat up in bed, blinking in the lamplight. "Please come with me," I said. "I think there's someone down in the kitchen."

She said nothing, just swung her feet out of bed and reached for a gray wool robe, which hung over a chair back.

We went softly down the back stairs. At their foot I whispered, "Wait." I went into the room that had been Torrance's. Above the fireplace hung a brace of pistols, all that remained of the firearms that had once lined the walls of this room. I took one of them down. Whether or not it was loaded I had no idea. But then, I reflected grimly, neither would the intruder know. And if I could hold him at gunpoint, while Dilsey went for help—

Out in the hall again, I silently handed Dilsey the lamp. Holding the gun in my right hand, its muzzle pointed toward the carpet, I moved beside her to that latched door.

Swiftly I pushed back the bolt and swung the door open, while Dilsey held the lamp high.

"All right!" I called. "I have a gun. Come on out into the light."

No answer. No sound whatsoever. And no smell of lamp wick. If there had been such a smell, it had been dissipated during these past few minutes.

Most disconcerting of all, I had no sense of danger now, no feeling that someone lurked beyond the lamplight's reach.

Dilsey was looking at me. "Nobody down there, child. You just got too much working on your mind."

"But there was someone! I heard someone."

"Now how's he going to get in? Door's locked down there, and windows, too."

"He could have broken a window."

"All right. We'll see."

Lamp held high, she moved down the stairs. After a moment's hesitation I followed. If Dilsey—superstitious, unlettered Dilsey—was not afraid, then I shouldn't be.

When I reached the flagstone floor, I looked around me. The light of the lamp Dilsey held shone into all the corners. No one was there. The windows I myself had locked from the inside were smooth sheets of black glass, giving back the lamplight. I moved to the table and touched the chimney of the big lamp standing there. It was ice cold to the touch. So much for my illusion of a few minutes ago that I could smell the just-extinguished wick of this lamp.

But that still left the sound that I had heard as I emerged from the library. I was sure I had not imagined that. I looked at the pots hanging from the fireplace's stone face. Someone not familiar with this room might easily have struck one of those pots with his shoulder.

But if there had been someone in here, how had he gotten in, or out? I tried the door opening onto the steps that led up to the rear lawn, and then those shoulder-high windows through which my mother long ago had kept an eye on me as I played with my doll dishes. They were still locked.

I felt a growing conviction that I had made a fool of myself. Even if there had been an intruder—and it seemed obvious now that there had not been—why should I have thought that his presence had anything to do with Torrance's death? If someone had killed him, the last thing in the world he would do would be to risk apprehension by returning to this house the very next night.

A hissing sound came from the fireplace behind me, and then an explosive report, and then a clanging noise, as if something had struck the iron grate. Even as I turned around I knew what had happened. A gas pocket in one of the small logs in the banked fire had exploded, lifting a still fairly solid chunk of partially burned wood into the air and then letting it fall back onto the grate. Could it have been a similar sound that I heard earlier? I knew that it could.

Dilsey had been watching me. She said, "You see? Now put that pistol where it belongs, child, and go back to bed."

Chapter 10

ⅼⁿⁱⁱⁱⁱⁱⁱⁱⁱⁱⁱⁱⁱⁱⁱⁱⁱⁱⁱⁱⁱⁱⁱⁱⁱⁱⁱⁱⁱⁱⁱⁱⁱⁱⁱⁱ

Now, two days later, as I climbed beside Dilsey to the fanlighted doorway, I felt certain that I would no longer imagine nighttime intruders in this house. Torrance's death had been accidental, the coroner's jury had said, and I was more than ready to accept that. I only hoped the townspeople were. But even if not all of them were, even if from now on I saw a certain reserve in some people's eyes when they looked at me, at least I was no longer in any danger from the law.

Clara Todd opened the door for us. As Dilsey and I stepped past her she beamed at me and said, "We're that glad for you, ma'am. That it's settled, I mean."

I took off my cloak and bonnet and handed them to Dilsey. "Then you know the verdict already."

"Yes. Danny came running up with the news a few minutes ago." Danny Boyle was a ten-year-old cousin of the Todd sisters. "Would you like a nice cup of tea to warm you?"

"No, thank you. I'll wait until later." As I started up the stairs, I looked down the hall at the door of Torrance's old room. For the past three days I had been too distraught to think of loneliness. But now I realized how much I was going to miss him, that old man with the wicked twinkle in his eyes.

Two afternoons later, on a day of scudding clouds and chill wind, funeral services for Torrance were held in the new church, which had replaced God's Old Barn. Almost the whole town was there, or tried to be. When the pews were filled, people stood in the vestibule. By the time the service was over, though, rain mingled with sleet had

97

begun to fall, and so only a few people followed the hearse on its short journey to Oakland Cemetery, the new burial ground laid out only a few years earlier. As I stood there, head bowed, listening to the minister consign all that was mortal of Torrance Ravencroft to the earth, I was aware of John and Aurelia and Dora Ravencroft standing on the opposite side of the open grave. Their faces, decorously solemn, gave no clue to their thoughts.

Brian was not at the graveside, nor had I seen him at the church, and yet the thought of him was with me, more real than the actual presence of his parents and sister. I hated myself for that. Although few people would have believed it, I had come to love Torrance. At this last solemn moment all my thoughts should have been of him. Instead, I was thinking of Brian on that glassed-in side porch, his voice thick with angry scorn. "At that time I didn't know you were for sale."

The verger was beside me, handing me a small shovel. I dug into the mound of freshly turned earth beside the grave and let a few rain-softened clods fall on the coffin. Then, feeling sad and empty, I turned away.

Three days later, in his Main Street office, Gerald Winship read Torrance's will to the Todd family and to Dilsey and to me, the only persons named in it. To his coachman and his cook he had left five thousand dollars, the equivalent of more than ten years of their joint wages. Each of the Todd girls received five hundred dollars. Dilsey Turman had been left only two hundred because, as his will explained, he was sure that I, his wife, would see to it that Dilsey was always well provided for. All the rest of his property, both real and personal, was left to "my wife, Fiona MacWain Ravencroft." There was an additional sentence that brought a smile to my lips, even as it made me realize how much I was going to miss him. "It is my fervent wish," he had written, "that she will use this money to reward her friends, confound her enemies, and, in general, have as good a time with it as I have had."

The Todd family and Dilsey left right after the reading of the will, but I stayed there for a while. Seated behind his desk, Gerald Winship made a tent of his fingers and smiled at me over the top. "Well, Fiona, how does it feel to be young, beautiful, and in sole command of a fortune?"

After a moment, I said, "Bewildering."

"Maybe I can help with that. I was Torrance's financial advisor as well as his lawyer, remember."

"Yes, I know."

"Would you like me to act in the same capacity for you?"

"If you were able enough to suit Torrance, you certainly should suit me."

"Good. I'll go over all of Torrance's—I mean your—investments. Most of them are sound, but I'm sure a few should be liquidated. Then you and I will have a conference."

Not replying, I sat motionless. At the word "investments," an idea had flashed into my mind, bringing me a sense of power and heady excitement. I said, "Do you know if Brian Ravencroft has raised the money to repair and outfit his whaleship?"

"No, he hasn't. Now he's trying to sell it outright, but with the proviso that he remain in command for at least the ship's next three voyages."

"Then he's back in Sag Harbor?"

Gerald nodded. "He came back from New York two days ago and went straight to Tom Stacewood at the bank and tried to sell him the *Silver Dolphin*. Stacewood said no."

"Why? Surely a whaler is a good investment."

"People are superstitious. If a whaler has two bad voyages in a row, talk starts that the ship's a Jonah."

"But surely hard-headed businessmen don't believe that nonsense!"

"You don't understand. Once a ship has such a reputation it's hard to sign crewmen aboard her—experienced ones, at least. And whaling is not only dangerous work. It's highly skilled. With mainly green hands aboard, the prospects of any voyage would be almost hopeless."

"But would people still regard such a ship as a Jonah if she had a new owner and a new captain? Wouldn't that take the curse off it?" Before he could answer, I rushed on, "I've heard the *Silver Dolphin* has an owner's cabin. Is that true?"

"Yes. What is this, Fiona? Do you want to buy the *Dolphin?*"

"Why not? I can afford to, can't I?"

"Yes, you can afford to. Do you want me to make Brian Ravencroft an offer in your name?"

"Not in my name! I want you to be the proxy buyer. I want you to keep my name a secret until after the papers are signed. *Then* he will meet the new owner."

His eyes, dark in his saturnine face, looked at me quizzically. Suddenly I was sure he had some inkling of the bitterness between Brian and me. Maybe Torrance had told him about it, or maybe he had just picked up some gossip. Anyway, he knew.

He said, "And his proviso that he should retain command of the ship?"

"I won't have that! He can sign on as mate, but not as captain. I have someone else in mind."

Gerald said, after a long moment, "Well, perhaps Ravencroft will agree to that. It will depend upon how hard up he is." He smiled. "It seems to me that already you are obeying that last injunction in Torrance's will."

"You mean about having a good time with the money?"

"I mean about confounding your enemies. Very well, Fiona. I'll get in touch with young Ravencroft right away."

We both stood up and moved toward the door. Then I halted. "Do you still want to buy that land?"

"What land?"

"The land adjoining your house. The land Torrance was too contrary to sell you."

"Yes, I'd still like to have it."

"Then it's yours, at the going price."

He smiled. "Thank you, Fiona. I can see that you are taking Torrance's advice about rewarding your friends, too. All right, I'll be in touch with you about the *Dolphin*."

Two afternoons later, the clerk who worked in Gerald's outer office brought me a note and handed it in to Clara Todd. Seated in the front parlor, I opened it and read what Gerald had written:

Well, it's settled. I have bought the Silver Dolphin *for you, at Ravencroft's asking price. It was fair enough, and I didn't think you would want me to haggle. For a while he balked at giving up com-*

mand of the ship, but finally agreed. It's obvious he is very hard up indeed.

I made it clear that I am not the real buyer. I told him that if he wanted to meet the new owner, and decide then whether or not he wanted to sign as mate aboard the Dolphin, *he could do so at three o'clock Thursday afternoon, here in my office. If that is not satisfactory, let me know. But I thought you might rather like such an arrangement.*

I remain,

> *Yr. obed. s'v't,*
> *Gerald Winship*

I certainly did like such an arrangement! Pulses quick with grim triumph, I folded the note and thrust it into the bosom of my dress. I had gotten to my feet and started across the room when I heard the knocker strike.

I waited. After a moment, Clara appeared in the parlor doorway. "Captain Slater to see you, ma'am."

"Please ask him to come in."

Steven Slater walked into the room. He bent over my hand and then said, "I have come to proffer my condolences."

"Thank you, Captain Slater. Please sit down."

When we were both seated, I said, "Shall I ring for tea? Or would you prefer something else? Sherry, perhaps?"

"Sherry sounds very pleasant. Will you allow me to pour it?"

"Thank you. And I will have a glass of Madeira, please."

As he stood beside the liquor cabinet, pouring wine into thin glasses, I was aware of how handsome he looked in black broadcloth trousers and fawn-colored coat and waistcoat. And he was not only handsome. He was intelligent, well bred, and brave. Any whaling master had to be brave. What was wrong with me? Why was it that he awoke in me none of the tremulous excitement, the yearning, that Brian Ravencroft had aroused?

For a while Steven and I sat there sipping our wine and speaking the conventional praises of that most unconventional man, my late husband. Then I said, breaking a brief silence, "I assume you plan to command the *Capricorn* on her next voyage."

"If that is agreeable to you, ma'am. After all, you now own the controlling interest in the ship. I had planned to sail early next month."

"If I asked you to, would you let someone else be master of the *Capricorn*, so that you could command another ship?"

His gray eyes looked bewildered. "I'm afraid I don't understand."

"I have bought the *Silver Dolphin*. She will need some repairs before she puts to sea again."

"The *Dolphin*! Brian Ravencroft's ship?"

"Yes. Since it has an owner's cabin, I intend to go on her first voyage under my ownership."

He leaned forward. "I will be delighted to command the *Dolphin*."

"Best to think about it first. She is considered a Jonah."

"The ship's had bad luck, that's all. One good voyage will end that superstitious talk."

I nodded. "That is my feeling, too. Now about my going on the voyage. The problem is that I realize I must have some suitable female companion."

"There is your personal maid. I think I have heard you call her Dilsey."

"I had thought it would be more circumspect to have as a companion some woman who is not a servant. Besides, Dilsey will not go with me. I broached the matter to her last night. She said that an obeah woman once told her that a sea voyage would mean her death." I smiled ruefully. "She seems afraid that if she goes along we will all drown.

"Of course," I went on, "I could send another letter to my mother. I have already written her of Torrance's death. I could ask her to accompany me on the *Dolphin*. But it would take weeks for her to receive such a letter, and more weeks for her to travel from Scotland to Sag Harbor, even if she decided to come. And I'm afraid she would not."

With a twinge of sadness I recalled my mother's last letter, which had arrived almost a month earlier. Unlike her previous letters, it had made not the vaguest mention of returning to America. Instead, there had been quite a lot in it about a childhood friend, Donald Cameron. Donald's wife had recently died—

For all I knew, I reflected, my mother was by now Mrs. Donald Cameron.

Steven said, "Perhaps I have the solution. My Aunt Prudence might agree to be your companion. She has been on sea voyages before. Her late husband, my uncle Mathias Slater, was the captain of a New Bedford whaler." He hesitated. "She might expect some sort of compensation. She is not at all well off."

"I wouldn't dream of not offering compensation."

"One other thing. She is quite deaf. But I gather you are mainly interested in preserving appearances, rather than acquiring an interesting companion. And she is of such obvious respectability that any gossip would be stilled at the start." He paused. "Shall I write to her? The packet ship to Boston sails tomorrow morning."

"Please do."

I looked at his handsome, enthusiastic face. I had to try to destroy the hope I saw in his eyes. Not to do so would be selfish and unfair indeed. I said haltingly, "Captain Slater, there is something I must say before we proceed with plans concerning the *Dolphin*."

My tone brought apprehension into his eyes. "Yes, Mrs. Ravencroft?"

"I know this seems an—an unwomanly thing to say, but I have gained the impression that you find me attractive."

His face flushed under its tan. "That is the case, Mrs. Ravencroft. While your husband was alive I of course tried to conceal it. And I had planned to say nothing until after a—suitable interval. But that is indeed the case."

"If I liked you less, Captain Slater, I might let you go on entertaining plans about me. But I do like you, and respect you, and so I must tell you that I do not have that—that sort of regard for you, and never shall."

The color ebbed away under his tanned skin. For a moment his gray eyes looked stricken. Then a certain stubbornness came into them. "Never is a long time, Mrs. Ravencroft."

"Captain Slater! If it is because of personal considerations that you have agreed to take command of the *Dolphin*, then I must warn you that you are sure to be disappointed."

"Very well. You have warned me. But I still would like to command the ship. And with your permission, I will write to my aunt."

"Only if I am sure we understand each other."

"You have made yourself very clear, Mrs. Ravencroft."

"Very well. Now there is one thing more. Would you object to sailing with Brian Ravencroft as your second in command?"

"Ravencroft?" I saw astonishment in his eyes, but nothing more. Perhaps he had never been ashore in Sag Harbor long enough to hear much gossip. In any case, it was obvious that he had no idea that Brian had ever been anything to me but my late husband's nephew. "But would he consent to sail as mate, particularly on a ship he once owned and commanded?"

"I don't know. He may not."

"Well, if he does, I would certainly have no objection. He's an excellent whaleman, so I hear. It is just that he's had bad luck on his last two voyages."

He rose, and so did I. "I know that Gerald Winship handled your late husband's business affairs," he said. "Will he act in the same capacity for you?"

"Yes. As soon as the *Dolphin*'s papers have been transferred legally to me, you and Mr. Winship and I will confer about repairing the ship and outfitting her."

"Very well. Good-bye, Mrs. Ravencroft."

Standing at the parlor window, I watched him stride down the walk. He didn't look like a man who had been rejected by a woman, rejected even before he proposed to her. Instead, there was confidence in his straight back. And why shouldn't he be confident? He was too intelligent not to know how much he had to offer a woman.

If I became lonely enough, I reflected, I might give in to temptation and marry him. But I hoped not. A man like Steven Slater merited a woman who would love him unreservedly, the way I had loved Brian until the night I came to hate him.

On Thursday afternoon I went down to Gerald Winship's office well before three o'clock. Thus I was already seated beside Gerald's desk when Brian entered the outer office. Heartbeats rapid, I heard him speak to the clerk. Then he was standing in the doorway of the inner office.

I think he must have guessed the truth almost immediately, because after a second or two the surprise in his face gave way to grimness. Gerald crossed the room. "Good afternoon, Mr. Ravencroft." Then, when they had shaken hands, "Of course, you know Mrs. Torrance Ravencroft."

"Of course." Face still bleak, Brian gave me a slight, stiff bow.

"Mrs. Ravencroft," Gerald went on, "is the new owner of the *Silver Dolphin*."

"I surmised as much when I walked in here and saw her." Brian's face was like a dark mask now.

"Sit down, please." Gerald waved a hand toward a straight chair facing mine and then returned to his own chair behind the desk.

When we were all three seated, I said, "Mr. Winship has told me that when he last saw you, you had not yet decided whether or not to sail as mate aboard the *Dolphin*."

"No, I had not decided."

"Before you do decide, perhaps I had best tell you that I plan to occupy the owner's cabin."

I saw a flicker of surprise in his face. Then he said, with no expression whatsoever, "I see."

"Perhaps you should also know that Steven Slater will be the new captain of the *Dolphin*."

That did affect him. The leap of pain in his eyes told me what he must feel at the thought of another man in command of a ship that once was his.

But evidently Gerald had been right about him. Evidently he was hard up indeed. Because after a moment he said, his face enigmatic once more, "Very well, I'll sign on as mate."

Chapter 11

ᘑᘑᘑᘑᘑᘑᘑᘑᘑᘑᘑᘑᘑᘑᘑᘑᘑᘑᘑᘑᘑ

The *Silver Dolphin* was more than a month out of Sag Harbor and less than a hundred miles off the Brazilian coast when the lookout, from his precarious perch inside an iron ring bolted to the mainmast, first sighted whales.

For me, the first weeks of the voyage had been in many ways as exhilarating as I had hoped they would be. On a March morning of sleet and freezing rain, the ship had left Long Wharf, sailed around Montauk Point, and then pointed her bow with its figurehead of an arched silver dolphin, south and east. Too far from shore to see anything except sky and water, we sailed past the mid-Atlantic states and Virginia and the Carolinas. Gradually the weather warmed, and sky and sea more often than not were blue and, for the first time in my life, I saw flying fish, looking like dragonflies with the moisture on their outspread fins iridescent in the sunlight. I also saw dolphins. They played about their huge wooden namesake, sleek bodies arching in and out of the water, and looking so graceful that it seemed strange that anything so clumsy as a whaleship should have been named after them. Still farther south giant turtles swam close to the ship, their brown shells, extended necks, and awkwardly paddling legs visible through a foot or so of water.

We stayed east of the Caribbean, but even so the islands that made up the West Indies sometimes were in sight, enchanted-looking islands, emerald or deep blue or even mauve according to the time of day and the quality of the light, floating in a sea that also changed color, from indigo to light blue to aquamarine.

At night, always accompanied by Prudence Slater, I

would leave our cabin to stand on deck, inhaling a tropic breeze that seemed to me laden with a flower-and-spice fragrance from those islands, and looking up at the stars. How strange to see, blazing low on the black velvet southern horizon, not familiar Sagittarius, but the brilliant stars that make up the Southern Cross. Thanks to the celestial map of the southern hemisphere, which Steven Slater had shown me, I could pick out Archernan and Al Suhail and other navigational stars with the lovely names given them by Arab astronomers many centuries ago.

As I implied, whaleships are ungraceful vessels, built for sturdiness rather than speed. But the large ones are roomy, and the *Silver Dolphin*, at four hundred and ninety tons, was one of the largest ever to sail out of Sag Harbor. The owner's cabin, a few feet down the afterhouse alleyway from the captain's quarters, afforded enough room so that Mrs. Slater and I seldom got in each other's way. Each of us had a bunk bed, wardrobe chest, and washstand. Each bunk had a green rep curtain, which could be drawn for privacy. Thus, long after Prudence Slater's gentle snores filled the cabin, I could lie awake in my bed. With the lamp still burning in its gimbals, affixed to the bulkhead beside me, I would read one of the scores of books I had brought from the Madison Street house.

I liked Prudence Slater. She was a little butterball of a woman with a remarkably wrinkle-free face that looked years younger than her snow-white hair. The day that Steven Slater brought her to tea at the Madison Street house, she said, "My nephew tells me you are a great reader. I am glad, because I won't be much company for you as far as conversation is concerned. Quite deaf, you know. I can hear you if you shout, but you'll soon get tired of that."

I had feared that she might become bored, far away from home and whatever friends she had, and unable to communicate with me except with considerable effort from us both. But she did not seem bored. She passed her days reading her Bible, the only book she had brought with her, and knitting caps and scarves and baby bonnets for her grandnephews and -nieces, and sometimes, with me beside her, walking around the afterdeck. The ease with which she nodded to a lookout sliding down from the rigging, or to the blacksmith at his bench pounding a bent harpoon back into shape, always reminded me that she had made several voyages with her shipmaster husband.

A cabin boy brought us our morning tea each day, but at noon and again at five o'clock we ate with Steven Slater in his quarters. Once in a while at table she would ask a question—"What is our position now?" or "When we stopped and gammed with the *Union* today, what news did they have?"—and Steven, leaning close to her ear, would shout an answer. But most of the time she devoted herself to her food, leaving Steven and me to talk of whatever we chose, from books to navigation, and from Sag Harbor to those South Pacific islands that at long last I would see.

Not once did he say anything that could possibly be construed as lovemaking. And yet I knew, just by his manner, that each day he became a little more confident of me. Lying awake at night, I would reflect bleakly that perhaps he would have a right to that confidence if Brian Ravencroft were not aboard this ship. Perhaps without the constant knowledge of Brian's presence, I might find myself increasingly responsive to the ardor I read in Steven's face. Why had I offered Brian the mate's position, anyway?

I, of course, knew why. It had pleased me to humiliate him in return for his humiliation of me. I hadn't realized how disturbing it would be to have him nearby, day after day, week after week. I remembered now how my mother had warned me, in effect, that I might find revenge a two-edged sword.

Knowing that Brian had the early morning and early evening watch, I usually was able to avoid him in the daytime by not going out on deck until nine in the morning. By that time I could be almost certain that he would have retired to his cabin to sleep or to work on the ship's log. At night I again would avoid the deck until past nine, when I could be sure that the dark, pacing figure atop the afterhouse, dimly illumined by the binnacle light, was not Brian but the third mate, Mr. Owen.

Every few days, though, I would catch sight of Brian, face shadowed by his visored cap, shoulders wide in the short "monkey jacket" that all whaleship officers wore, because a longer coat, by becoming entangled in a rope attaching a whaleboat to its fleeing quarry, might pull a man overboard.

Once I saw Brian drilling the five-man crew of his whaleboat. Around ten that morning I had been standing at the rail, gaze fixed on the glassy, foam-marbled water that seethed past the hull, unaware that Brian was even on deck. Then I heard the shrilling of a whistle and looked over my shoulder. Brian stood about midship, the whistle to his lips.

Noise and motion erupted all over the deck. I saw his crew streaking toward the rail—two young Sag Harbor boys who had signed on as "greenies," two Kanakas, and a Sagaponack Indian, six and a half feet tall, who, according to Steven Slater, was the best harpooner in the entire whaling fleet. Brian had joined his crew now. Moving almost too rapidly for my eye to follow, the men lowered a whaleboat and slid down the falls. Then, with Brian standing in the stern, long steering sweep in his hand, the oar-propelled boat shot through the water. Someone—perhaps the harpooner—tossed what looked like a beer keg with a rope wrapped around it into the sea. That, I realized, was supposed to be the whale. After standing statue still in the bow for a moment, the tall Indian tossed his harpoon at the floating keg. As soon as it struck, he and Brian changed places, maneuvering past each other with almost dancers' grace in the narrow boat. With Brian standing in the bow, the other crewmen, using paddles now instead of the long oars, brought the boat close to the keg. Lance in hand, Brian went through the motions of driving the metal as deeply as he could into the whale.

They had taken the keg aboard and were coming back now, their long oars making the boat, as graceful as its mother ship was clumsy, seem almost to fly over the water. Then, as the boat drew closer, I saw that Brian was looking straight up at me. I turned and went to my cabin.

On still another occasion, an instant after I had left my cabin to go on deck, I saw a man moving toward me along the narrow passageway. Since the light was behind him it took me a second or two to realize, from his broad-shouldered silhouette, that he was Brian. I stopped short, and so did he.

Pulses swift with anger, I stared at him. Obviously we could not pass each other without touching. I was about to retreat to my cabin when he said, "My apologies, Mrs. Ravencroft," and turned and retraced his steps. Emerging onto the deck, I walked past him with a brief nod and then moved to the rail. I did not look around until I heard his footsteps along the passageway, moving toward Captain Slater's cabin.

But it was not until the day the *Silver Dolphin* sighted whales that I realized just how rash I had been to embark upon a voyage that included Brian.

It happened about six in the morning. Shouts and the pound of running feet dragged me up from deep sleep. Red sunrise light filled the cabin. Somewhere frenzied voices were shouting "She blows! She blows!" and then "Breaches!" Heart hammering with excitement, I got out of bed.

Despite her deafness, Mrs. Slater must have become aware of the uproar because she sat up in bed and asked, in the flat voice of the deaf, "What is it, what is it?"

I moved across to her and bent close to her ear. "I think they've sighted a whale."

"Good!" She threw back the covers on her bed.

It took us at least a quarter of an hour to wash, dress, and comb our hair. There was no sound from the deck now, and so I knew that all four boat crews must be out on the water. Mrs. Slater and I hurried down the passageway and out onto the deck.

I gasped. It was not *a* whale the lookout had sighted but a pod of them, at least a dozen. Ahead of us, over a wide arc of sunrise-dyed water, I could see the flash of spouts again and again, as if invisible stones were falling at random into the ocean. Now and then, through the choppy water, I caught glimpses of the whales themselves, black, elongated shapes that looked enormous, even at a distance. And I could see other moving shapes, tiny by contrast, that I knew must be the whaleboats.

At my elbow someone said, "Beg pardon, ma'am."

I turned and saw Tommy, the cabin boy who brought Mrs. Slater and me our tea each morning. Fifteen years old and nearly six feet in height, Tommy seemed to have a child's ingenuous, freckled face attached to a man's body. In his hand he held a telescope.

"Cap'n said that when we sighted whales I was to fetch this glass from his cabin and give it to you, ma'am."

"Thank you." How like Steven to be that thoughtful.

Tommy said, handing me the telescope, "Look about ten points to starboard, ma'am. You'll see the cap'n. Fast to a big 'un, he is."

Tommy was right. When I pointed the glass in the direction he indicated I could see the fragile boat and the long stretch of hempen rope that held it to the harpooned whale. The creature, maddened by the iron sunk into its body, was towing the whaleboat at a greater speed than the *Dolphin* could achieve with all canvas set and a following wind. In the bow I could see Steven, fair head glinting in the sunlight as he waited for the moment when, like a matador, he could plunge the lance lethally deep into the lungs of the exhausted whale.

I asked, "Where's Mr. Ravencroft's boat?"

"The mate's? Swing the glass over portside. There! That ought to be it."

It was. I saw the boat alongside a whale several times its own length. I saw the Indian harpooner standing at the tiller in the stern, and Brian in the bow, lance upraised, aiming at a spot not far behind the eye in the enormous head. Brian lunged.

Quite suddenly, everything went wrong. I saw the boulderlike head turn, ramming the boat, spilling men into the sea. Then the head had disappeared beneath the water and the mighty flukes, perhaps twenty feet across, were raised skyward. I saw them descend upon the overturned boat and the helpless, struggling men. There flashed through my mind then all those stories of boat crews wiped out by one blow of a whale's flukes—

I felt someone take the telescope from my hand, heard Mrs. Slater say, "Grab hold of her, boy!" Then unconsciousness closed in around me like a dark gray fog.

I came groggily awake to find myself stretched out on my bunk, with Mrs. Slater sitting beside me. I looked at her dazedly for a moment and then cried, "Are they dead? Are they all dead?"

She must have guessed my question. She said, taking my hand and holding it between both of her own, "I don't know. The cabin boy will come and tell us as soon as there is any definite news."

I could hear many voices on deck now. Plainly, at least some of the boat crews were back aboard. I sat up in the bunk, intending to go find out for myself what was happening, but with surprising strength Mrs. Slater pushed me back against the pillow. "Stay here! Those men have their hands full without us getting in the way."

Their hands full. I thought of calloused, sun-browned hands lifting Brian's broken body from the water. And with a twist of agony I remembered the first time when, in a hansom cab carrying us toward the Brooklyn ferry, Brian's arms had gathered me close and Brian's lips, warm and tender, had come down upon mine.

Footsteps along the passageway. Someone knocked and then, after a few seconds, came into the room. I turned my head on the pillow and saw that it was not the cabin boy, but Steven Slater. He walked over to the bunk and stood looking down at me.

"I hear that you saw that whaleboat stove in. I'm sorry. I realize now that I shouldn't have given Tommy standing instructions to bring that telescope to you. But I had no idea—"

"Please!" I whispered. "The men in that boat. Are they all right?"

He hesitated and then said, "Most of them, although they were half drowned by the time the second mate's boat picked them out of the water. But one man has a broken leg, and another—well, we couldn't find him. Probably the whale's flukes broke his back or his neck, and he stayed under."

"Was it Brian?" Sitting up in bed, I grasped Steven's arm. "Was it?"

He looked down at me. When he finally spoke, his voice had an odd, remote tone. "No, the mate managed to swim clear. It was that Indian harpooner who drowned. Best harpoon man I ever sailed with." Then, careless of his aunt, whose puzzled and faintly alarmed gaze went from one to the other of us, he said in a flat voice, "So that's why I've had no chance with you."

With relief flooding all through me, I was unable to speak. He said "Why didn't you tell me you were in love with someone else? You needn't have told me it was Ravencroft. You could just have said—"

"But I don't love him! I hate him!" The flood of almost unbearable longing and regret I had felt only minutes ago was gone now. I was remembering things. Brian in that sordid room, saying he was crazy about me. Brian on the Main Street sidewalk, remarking that perhaps he should call me Aunt Fiona. Brian last New Year's Eve, telling me that in the past he hadn't realized I was "for sale."

Steven said, "It seems a strange kind of hating, Fiona, that could make you look terrified at the thought that he might be dead."

It was the first time, I realized, that he had called me by my first name. "I know," I said miserably. "It's as if part of me stays—stays attached to him even though the rest of me wishes I'd never met him. But I shouldn't have offered him the mate's position on this ship, especially not when I intended to be aboard also."

His tone was wry. "Well, I guess love can make all of us do strange things. For instance, I would like to manage it so that a block and tackle would fall on my first officer a few days from now. I don't imagine I'll do it, but I would certainly like to. Well, good-bye, Mrs. Ravencroft, I'm needed on deck."

Chapter 12

Partly because I was ashamed of myself, and partly because I still felt shaken, I did not join Steven Slater and his aunt for dinner that night, but ate from a tray Tommy brought to me. The next night, though, I did have dinner in the captain's cabin. Although I was aware of hurt and accusation deep in his gray eyes, his surface manner was as pleasant as ever. Before the pod of whales had scattered and fled, he told me, the boat crews had taken five of them, including the wounded whale that had killed the harpooner. The yield of the dead whales, which had been towed to the ship and then chained so that they lay parallel to the hull, might be more than four hundred barrels of oil.

By that time, the crew was trying out the catch—that is, rendering the oil out of the blubber in huge iron cooking vats set in a brick frame. All my life I had heard that trying out was a messy and unpleasant business, so unpleasant that I had no intention of going on deck until it was over. But even in my cabin I was aware of the greasy smell of cooking blubber, and I had a mental picture of the deck drenched with oil. On the third afternoon after the whale hunt I heard something bump against the side of the ship. I looked out a porthole and saw that the carcass of a cut-adrift whale was moving past, just below the surface of the water. The men up on deck had stripped the enormous creature of everything that could bring money. Because of whaling stories I had heard since I was a little girl, I knew that the crew must have first severed the giant head and brought it aboard in two sections, since it was too large for even a block and tackle to lift in one piece. I knew that the braincase had been opened and the spermaceti, a highly valuable substance used for making fine candles, had been ladled out. After that the blubber had been removed from the body of the whale in chunks large enough to kill a man if they fell on him. And then the huge carcass had been cut adrift.

I thought of that pod of whales, as I had seen them in the morning sunlight, spouting plumey white fountains and sometimes arching into the air like their graceful small cousins, the dolphins. So that some men could spend money at places like Josie Carpenter's, and others could build mansions in New Bedford or Nantucket or Sag Harbor, hundreds of thousands of those huge but harmless creatures had become like that ugly mass I had just seen floating past. Feeling sickened and ashamed—after all, that whale oil up on deck would make me richer, too—I turned away from the porthole.

Prudence Slater had looked up from her Bible. She said, eyeing me sharply, "What's wrong?"

I hesitated. Then I crossed to her side and bent down. "The whales!" I shouted. "It seems a shame to kill them just for barrels of oil."

Her gentle face grew stern. Too late, I remembered that she was the widow of Captain Mathias Slater, who had sailed in whaleships all his adult life. She said, "It isn't just the whales that get killed, my girl. So do men. You ought to know that, after what happened a few days ago."

But the whales don't start the violence, I wanted to say. Whales don't hunt men. Perhaps something of what I thought showed in my face, because she said, "It's a law of nature and of God. Creature preys upon creature. And as for man—well, it is right here in Genesis." Rapidly she turned the thin, rustling pages. "This is what God said to Adam and Eve. He said, 'Have dominion over the fish of the sea, and over the fowl of the air, and over every living thing that moveth upon the earth.'"

I nodded. To me also those words had been familiar ever since my early childhood. It was absurd, perhaps even wicked, to feel rebellious against them. And yet I couldn't help thinking that perhaps the Almighty could have arranged things a little differently.

"Besides," Mrs. Slater said, "if you don't realize al-

ready what seagoing men go through to get that whale oil,
just wait until we reach the Horn."

I knew I wouldn't have long to wait. Already the air
had grown much colder. Strange to think that it was now
May, and that back in Sag Harbor the air was sweet with
lilacs, and orioles were building nests in newly leafed-out
elm trees, and the transplanted wild iris were blooming in
the backyard of that little house where I was born. Here,
somewhere off the coast of Argentina, it was early winter.
One morning, about a week after that conversation with
Mrs. Slater, I awoke to see through the porthole that snow
was pelting the greenish-gray water. The snow proved to
be only a flurry, but during the next few days the sea and
sky remained gray and the air grew increasingly chill.

Less than three weeks after that first whale chase the
Dolphin encountered another pod, this time not of sperm
whales—we were by then in waters too cold for that spe-
cies—but the even more dangerous southern right whale.
I stayed in my cabin all during the hunt, and so it was
through Tommy that I learned that Brian's crew, in one of
the two spare whaleboats, had accounted for three of the
five whales taken. "That Mr. Ravencroft!" he said admir-
ingly. "The chances he took! All but climbed on the whale's
back, he did."

I could imagine how grimly determined Brian must
be, after that episode that had resulted in a drowned harpooner and a stove boat, to prove that the accident had been
in no way due to his incompetence. And perhaps something
else was spurring him on. Perhaps Steven Slater had let
Brian see some of the bitter hostility I had perceived in his
face when he spoke of arranging to have a block and tackle
fall on his first officer. If so, Brian, already humiliated by
sailing as mate on a ship that once had been his, would be
doubly determined to prove himself a better whaleman than
the *Dolphin*'s new master. I thought of those two men,
forced to go on working together in the weeks and months
ahead, despite their mutual hostility. Again I felt ashamed
that, in my desire to even the score with the man who had
wounded and humiliated me, I had made an unhappy situation for Steven Slater, too.

But in less than a week after the five right whales
were tried out we had started around the tip of South

America. After that I had no room in my thoughts for anything except the terror that the next sledgehammer blow of a gigantic wave, the next typhoonlike blast of shrieking wind would send the *Dolphin* plunging into fathoms of icy water.

Nearly forty-eight hours before the ship altered course to sail around the Horn, Mrs. Slater had suggested that we go up on deck. Through the fading light of a gray afternoon she pointed at a smudge on the western horizon and said, "That's Los Estados Island. Best take a good look, my dear. It's apt to be the last land you'll see for considerable time."

She was indeed right. By midmorning the next day the skies were almost black. Through the cabin porthole I saw that the long, smooth south Atlantic swells had changed to gray-black cliffs of water, topped with ragged spume, that slammed the *Dolphin* again and again, until she shuddered like a live thing. Just before noon Tommy came to our cabin. "Cap'n says best not to join him for dinner and supper until we're around the Horn, ladies. Ship tossing like this, you might fall and get hurt. I'll bring your grub." He added apologetically, "It's apt to be cold most of the time. Cook can't manage a fire if the gale gets worse."

I cried, clinging to the corner of my washstand, "Worse! How could it get worse?"

"It can, ma'am," he said, still in that apologetic voice.

It did. For four days and nights I could sometimes hear, through the hammer blows of waves and the howling of the wind, the groaning of the ship's timbers. Both Prudence Slater and I stayed fully clothed and in our bunks most of the time, and not just to ward off the Antarctic chill. To move about that tossing room was to risk broken bones.

The nights were indeed terrible. Because Mrs. Slater warned that an especially severe roll might dislodge the oil lamps from their gimbals, and thus cause a fire if the lamps were lit, we passed the nights in darkness. Even so, I found the days more horrifying, because then I could see through the porthole the towering green-black seas, studded with huge chunks of ice. I tried my best to read in the gray light that came through the streaming portholes. In her own bunk, Mrs. Slater read the Bible. Although her face looked pale and tense, she seemed far less frightened than I was. But then, this was her third trip around the Horn. And besides,

I reflected wryly, she had the added advantage of deafness.
The maniacal screaming of the wind and the crash of tons
of ice-laden water on the decks would be for her mercifully
muffled.

Wretched as I was, I knew that, compared to the men
on deck, Mrs. Slater and I passed our hours in cozy comfort.
When Tommy brought our meals—meals for which we
would have had little appetite, even if they had not consisted
mainly of bully beef and hardtack—he told us of what was
happening throughout the rest of the ship. Because of a leak
in the steerage, pumps were going night and day. Spars
were coated with ice, so that men in the rigging knew there
was constant danger that a misstep would send them plunging to the deck. Sleet cut their faces, and made the tilting
deck treacherous as a skating rink. The bowsprit had been
carried away, leaving the boom to slam against the bow,
and men had been sent overboard into the ice-laden water
to repair the damage.

On the sixth day after Mrs. Slater and I had gone on
deck to look at Los Estados Island, the wind suddenly
veered. Fog closed in. By ten in the morning I could see
nothing outside the portholes except dark gray smother,
although I could still hear and feel the pound of gigantic
waves against the ship. When Tommy brought us our noon
meal he reported that even "the old hands" said it was the
thickest, coldest fog they had ever experienced.

After two days of windless fog, although the ship still
rolled heavily, the seas were no longer mountainous. In
midafternoon Mrs. Slater and I ventured on deck for a few
lungsful of fresh air. We found ourselves in a strange world.
Water dripped like rain from the rigging, and fog was so
thick that the masts seemed to disappear at a point only a
few feet above the deck. We heard voices of men in the
shrouds and farther down the deck, but the men themselves
were at best dim, ghostlike shapes. For several minutes the
only face we saw was that of the helmsman, looking like
a death mask in the greenish glow of the binnacle light.
Until now I had considered the fog a vast improvement over
the shrieking gale. But here in this world of midday darkness
and dripping water and dim, looming shapes, I began to
remember stories I had heard of fog-shrouded vessels col-

liding with old wrecks afloat in these bleak waters, or with ships homeward bound from the Pacific.

Then I saw a man coming toward us, wide shoulders taking shape through the fog. The pulse in the hollow of my throat beat faster. After a moment, though, I saw that he was Mr. Owen, the pleasant third mate who, at almost forty, was the oldest officer on the ship. He said, "I hope you ladies have not been too uncomfortable."

I said, "We are managing," and then added, "How much longer do you think it will be?"

"Until we have rounded the Horn? Well, we are making little headway in this fog. But once it lifts, it should not take us more than four or five days."

The wind came howling back the next afternoon, ripping the fog to tatters. But even though it brought both mountainous seas and heavy snow, I was glad of the wind because it meant a speedier exit from this hellish region of raging wind and water.

Early in the afternoon four days later—days of gradually diminishing wind and waves—Steven Slater came to our cabin. He stood with his cap in his hand and his legs braced against the still-heavy roll of the ship. His eyes were so bloodshot and he had lost so much weight that I wondered just how many hours of sleep he had allowed himself these past two weeks. His manner, though, was as calm and courteous as if we were meeting in some drawing room on Sag Harbor's Captains' Row.

"We have passed the Horn, ladies. I hope you will give me the pleasure of your company at supper tonight."

Chapter 13

ᖴᖴᖴᖴᖴᖴᖴᖴᖴᖴᖴᖴᖴᖴᖴᖴᖴᖴᖴᖴᖴᖴᖴᖴᖴᖴᖴ

O n an afternoon five weeks later we anchored just before sunset outside the coral reef of Oluca Island. Since in the tropic night descends almost as soon as the sun is gone, Steven Slater had ordered that everyone must stay aboard ship until the next morning.

At supper the night before, he had told me of his intention to stop for several days at Oluca, a French possession in the Society Islands, so that he could buy fresh supplies from the trader there, and so that the crew could have a much-needed rest.

"But aren't you afraid of losing some of your men?" I had heard that quite often whaleship crewmen, rebelling against their hard life, had chosen to hide in some tropical island's interior until the ship sailed without them.

Steven smiled. "The *Dolphin*'s hold is more than half full of whale oil." During our voyage of several weeks from Cape Horn to these equatorial waters, the ship had taken not only sperm whales but several finbacks too, whose highly valuable oil was used to lubricate fine watches and other delicate instruments. "That means that even the greenies aboard, who'll have only a one-three-hundredth share of the profits, will be prosperous men for at least a little while after we get back to Sag Harbor. No, no one will desert."

Now I stood at the ship's rail, watching the blazing colors fade from sea and sky, watching the green island, with its crescent of palm-fringed beach, become a black silhouette against the last ashes-of-roses glow in the west. Soon even that bit of sunset light was gone, and the sky had become a deep blue bowl, illuminated by a half moon, and with the Southern Cross brilliant above the horizon. On the island's beach I saw a fire, only a small glow at first, but soon a bonfire whose flames wavered in the soft breeze. Then I heard the throb of drums and voices singing. The music was like nothing I had ever heard before, meltingly soft and sweet and yet sad, too. My throat tightened, and I felt a vague ache in my heart, a longing for all I did not have and might never have.

"Fiona."

With a start I turned and looked at Brian. I had assumed that at this hour he would be up in the darkness of the afterhouse deck. Too late I realized that aboard an anchored ship the officers would not need to stand regular watches.

"Fiona, listen to me."

His big square hand reached out and covered mine as it lay on the rail. I jerked my hand free, said, "How dare you?" in an even voice, and started to turn away.

He caught hold of my arm just above the elbow. "All right! Call your Captain Slater and have him keep me in irons for the rest of the voyage. But first I'm going to say something I've wanted to say for three years now, something you've never given me the chance to say. It's just this. I'm sorry, Fiona. I was a fool to take you to that tavern that night, and I'm sorry."

I did not answer, but apparently he sensed that I no longer intended to go to my cabin, because his hand fell from my arm. I turned back and looked at the red-gold beach fire and its long, wavering reflection in the lagoon's waters.

"I insulted you grievously," he said. "I knew that. I knew it almost as soon as I had done it. But after all, I did you no harm otherwise."

No harm! Before that night when he had treated me like a slut, he had made me love him. Even after I had come to hate him, the memory of the love I'd had for him made the feeling I could have for anyone else—even as fine a man as Captain Slater—seem a poor, pallid thing. And yet he claimed he had done me no harm.

"Anyway," he went on, "you have your revenge. You have it every day. I built the *Silver Dolphin*. I was her

captain. Do you know what it does to me to have to take
orders aboard what I still feel is my ship? Do you know
what a constant, daily, hourly humiliation does to a man?"

I felt a twinge of guilt and bitterly resented him for
making me feel it. "Then why did you sign on as mate?
You must have known what it would be like."

He said, after a long moment, "I needed the money.
And if the *Dolphin*'s luck holds up for the rest of the voyage,
I may have enough to buy a controlling interest in a new
ship. But as I said, Fiona, you've had your revenge. I'm
not suggesting that we be friends. I don't suppose we can
ever be that. But at least let's stop being enemies. After
all, we're going to spend months more aboard this ship. So
please, Fiona."

"Very well. We're not enemies." Then because his
voice, as he spoke those last three words, had held the tone
that used to shake me like a wind, I added quickly, "How
many people are on Oluca?"

"About three hundred natives. And of course there's
Miguel Costa, the trader. He's a Portuguese who deserted
about fifteen years ago from a Boston merchant ship. He
has a native wife and a half-dozen children. Costa's a rascal.
Maybe no more so than other traders in these islands, but
still a rascal. After the missionary couple who'd built a
bungalow near his store moved out, Costa started renting
it at fancy prices to sea captains or anyone else who wanted
to stay on solid land for a while. And of course he turns
none of that rent money over to the missionaries."

"Where did they go?"

"The missionary couple? To the other side of the
island. They have a school there and a little village made
up of their converts."

"But why did they move?"

"I suppose because they wanted their converts to stay
converted. And that would be hard to manage with somebody like Costa close by, not to mention the crews of the
whalers and merchant ships that anchor outside this lagoon."

And also not to mention the music of the other islanders. It was still floating across the water, lovely and
sad and sensual, bringing me the memory of how once I
had hoped that the man beside me would hold me in his

arms on just such an island, and on just such a night as this one.

I said abruptly, "Well, good night," and turned toward my cabin.

Around ten the next morning, two crewmen in a small dory rowed Steven Slater and me away from the ship. At my feet was my portmanteau, a canvas-wrapped bundle of books, and another bundle containing sheets and towels and a light blanket. Thus equipped, I intended to set up housekeeping for a few days in that missionary-built bungalow Brian had mentioned. I had tried to persuade Prudence Slater to come ashore with me, but she had refused. "As you know, I often accompanied my husband on voyages. But except for one occasion on the first voyage, I never went ashore on the Pacific islands. I found the behavior of the crewmen and the native women too offensive. You may go ashore if you like, my dear, but I shall stay here."

"Very well. I'm sorry you won't be with me." I knew that she had expected me to say that I, too, would stay aboard, now that she had given me her reason for doing so. But ever since childhood I had wanted to see an island like Oluca. Now, after this long and often hideously uncomfortable voyage, I was not going to forego my dream. After all, if I saw something that offended me, I could turn my head away.

The little boat skimmed over blue water sparkling in the sun, over a reef of ivory-colored coral clearly visible a few feet below the surface of the limpid green water. Before the dory moved on across the lagoon I caught a glimpse of a cloud of fish, multicolored as a rainbow, hovering beside the reef. When we were near the shore, brown young men in bright loincloths waded into the water and drew the boat up onto the sand.

Steven and I stepped out onto the beach to become the center of a small crowd. More tall, sturdy young Polynesian men. Pretty girls with their luxuriant black hair hanging down their backs. Older women, ranging from plump to downright fat, but all cheerful looking. Apparently

none of these people had ever seen a redheaded woman
before, because they pointed at my hair, chattering away
in a mixture of English and Polynesian, and two of the
older women reached out to touch it.

With the crewmen carrying my belongings, and with
the crowd trailing after us, we walked up the beach toward
a bungalow visible inside the first line of palm trees. "That's
the trader's place," Steven said. As we neared it, a dark-
haired man, barefoot and wearing none-too-clean white cot-
ton trousers and shirt, came down the bungalow steps to
meet us. He was about forty-five, still husky of shoulder
but with a waistline gone to fat. Behind him in the doorway
stood a large native woman with a baby in her arms and
two small children clinging to her skirts.

"How good to see you again, Captain Slater!" The
trader's English held only a trace of Portuguese accent.
"Your men who were here early this morning told me that
you are in need of tea, flour, jerked beef, and rum, among
other things. Fortunately merchant ships have delivered
cargo here twice this month."

"Fine. But see to it that I get no short weights this
time."

"Captain, you know I have never cheated you!" Miguel Costa's injured air was so patently false that I almost
laughed. Plainly, just as Brian had said, he was a rascal.
But he was an engaging one.

Now he was beaming at me. "And this is the lady
who is to occupy my fine bungalow?"

"Yes, this is Mrs. Ravencroft. Please show her the
bungalow now."

With the crowd still trailing along, Costa led us
through a small group of native houses thatched with palm
leaves and set on low stilts. In the cleared spaces between
the houses naked brown children played and chickens
scratched and a sow nursed a row of piglets. Before the
largest of the houses stood a tall, white-haired native wearing a necklace made of shells. Even before Steven introduced us, I realized he must be the village chief. Plainly
he had felt it beneath his dignity to come down to the beach
with the other villagers. Instead he had waited for us to
come to him.

We moved through the rest of the village and then

into a grove of coconut palms. In its midst stood a bungalow, thatch-roofed and bamboo-sided, which looked identical to those in the village we had just left. Costa spoke a few sharp words in Polynesian, the small crowd of natives stepped aside, and he led Steven and me into the bungalow. Its floor was of wide hardwood planks, and its furniture consisted of a wooden chair, a wooden-frame bed with a canvas-covered mattress, and a washstand that held an oil lamp as well as a pitcher and basin. Miguel Costa punched the mattress with his fist. "Genuine chicken feathers inside!" He moved to one of the two windows cut into the bamboo walls and let down a rolled-up blind of what looked like woven palm fronds. "See, everything just like back home, and only three dollars a day."

"Three dollars," I exclaimed. "Why, one can have the finest hotel room in New York City for less than that."

"Yes, lady." He gave me that rascally and yet somehow winning smile. "But on Oluca this is the only hotel room."

With an effort I managed not to return his smile. "All right," I said. "I'll take it."

During the next week I came to regret that decision. Oh, not during the days. The days were lovely. It would have been enough just to walk about on solid earth rather than an ever-moving deck. But in addition there was the silky sanded beach, where I often spread out an old shawl from my portmanteau and sat for an hour or so, either reading or just looking out over water that changed from blue to aquamarine and then back again. One morning I walked along the beach, clear to a sheltered cove on the other side of the island, and introduced myself to the missionaries, a Mr. and Mrs. Heathcote from Philadelphia. An earnest, kindly pair in their late thirties, they showed me the village inhabited by their converts, where the men wore not loin cloths but lavalavas reaching below the knees, and the women were enveloped from neck to instep in loose-fitting dresses. When I was ready to leave they pointed out a path that would lead me to the other side of the island and described the ferns and varieties of tree orchids I would see along the way.

Yes, the days were as enchanting as I had hoped they would be. It was the nights that made me wish I had never

come ashore on this island. The days belonged to the young
men pearl diving from their outrigger canoes in the lagoon,
and to the children playing in the dirt, and to the plump
married women chatting back and forth as they sat in village
doorways. The nights belonged to the throbbing drums, and
the singing voices, and the soft-eyed native girls, and the
crewmen off the *Dolphin*. More than once, as I lay awake
in my bungalow, I heard feet running through the palm
grove. I would hear a girl's squeal of mock protest, and a
man's low voice, and her provocative laugh, and then silence. And although I knew that I should feel repelled, or
at least shocked, all that I felt was a terrible loneliness.

Brian, I knew, was not on shore at night. I caught
glimpses of him during the day, going in and out of the
trader's bungalow, or inspecting the two whaleboats, which
had been brought up on the beach to have their seams
caulked. I had observed, though, that he and any other
officers who had come ashore were rowed back to the ship
in the late afternoon. Also, just at sunset, I had seen two
outrigger canoes, each carrying two girls, move out across
the lagoon to the anchored ship. Did one of those girls, in
spite of the proximity of Prudence Slater in the owner's
cabin, share Steven's berth? Perhaps. The idea did not dis-
turb me. It was the thought of Brian holding a naked brown-
skinned girl in his arms that filled me with bitterness and
pain.

Well, I kept reminding myself, very soon now we
would be away from this beautiful but hateful place.

The village had decided to hold a feast the night before
the *Silver Dolphin* was to sail. As the trader's fat wife told
me when she brought my morning tea, the feast would be
Oluca's way of saying aloha to us. By then I knew that
word, which Steven told me was used widely throughout
the Polynesian islands, and which means both welcome and
farewell. It was also a word that occurred frequently in the
most haunting of the songs I had heard the night the ship
dropped anchor out beyond the reef. After lunch, when I
walked down to the beach, I saw at least a score of young
men and women preparing the long trench in which the
festive food—fish and shellfish and pig—would be cooked
over heated stones.

The feast began during the brief tropic dusk, with a

streak of sunset red lying along the western horizon and a full moon rising in the east to send a shimmering path over the sea. Oil-soaked torches, attached to bamboo poles that had been sunk in the ground at intervals along both sides of the trench, seemed to burn more brightly as the last of the daylight faded. The chief sat cross-legged on a woven mat of dried grass at one end of the trench. Steven Slater and I, seated on similar mats, occupied the places of honor on either side of him. Next to me was Mrs. Costa, the trader's wife, and next to Steven was Miguel Costa. The rest of the space on both sides of the trench was occupied by the *Dolphin*'s three mates and her crewmen and by what seemed to me every villager over the age of fourteen.

The Costas had supplied tin plates and forks for those at our end of the trench, so that we would not have to snatch our food with our fingers from the heated rocks and then drop it into coconut-shell bowls. They had also supplied rum and some sort of white wine, dry and heady, to supplement the native drink, made from the fermented juice of various plant roots.

I knew that the food was good, from the ginger-flavored pork to the fish baked in banana leaves to the little red baked bananas themselves. But I really couldn't enjoy it. I was too taken up with the effort of not looking at Brian, farther down along the row of people opposite me.

As the feast went on, the talk and laughter grew louder. At the far end of the trench a girl began to sing that song I found so disturbingly beautiful. After a moment a native drum joined in, and a sort of stringed, lutelike instrument, which I had heard almost every night this past week. Miguel Costa was holding a wine bottle toward me again. As I had far too often, I extended one of the thick glasses with which the Costas had supplied all of the island's visitors, and he filled it almost to the brim. Although I did not look at Steven Slater, I sensed that he was watching me with puzzled anxiety. I did not care. The wine helped ease that tight feeling in my chest, a feeling that had seemed to grow a little worse each day this past week.

The wistful melody had given way to another song, a kind of chant. The drum quickened its beat. Many of the girls were on their feet and dancing now, graceful bare arms raised, lithe bodies swaying. After a minute or so, they began to stretch out their hands to members of the *Dolphin*'s crew in smiling, wordless invitation to join the dance. Many of the men did, stomping the ground in ludicrous, drunken imitation of the girls' sinuous movements and eliciting shouts, some derisive, some encouraging, from their equally drunken shipmates.

A girl was dancing close to Brian. Although still seated on a mat, he had turned away from the food-filled trench to watch her. She extended slender brown hands, fingers wriggling an invitation to dance with her. Smiling, he shook his head. But his dark-blue gaze was so admiring that I did not wonder that she stayed there, dancing just for him, rather than seeking a partner from among the other men.

I recognized the girl. She was one who had stood in the prow of an outrigger canoe as it moved across opalescent water toward the ship two nights before.

Suddenly I could stay there no longer. I leaned toward Steven, trying to pitch my voice so that it would be audible beneath the throbbing drum, the singing, the intoxicated laughter. "I—I don't feel well. I think I'll go to my bungalow. Will you explain to the chief and to the Costas?"

He looked worried. "I had best come with you."

"No! I mean, no thank you. It's just too much wine, and all the noise. I'll be all right."

"Very well," he said, after a moment. He came around the end of the trench and helped me to my feet. The chief was looking at us with puzzlement plain in his dignified face. I gave him an apologetic smile, and Steven said a few words in Polynesian. The Costas, though, were so absorbed by the revelry farther down the two lines of feasters that I'm sure they did not even notice when I slipped away up the path to the village.

In the bright moonlight the cluster of small houses was silent, seemingly deserted. Aware that my gait was far from steady, I moved on, hoping that once I was in my bungalow I would not be able to hear those laughing, singing voices.

Inside the wind-stirred palm grove, moonlight and shadow made moving patterns on the earth. I realized that I must be very drunk indeed, because when I looked at those shifting light-and-shadow patterns the earth seemed to move beneath my feet, as the ship's deck had done for so many weeks. With an impulse toward tears, and with footsteps that were slower and more careful now, I moved toward the dark bungalow.

Footsteps behind me. I turned. A moving patch of moonlight showed me the visored cap shadowing the face, the uniform with its whaling officer's short jacket. I said, feeling more tearful than ever, "Oh, Captain Slater." My tongue felt oddly thick. "I didn't want to spoil the evening for you. I told you not to—"

"I'm not Captain Slater," Brian said, and kept on walking toward me.

Anger mingled with my urge to weep. "What do you think you're doing?" At least I believe that is what I said. Afterward I was never quite sure what words the two of us had used that night. "Now go away and leave me alone."

"No." He had stopped in front of me. "You don't want me to do that."

"Don't want you to! What on—"

"Fiona, listen to me!" His hands had shot out and grasped my upper arms. "I was a fool once. But you've been an even bigger fool ever since. How long are you going to keep it up?"

"Let me go!" I tried to pull away from him. His hold on my arms did not slacken. "If you don't let me go," I threatened, "I'm going to scream and scream and—"

"Yes, you can do that. Slater or someone will hear you. He has the power to keep me in the brig all the way back to the States, and I'm sure he would do so with the greatest of pleasure. So go ahead and scream."

I stood silent, miserably aware even in my tipsiness that I did not want that to happen to him.

"Oh Fiona!" One of his arms went around me, pulling me close against him. With his other hand he tilted my chin and then brought his lips down on mine. I twisted my mouth free and said desperately, "You're not fair! I've had too much wine—"

"Don't talk to me about fair!" His hand forced my face back toward his. "Not after I've waited all this time."

Again his mouth covered mine. I fought him, pushing against his hard shoulders with the heels of my hands, trying to wrench my lips free from the demanding pressure of his.

But even as I fought I was aware that his kiss, and his arm holding me pinned to him, had set up a wild clamor in my blood.

And then it was all too much for me. Not just my tipsiness, and the moonlight, and his lips that had left my mouth now to kiss my throat. I think that it also must have been the accumulated strain of those years in which, whether I loved him or hated him, he had been the emotional center of my life. The last of my resistance crumpled under a great wave of loneliness and desire. I made a whimpering sound and wound my arms around his neck. Again he kissed my mouth, and I became dimly aware that my lips had become soft and accepting beneath his.

He lifted his mouth from mine and looked down at me through the moonlight, dark gaze searching my face. As if from a distance I heard his soft, triumphant laugh. Then he bent and lifted me into his arms. I made no effort at all to stop him.

When I awoke in the morning I was alone in the bed. For a merciful moment or two I was aware only of the bright sunlight flooding through the windows, and of a slight ache behind my eyes. Then I became aware that I lay naked beneath the sheet.

Memories of the past hours, disjointed and shameful, tumbled through my mind. Brian undressing me. Brian lying beside me in this bed, head propped on one elbow, dark face looking down at me, with a smile curving that full lower lip. Brian's hand caressing me from throat and shoulders to thighs. And, finally, my body's complete acceptance of him, not once but several times.

Now I lay here alone, hearing once more in my imagination that low, triumphant laugh with which he had lifted my drunken self into his arms there in the palm grove. I felt a humiliation more scalding than I had known it was possible to feel. To over-thirty Brian Ravencroft—far from rich now and reduced to taking orders aboard a ship where he had once given them—to that Brian I had granted what I had refused to a younger, highly successful Brian. Perhaps he had been sure I would, even as he followed my uncertain footsteps through the silent village. How triumphant he must feel. For him, last night had made up for everything, including the afternoon when he had learned that I was the new owner of the ship he had built.

Even in my most bitter moments these past few years I had not thought Brian capable of taking advantage of a woman who, out of unhappy loneliness, had indulged too heavily in drink. Now I knew that he was capable of it.

And I knew something else. I could not spend any more days, let alone weeks or months, in Brian's company aboard the *Dolphin*. I lay there, forcing my distracted thoughts into some sort of order, until I had decided what I must do to salvage at least a little of my self-respect.

About an hour later, in an outrigger canoe manned by a young native boy, I approached the starboard side of the *Dolphin*. A crewman, idling at the rail, sighted me, let down the rope ladder with its iron rungs and, hands reaching down, helped me onto the deck.

The first person I saw after I stepped aboard was Prudence Slater. Seated on a stool near the now-idle try works, she was knitting something dark green, a shawl, perhaps. Then, with an almost physically painful leap of my heart, I saw Brian. He stood over by the midship rail on the port side, and he was talking to Mr. Owen, the third mate, and Mr. Sanford, the ship's blacksmith. And, just as Brian had laughed in triumph when he saw complete surrender in my face the night before, all three of those men were laughing now.

Laughing at what had happened to Fiona MacWain Ravencroft, widow of a man old enough to be her grandfather. Fiona, who had dared to buy the *Dolphin*, and dismiss the ship's former captain, and travel in the owner's cabin to this beautiful and treacherously seductive part of the world. I felt not just my face but my whole body burning with shame.

The blacksmith had seen me. He said something to the other two. Brian turned, a startled look on his face. Then, smiling, he moved toward me. I waited, somehow holding my head high, until he was quite close. Then I said, in a voice as cold and curt as I could make it, "I want to see you in my cabin, right now."

His smile vanished. After a moment he nodded. Aware that he followed, I moved down the afterhouse passageway to my cabin. When we were both inside the room with the door closed, I said to him, "I am not sailing on the *Dolphin* today."

He stared at me. "Not sailing! What are you going to do?"

Again I made my voice as cold and contemptuous as I could. "That is no concern of yours."

"Fiona! What's wrong? I'd have thought, after last night—"

"Last night," I said bluntly, "I was drunk. Did you dream that I would have let you touch me otherwise?"

An angry flush made his dark face even darker. Then, as he stared at me silently, the color drained away, leaving him with a gray look.

"If you'd been a gentleman," I went on, "it would never have occurred to you to take advantage of the fact that I'd had too much to drink. But you Ravencrofts have never been much hampered by ethics, have you?"

Still he did not answer but just stared at me, lips compressed, and his pupils so expanded now that his eyes looked not dark blue but black. "That's all," I said curtly. "You can go now."

He moved to the door. Then, hand on the knob, he turned to face me. "Rest easy, Mrs. Ravencroft. If I can help it, I'll never come near you again."

I waited until I heard his footsteps die away down the corridor, and then waited some more until my hammering heartbeats slowed. Then I went down the passageway and tapped at Steven Slater's door. He called, "Come in."

I found him seated at his desk with the ship's log spread out before him. Quickly he got to his feet. "Good morning." His manner was as courteous as ever, but a strained quality in his smile made me think that he suspected why his first officer had left the feast and not returned. Well, that look in the eyes of this young man, a man whose good opinion I valued, was just another penalty I would have to pay for my stupidity.

He indicated a chair. When we were both seated, I said, "I am not sailing with you. I shall stay on Oluca until I can get passage home on another ship—a ship whose captain has brought his wife with him, of course."

I knew that there would be such ships. During our

week's stay on Oluca a homeward-bound Nantucket whaler and a Boston merchantman had anchored outside the reef long enough to take on supplies. And according to Miguel Costa two Sag Harbor–based ships, both heading home, had stopped at the island earlier that month. None of those ships had carried women passengers, but Costa had told me that not infrequently the ships that stopped at the island had not only captains' wives aboard but their children as well.

Steven looked astounded. "But you can't stay there in that bungalow for days or even weeks, not when the only other white person nearby is that ruffian of a trader!"

"I will stay there only tonight. Tomorrow I will go to the missionary couple on the other side of the island. Their bungalow has an extra bedroom. I am sure they will let me stay with them."

He said, after a moment, "Why are you doing this? Has somebody aboard this ship offended you?" His tone hardened. "If so, I will make sure that you do not even see him for the rest of the voyage."

I knew what he meant. Brian, confined to the brig, with the second mate promoted to first, and Mr. Owen promoted to second, and one of the harpooners promoted to Mr. Owen's position. For a moment I relished the thought. But even if I did not see Brian, I would still be aware of his presence aboard the ship.

"If you don't mind," I said, "I would rather not discuss my reasons for remaining behind. Let us just say that I have not found life aboard a whaleship completely to my taste."

After a moment he inclined his head.

"But I do worry about Mrs. Slater," I added.

"You needn't. This will be far from the first time my aunt has been the only woman aboard a whaleship."

"If I write a note of explanation, will you give it to her?" I did not relish the thought of shouting in her ear for several minutes.

He nodded.

"As soon as I've written the note, I'll pack all my belongings still in my cabin. Will you please have them sent ashore in one of the whaleboats?"

"Of course. But I wish I could dissuade you."

I managed to smile. "I'll be all right. Why, probably I'll be back in Sag Harbor well before you are."

"Probably. We may be out here in the Pacific whaling grounds for any time from another few weeks to several months. It all depends upon what luck we have."

We were both silent for a few moments. Then I said, "I'd also like you to carry a message to Gerald Winship, empowering him to keep managing my business affairs for as long as I'm away." I hesitated, and then went on, "I intend to instruct him that Brian Ravencroft is not to sail again on the *Silver Dolphin* or on any other ship in which my husband left me an interest, if he can possibly be prevented from doing so. If—if by any chance you sail again before I return to Sag Harbor, I hope you will remember my wishes when choosing your officers."

Steven Slater said grimly, "That is one thing you can be sure of."

When I left my cabin to move onto the deck about forty-five minutes later Brian was nowhere in sight. Prudence still sat beside the try works, though, gaze lowered, hands plying the long bone needles. I felt ashamed of myself for not saying good-bye to her. But my decision not to do so sprang from more than the fact that it was difficult to communicate with her. I knew I would not be able to fob off on her the vague explanation that I had not found whale-ship life to my taste. Steven had been compelled to accept it, but his aunt would ask questions, looking right through me with those calm, experienced eyes as she did so.

With the aid of a crewman—not the one who had helped me aboard but one of the young "green hands"—I descended to the waiting outrigger canoe.

That night, after the trader's wife had brought my dinner, the last dinner I would have in that bungalow, I went outside. I walked through the palm grove and the village, now filled with the sound of talk and laughter and the smell of fish and taro root cooking over open fires, to the deserted beach. Standing there I looked out over water stained with faded sunset color to the spot where, until midafternoon, the *Dolphin* had lain at anchor.

"Hello, lady," Miguel Costa's voice said.

I turned, aware that he had called out while still some distance away, so as not to startle me. I answered his greeting, and he crossed over the soft sand to stand beside me. "Then you are leaving us tomorrow."

"Yes, right after breakfast. I've engaged two of the village boys to take me and my belongings around to the missionary settlement in their canoes."

The trader sighed. "A sad business."

"Well, Mr. Costa, I should think you would have to agree that it will be far more suitable for me to stay with Mr. and Mrs. Heathcote."

"Of course, of course! I did not mean that. I mean it was a sad business about you and the *Dolphin*'s chief mate."

I stiffened with incredulous shock. Whatever he knew or had guessed, how dare he mention it to me!

"A sad business for me, too," he went on.

Bewildered now, I said, "I haven't the slightest idea what you're talking about."

"Why, the wine he was going to buy so that everybody aboard the *Dolphin* could drink your health! Twenty bottles of very expensive wine I bought off a French merchantman more than a year ago and haven't been able to sell. And now I've still got it on my hands."

After a long moment I said, very slowly, "Mr. Costa, will you please tell me just what happened about—about the wine?"

"Of course. This morning I had just gotten up when here was the chief mate hammering on my door. He said he wanted me to put my best wine, as much of it as I had, aboard the ship before she sailed. You and he would be getting married, he said. I asked when, and he said you hadn't set the date yet, but as soon as the ship was at sea the captain would have the right to tie the knot. Happiest looking young fellow I ever saw in my life. Then just before noon he sent a note ashore by one of the crew saying he wouldn't need the wine after all. Then when I learned the ship was going to sail without you—"

He broke off. "Hey, lady! Don't look at me like that. I guess I been talking way too much, huh?" Then, defensively, "But you asked me about the wine."

I somehow managed to say, "It's all right, Mr. Costa. But if you don't mind—"

"What? Oh, I see. You don't feel like company just now. All right. I'll see you in the morning, and we'll settle up for what you owe me for the bungalow."

He moved away. I stood looking out over the rapidly darkening water to where the *Dolphin* had lain. I felt a strange mixture of joy and poignant regret. If only I could turn time back about nine hours, back to a moment before I had stepped aboard the ship to lash him with perhaps unforgivable words.

Why had I assumed that he had taken me coldly, calculatedly, contemptuously? True, there had been that episode at the tavern north of New York City. But yesterday evening he had said that he had behaved like a fool that night. Why hadn't I realized that Brian Ravencroft, like anyone else, could change over the years?

And why had I leaped to the conclusion this morning that his laughter and the third mate's and the blacksmith's had been salacious laughter, directed at me? Oh, perhaps I had reason to, considering my shamed awareness that I'd had too much wine the night before, and my memory of Brian's low, exultant laugh as he lifted me from my feet. But I realized now that the overwhelming probability was that they had been laughing at something that had nothing whatever to do with me.

I thought of the *Dolphin*, miles away now over the dark water. I could have been aboard her, excitedly conferring with Prudence Slater about what I would wear for my shipboard wedding. And later on, after I had transferred my belongings to Brian's cabin, the old dream would have come true, the dream of sailing tropic seas as Brian's wife.

But the dream could still come true, I told myself feverishly. With any luck at all, I would be waiting on Long Wharf when the *Dolphin* dropped anchor there. Perhaps it would be even better that way. Granted, Steven Slater would have performed the marriage ceremony with as good a grace as he could muster. Nevertheless he would have found it both humiliating and painful, and the knowledge of what he felt would have shadowed my own happiness. Better that Brian and I be married in Sag Harbor, in that lofty-spired structure that had replaced God's Old Barn, which the townspeople had begun to call the Old Whaler's Church.

The moon, rising later than the night before, now loomed red-gold through the horizon mist. Up beyond the first line of palms a drum began to throb an accompaniment to a girl's singing. Beauty hurts when you're alone. I turned my back on the moon and started walking along the beach, hoping to escape that singing voice.

Tomorrow night I would be on the other side of the island, away from this disturbing music and the soft, sensuous laughter of young men and women. And in another few days, pray heaven, I would be aboard a Sag Harbor–bound ship.

Chapter 14

∞∞∞∞∞∞∞∞∞∞∞∞∞∞∞∞∞∞∞∞∞∞

On a morning eight months later—eight tormenting, endless months—the Sag Harbor merchantman upon which I had finally obtained passage rounded Cedar Point and sailed toward Long Wharf.

For the first week or two after I had taken up residence with Mr. and Mrs. Heathcote I had felt confident that soon I would be on my way home. In fact, I had felt so confident that I had even been able to enjoy helping Mrs. Heathcote teach the English alphabet to small children and give the women sewing lessons, so that they could make the modest dresses they wore. What matter that as yet no ships at all, since the *Dolphin*'s departure, had lain at anchor beyond the lagoon on the other side of the island? Soon ships would arrive.

And they did. During the weeks that followed, boys from the village near the trading post brought me word of more than a dozen visiting ships. The trouble was that none was suitable to my purpose. Most of the whalers had so little oil in their holds that they could not hope to head back toward Sag Harbor—or New Bedford or Nantucket—for many months. Most of the merchant ships were en route to Hong Kong or Australia, rather than home. And of the ships that were headed in the right direction, not one had officers' wives aboard. Even if I had been willing to take passage on any of those ships, a lone young woman among at least a score of strange men, no captain would have allowed me to do so.

When more than two months had passed, I decided that at least I could send letters by the next homeward-bound ship. Even if I did not arrive in Sag Harbor before the *Dolphin*—and I still had every hope that I would—my letters surely would do so. Accordingly, I wrote to Gerald Winship, countermanding my order that Brian should never sail again aboard any ship in which I had a controlling interest. And I wrote to Brian. In fact, I wrote about a dozen letters to him—some abject, some defensive, some far, far too bold—until I finally composed one that satisfied me. I felt that my letter, without too much sacrifice of dignity, conveyed to him my love, my regret, my hope that we could "both stop being fools, and be happy together." Six weeks passed before another homeward-bound ship, a Boston merchantman, dropped anchor at Oluca, but at least I was able to send my letters on their way.

Another tormenting two months passed before the sort of ship I'd been waiting for arrived. She was the merchant vessel *Phoebe Claymore*, one of the few ships that still carried on Sag Harbor's once-thriving trade with the Far East and the Carribbean. She was bound for home. And she carried the wife and two small children of the first mate, a New Bedford man. Pray heaven, I thought, as a dory carried me and my belongings out to the *Phoebe*, pray heaven that the *Silver Dolphin* had encountered very poor luck, so poor that she was still in the south Atlantic, or even here in the South Pacific, vainly hunting whales.

The return voyage was not a pleasant one. To make room for me, the third mate moved in with the second mate, thus leaving me his own cabin, which was cramped and ill ventilated. I did not hit it off well with the first officer's wife, a thin blonde young woman. She was shocked, or pretended to be, that I had lived all that time on that island without a husband's protection, even though I reminded her more than once that I had been living with a missionary couple. And I found that her shrill scolding of her children and her disparaging remarks about her husband got on my nerves. Furthermore, the rounding of the Horn seemed to me as terrible as it had been the first time. No, not quite, because this time I had known what to expect. Nevertheless, the demonically howling wind and the towering, ice-laden waves were like a prolonged nightmare. But at least I knew that each day, each hour, brought me nearer to home.

Once around the Horn we moved northward through

gradually warming air. To my intense frustration, we stopped for a week in Jamaica, so that the *Phoebe* could discharge tea from Hong Kong, take aboard rum, and have repairs made to pumps that had never worked properly since our arduous passage around the Horn. But at least there was a sleek trading schooner tied up alongside the *Phoebe* at the wharf in Jamaica Bay. After I learned that the schooner was sailing the next day, and that Sag Harbor was among her ports of call, I again wrote to both Brian and Gerald, giving the approximate date of my arrival, and sent the letters over to the schooner's captain. That graceful ship, so much swifter that the square-rigged *Phoebe*, would reach Sag Harbor at least two weeks before we did. Thus, if the *Silver Dolphin* had reached home before me, I almost certainly would see Brian waiting on Long Wharf.

Now, as we glided over the calm waters of Sag Harbor Bay, I could see the flag on Beebee's Mill, announcing our arrival. Through the expectant pounding of my heart I could hear a rattling noise as crewmen, up in the rigging, took in sail for the last long glide to Long Wharf.

And then we were there, and with my hands gripping the rail I scanned the upturned faces, most of them familiar to me, of townspeople who had flocked down to the wharf. My gaze found Gerald Winship's thin, dark face, and I smiled at him as he lifted his tall beaver hat. Then my eyes went on searching.

He wasn't there.

Well, I told my anxious heart, that did not necessarily mean that he had come home and sailed on some other ship, perhaps without receiving either of my letters. It might mean that the *Silver Dolphin*, after leaving Oluca, had been plagued with all the ill luck I had wished for her, luck so bad that she was still out there somewhere on one of the world's oceans, trying to fill the empty spaces in her hold.

The gangplank had thumped down. Carrying my portmanteau—my trunk and my box of books would be delivered later to the Madison Street house—I descended to the wharf. Smiling, Gerald took the portmanteau from my hand. "You're looking splendid, Fiona. You're thinner, but you look fine."

"So do you," I said, as we moved along the wharf. And he did. It was not just his shiny new beaver hat and his frock coat of fine broadcloth, but his general air of well-being.

He laughed. "Perhaps my new prosperity is becoming to me. Remember that land you sold me, those hundred acres adjoining my own property? Well, not two months later a New York real estate firm offered me a whacking big sum for it. I sold them my original property, too. I think they expect that a railroad will be built out to eastern Long Island, and they hope that spot between Sag Harbor and Bridgehampton will become the terminal. Well, here's my carriage."

It too looked new. Roofed but open sided, it was the sort of light, four-passenger vehicle that had become popular, now that it was fashionable for younger men to handle the reins themselves, rather than employ a coachman. "Did you buy this with part of your profits?"

"That I did. I also bought the old Wellville house on Latham Street, practically around the corner from your house."

When he had placed my portmanteau on the rear seat, handed me into the front, and gotten in to sit beside me, he said, "I really feel I should give you part of the profits."

"I don't need them."

Reins in his hands, he turned to me smilingly. "I guess you don't, especially after the *Dolphin*'s last voyage. You certainly brought her luck, even if you did let her come home without you."

My heart gave a painful leap. "Then the *Dolphin* came back?"

"Six months ago, with every barrel aboard her filled. Captain Slater told me that off Peru, a couple of weeks after they left you on Oluca, they hit a spot where the whales practically swam into the try pots. They filled the hold and headed straight for home.

"Now what do you say," he went on, as the white horse drawing the carriage broke into a brisk trot, "that we drive along Main Street and then circle over to Madison Street? We had a hurricane while you were away and it uprooted some big trees along Captains' Row. You might be interested to see that. And I can talk to you about business matters as we drive along."

"All right." Then, from a constricted throat, "Has the *Dolphin* sailed again?"

"Yes, under Captain Slater, six months ago. If she has the same sort of luck she had last time out she should be home soon."

"And—and Brian Ravencroft? Did he sail with her?"

Gerald turned an astonished face toward me. "Of course not. For one thing, Captain Slater had given me that note from you, saying that under no circumstances was Ravencroft to sail on the *Dolphin*. True, afterward you sent me a letter countermanding that order, but it didn't arrive until weeks after the *Dolphin* had sailed again. And anyway, Ravencroft had told me the day he came back from that voyage you were on that he would not sail again on any ship in which you held an interest."

I said painfully, "Then he sailed on someone else's ship."

"No. Listen, Fiona." There was embarrassment and concern in his voice now. "I know it is none of my business, but it's easy to guess that there was some—some sort of trouble between you and young Ravencroft on that voyage."

"Yes. But from Oluca I wrote him a letter that should have set things right. I sent it at the same time as I sent that letter to you, so if he was still here he should have gotten it. Was he?"

"Yes, he was here."

"Is he here now?"

"Yes. See that hole at the edge of the sidewalk? That's where one of the trees felled by last September's hurricane stood. It was a big elm, at least forty years old."

"Oh," I said mechanically. "That's too bad. But tell me about Brian. What is he doing?"

"Well, his share of the profits from that voyage was substantial, of course, and his father's prospects have been looking up, too, and so they plan to start a new packet-ship service between Sag Harbor and Boston and other New England cities. I guess they think it will be less risky than whaling." He paused, and then added with a rush, "Besides, I hear that Pamela doesn't want Brian to go to sea any longer."

Terror tightened my nerves. "Pamela! What Pamela? And what does she have to do with it?"

"Pamela Stacewood. I mean, that used to be her name. Brian married her about a month after the *Dolphin* got back."

Stunned, I turned my head away and stared at the houses we were passing. I had been gone from Sag Harbor for thirteen months. It was April now, with daffodils and a few early tulips bright behind picket fences, and willow trees trailing graceful yellow-green branches at the curbside. April, the month of renewal. But Brian was married, and I, at twenty-four, felt old and finished.

Chapter 15

B efore leaving Sag Harbor I had given the Todd family
an indefinite leave of absence. Dilsey, though, had
stayed on in the Madison Street house while I was gone.
Before Gerald and I were halfway up the steps she had the
door open. As soon as we were inside the house she said,
"Oh, child! I'm so glad to see you," and burst into tears.

"And I'm glad to see you." Arms around each other
we both wept.

After a moment I moved away from Dilsey's embrace
and daubed at my eyes with a handkerchief. I tried to smile
at Gerald. "You'll have to forgive this display of emotion."

He returned my smile. "Why, it's only natural." But
something in his eyes told me that he knew my tears sprang,
not just from the joy of reunion with a beloved servant and
friend, but from a far less happy cause. He went on, "I'll
leave you now. Do you want to come to my office at three
tomorrow? We can go over certain matters in detail, such
as your profits from the *Dolphin*'s last voyage."

That "lucky," too-brief voyage, which had brought
me money I did not need and made me lose all that I had
ever really wanted. "Yes, I'll be there."

When he had gone, Dilsey and I went up to my sitting
room and bedroom on the second floor. On a table beside
a window, its freshly laundered curtains stirring in the light
spring breeze, stood a green glass bowl filled with fragrant
poet's narcissus. Dilsey said, "Mr. Winship told me two
weeks ago that you'd written from Jamaica you would be
home soon, so I kept putting fresh flowers here every few
days."

"They're lovely."

She looked at me with sorrowful brown eyes. "Mr. Winship told you, didn't he?"

I didn't pretend not to know what she meant. "Yes, he told me."

"Didn't I warn you? Didn't I tell you if you kept driving him away from you, someday he'd—"

"Dilsey! Now don't start that!"

"You was such a smart little one. How is it you grew up so stupid, cutting off your nose all the time to spite your face?"

"Shut up, shut up!" Then: "Oh, Dilsey! I shouldn't scream at you. I'm sorry, I'm sorry."

"I'm sorry, too. It's only because I love you that I keep pecking away at you. Ever since you was no bigger than a minute I've loved you like you was my own child, and never mind about different colors."

"I know you have. And I've loved you."

She said, after a long moment, "You want to hear about it, leastways as much as I know?"

"Yes." I knew I would be hearing plenty about the Brian Ravencrofts from others. Better to hear it first from Dilsey.

"They say the marrying was a lot more her idea than his. Fanny Stopes, who was a maid to Miss Pamela for a while, told the Grants' cook and she told me that Miss Pamela had been crazy about him even when she was young enough to have her hair hanging down her back."

I felt a dull astonishment. I'd had reason to know that Pamela was capable of malice, or at least had been when we were both children. Later on, though, I'd felt that there could be little beside pleasure in her own appearance behind that perfect face. Certainly I hadn't thought her capable of an enduring passion. But then, I reflected wryly, I hadn't shown much ability to read the human heart.

"They say they're not happy, not happy at all."

I felt gratification, and then almost immediately I was ashamed. If I loved Brian, and I did, then I should not want him to be unhappy, whatever the cause. I said, "What is the trouble between them?"

"Trouble? No trouble, except that the man don't love his wife." When I didn't answer, she asked in a matter-of-fact tone, "You going to hire the Todd family back? Maybe you could, even though they're working for the Satherlees now."

"I don't know," I said dully. "I haven't had time to think about it."

"No real need to hire them. I could manage, since there's just the two of us."

The two of us. Two women alone in this big, silent house. Would we still be alone here five years from now, ten, twenty?

Dilsey said, as if she had caught an echo of my thoughts, "There's three letters from your mother down in the library. She wrote to me, too, and the Grants' cook read it to me. I guess your mother won't be coming back here. She got married."

"To a man named Donald Cameron?"

"That's the name."

Silence settled down. Then I heard the knocker strike. Dilsey moved to a window overlooking the street. "There's a wagon down there with a trunk. I guess it's yours from the ship. I'll go down and have them carry it in, and then fix us some food."

Two weeks passed before I saw Brian.

I kept to myself during those weeks, venturing out only to confer with Gerald at his office, and declining several invitations that were handed at the door to Dilsey. Then, midway of the second week, I decided to accept an invitation from the Corbells, whaleship owners who occupied one of the largest houses on Captains' Row, even though I knew that there was an excellent chance that Brian and his wife would be there. After all, I could not avoid him forever. Better that I choose the ground for our first meeting since my return, rather than find myself facing him at some completely unguarded moment.

The Corbells' party was an evening reception. In the small cloakroom off the wide entrance hall I took off the pale yellow velvet cloak that matched my bare-shouldered gown and left it with a maid. Then I crossed the hall to a drawing room so large that it often served the Corbells as a ballroom. Light from wall lamps and from an enormous crystal chandelier set with scores of candles shone on groups of men and women in evening dress, some of them seated on chairs and sofas upholstered in brocade or velvet, others standing. Against one wall was a table, presided over by a manservant, which held a large bowl of fruit punch as well as stronger potions in decanters. On the opposite side of the room was a buffet table with two maids standing behind it.

I saw Pamela first. Lovely in rose-colored satin, she stood chatting with two other young matrons and several young men. Then I saw Brian, one of a group of men near the punch-bowl table. As if feeling my gaze on his profile, he turned his face toward me.

For a moment our smiling gazes locked. Then I saw my plump, elderly hostess moving forward to greet me. Soon I was surrounded by people. Their manner was courteous—in some cases even warm—as they welcomed me home. But I saw avid questions in even the friendliest eyes. I of course could understand that. Already an object of curiosity because of my background and my marriage to Torrance, I had rendered myself a target for even more gossip by remaining behind when the *Dolphin* returned from the South Pacific.

A maidservant held out a tray laden with glasses of punch. I took one and began to move about the big room, greeting acquaintances and not looking once in Brian's direction. Then, heart beating fast, feeling sure that it would not take him long to join me, I moved to one corner. Back turned to the room, I looked up at the portrait of a fat woman in a powdered wig, a portrait of Mrs. Corbell's grandmother, to judge by the strong resemblance.

With at least fifty people laughing and chatting in the room, I sensed rather than heard his approach. I remained motionless until he said, "Fiona."

I turned. "Hello, Brian."

We faced each other bleakly. He appeared far older than when I had last seen him, not just because of the flecks of gray at his temples but because of the look of settled unhappiness in his eyes. Finally I said, "Did you get my letters?"

"Both of them. But by the time even the first one reached me it was already too late."

Too late, because by that time he had married. Against my own volition I said in a low, shaking voice, "Why did you do it?"

"I shouldn't think you'd find that hard to guess." His voice was harsh. "I had passed my thirty-second birthday, it was high time I married, and I'd lost all hope of you. And here was a beautiful and well-connected woman who made it plain that she *did* want me." His voice grew even harsher. "And if you can blame me for that, then to hell with you."

"No, I don't blame you." My throat closed up momentarily. Then I said, "Oh, Brian! What are we going to do?"

"Do? Why, just go on living our separate lives." Again his tone roughened. "I imagine you'd think that becoming my mistress now wouldn't be good enough for you, and although it may strike you as strange, I would feel the same way about it."

For a moment more we looked at each other bleakly, hopelessly. Then I stiffened and said in a low voice, "Your wife is coming this way."

She was accompanied by the two somewhat older women with whom I'd seen her chatting. She said, eyes dangerously bright, and with one hand beating a little ivory fan against the low-cut bodice of her dress, "Fiona! Welcome home!"

"Thank you, Pamela," I managed to say, and then added, "Good evening, Mrs. Clay, Mrs. Garret."

"We were just saying," Pamela went on, "that you must have found that island fascinating indeed to have stayed there all that time." She leaned toward me, with the ivory fan beating even faster. "Tell me, are the native young men as handsome as I've heard?"

I felt the blood rush to my face. Then, before I could make the sort of retort her malice deserved, I saw that, although her lips were curved in a vicious little smile, there was suffering in the depths of those wide-spaced blue eyes.

Had her husband told her that he loved me? Probably not. Probably it was only instinct that had told her. But she knew.

After a moment I said, in a neutral tone, "Yes, the Polynesians are a handsome race. Will you excuse me now? I see some people across the room I must speak to."

Without looking at Brian, I walked away. And half an hour later, still without looking at him, I said my farewells to my host and hostess and left.

As spring gave way to summer, my life settled into a routine, comfortable and empty. I rehired Joseph Todd as coachman-gardener, and would have rehired his wife and daughter too if they had expressed dissatisfaction with their positions at the Satherlees. But they seemed quite content, and I was content to do without their services. In fact, I welcomed the chance to help Dilsey by keeping my own bedroom and sitting room in order, and even by cooking an occasional meal in that cellar kitchen where my mother had toiled so long ago. Such activity helped fill up my days. The rest of the time I read, or wrote long letters to my mother, or rode through the village and its surrounding woods on Satin, the bay mare that Torrance had given me, and that I had boarded at the livery stable near the waterfront while I was away. Once a week I gave an "at home"—Brian and Pamela never came to those gatherings—and I accepted at least half the invitations that came my way.

Sometimes at evening parties I saw not only Brian and Pamela, but the elder Ravencrofts and Dora. Usually Dora stayed close to Brian, sometimes even clinging to his arm. She not only looked happier than she had a few years before, but younger. Perhaps she was glad to see her brother married to a woman of whom she need not be jealous, a woman he did not love.

At those parties Brian and I never spoke more than a few polite words of greeting. After that painful exchange of ours in the Corbells' drawing room, what was left for us to say?

In a way, though, he did say something more to me. One day in late May I found a small package waiting for me at the village post office. Its printed return address was the most fashionable store in New York City. Even though it had been addressed to me in a feminine hand—undoubtedly a shop attendant's—I somehow had an intuition as to who had sent the package.

I did not open it until I reached my bedroom. There

was no card inside, just a white box holding a scent bottle with a cut-glass stopper and a label that said "Parfum Tropique." The moment I opened the bottle I knew with certainty who had sent it. As I inhaled the heady fragrance I was back in that moon-flooded palm grove on Oluca with Brian's arms around me.

With a not-quite-steady hand I set the bottle on my dressing table and lifted from the bottom of the box a white card, printed in both French and English. This "haunting fragrance," the card said, had been made from a distillation of frangipani, a plant native to the tropics.

Perhaps he had seen this perfume advertised in a shop window or in a New York newspaper. Perhaps he had learned of it some other way. In any case I could imagine him going—perhaps not quite sober?—into that fashionable store, and arranging to have this package sent to Mrs. Torrance Ravencroft.

I knew that for both our sakes I must not wear this scent at any gathering where I might meet Brian. Perhaps already he had regretted the impulse that had caused him to send it to me. In fact, I knew I really should throw the bottle away. But of course I knew that I wouldn't. I would keep it on my dressing table. And sometimes I would lift the stopper and inhale, so that through the most evocative of the senses I could relive that night on Oluca.

As the summer wore on, I heard Brian's name more and more frequently at all feminine luncheons and tea parties, at least when Pamela Ravencroft was not among the guests. Nearly all of the talk was about an Addie Crane, a woman Pamela's husband had "taken up with." She was a woman of thirty-odd from "up the island"—Riverhead, to be exact—where her late husband, dead less than a year, had run a tavern. How Brian had first met her no one seemed to know, but probably the stage upon which he frequently traveled to New York had stopped at that Riverhead tavern. Anyway, she now lived in a little cottage in Redwood, that sparsely settled stretch of land along Sag Harbor Cove, without visible means of support and with Brian Ravencroft as a frequent visitor. I found that I was not jealous of this Addie Crane. Just as these parties were my means of getting by despite loneliness and vain regrets, Addie Crane was his way of getting by despite a loveless and, no doubt, increasingly rancorous marriage.

Although the gossiping women at those parties tried not to show it, I sensed that a great deal of their attention was centered upon me as they talked of the woman in that Redwood cottage. That could mean only that Sag Harbor people had at least the suspicion that something had happened between Brian and me on the island of Oluca. I was sure that neither Brian nor Steven Slater had talked. But there had been a score of officers and crewmen who had seen Brian leave that native feast, not to return, almost as soon as I had left it.

But, I reflected cynically, having my name bandied about apparently hadn't affected my social standing too much. I not only had plenty of invitations, I had suitors. Two of the town's most eligible young men came frequently to my "at homes," hovered about me at other people's parties, and gave every indication that with the slightest encouragement both would ask for my hand. At night, lying awake, I often smiled at the irony of it. Several years before, when I had been a maiden unsullied, no young Sag Harbor man of good family had chosen to court the daughter of Duncan MacWain, convict, and Martha MacWain, cook to Josie Carpenter. But now that I was what everyone, had they known the truth about me, would have had to call a fallen woman, I was quite acceptable.

One afternoon in late June Gerald Winship paid me a visit. The *Silver Dolphin* had docked that morning after another highly successful voyage. "It took Slater only eight months this time to fill the holds to capacity! That young man is making himself rich and you richer."

I smiled. "I've gathered you are still doing quite well yourself."

"I certainly am," he said with frank pleasure. "I made a twenty-five percent profit on the stock exchange shares I sold last week. But how did you know about it?"

"I didn't, specifically. But at the Grants' a few days ago we were all talking about the boat the Sag Harbor boatworks had just built for you."

The talk had been somewhat disapproving. To Sag Harbor people, ships and boats, through which the town had obtained its wealth, were a serious matter. But now Gerald Winship had ordered a boat whose only purpose was pleasure. A thirty-five-foot sailboat, it had a cabin with a settee that could serve as a single bed and enough seating capacity for a half-dozen people.

He laughed. "I'm taking her out for the first time next Thursday. I'll be able to sail and fish all over eastern Long Island waters, from Peconic Bay to Montauk. And if, in the late afternoon, I decide not to come back to Sag Harbor Cove—I'm going to keep her docked at an old wharf there— I can drop anchor in some inlet and stay there until morning."

I poured sherry, and we drank a toast to the *Silver Dolphin*'s homecoming, and to the maiden voyage of the *Sprite*, which was what he had named his sailboat.

I felt dismay but no surprise when Steven Slater called upon me the next afternoon, his tanned face holding a blend of nervousness and optimism. For a while as we sat in the sun-flooded parlor we talked of the *Dolphin*'s last voyage. Then he said, "As soon as she's caulked and equipped with some new canvas she'll be ready to sail. Are you going to send her to sea again soon?"

"I suppose so, if Mr. Winship advises me to."

"Would you mind if some other skipper commands her this time? I've been at sea almost continuously for several years now."

"I quite understand. Of course you'd like to stay ashore awhile."

"It isn't just that." While I watched apprehensively, he got up, walked over to the unlighted fireplace, and stood looking down into it for several minutes. Then he turned back to me. "The truth is that I don't want to make another voyage until I can take you with me, as my wife."

"Please!" I said in a low voice. "Please don't say things like that."

He looked distressed now, but his jaw was stubbornly set. "Why not?"

"I thought you understood why not, that day aboard the *Dolphin* when I thought Brian Ravencroft had been hurt."

"But he wasn't married then! Now he is."

I wondered who had told him. Gerald probably.

"Please listen to me. As I once told you, it would not be fair of me to marry you. You deserve a wife who can give you the kind of love that I cannot."

"Shouldn't I be the best judge of what is or is not fair to me?"

Not knowing what else to do, I shook my head.

A strained silence settled down. After a while he gave a wry little laugh. "Perhaps it is time I started believing you."

"It is." Even though he was at least two years older than I, I felt a decade older than he at the moment. "The world is full of young women who would swoon with joy at the thought of marrying a man like you."

He said, still in that wry tone, "And there are such young women here in Sag Harbor?"

"Surely you must realize there are."

"Well, perhaps I shall stay ashore for several months, and spend at least part of my time in this village. After all, I have very comfortable quarters at Mrs. Markley's boarding house."

He left soon after that. I had a feeling, not unmixed with regret, that I had heard Steven Slater ask me for the last time to share his life.

The next afternoon, a Sunday, Gerald Winship called upon me. Perhaps, he suggested, I would like to see his sailboat. In his open carriage we drove leisurely through narrow village streets, where scarlet roses rioted over split-rail fences, and then along much-wider Main Street to Glover Street. Soon we were moving along a narrow road, bordered by oaks and maples and scrub pine, through the stretch of land known as Redwood.

A roan horse and its rider were coming toward us. A moment later I saw, feeling the leap of the pulse in the hollow of my throat, that the man was Brian. When he drew abreast of us he gave a formal nod, his lips smiling but his dark blue eyes remote, and rode on. Neither Gerald nor I spoke of it, but I was sure he knew as well as I did that an Addie Crane lived somewhere farther along this road, and that undoubtedly Brian had been visiting her.

When Gerald finally did speak it was with seeming irrelevance. "I know you may tell me this is none of my business. But didn't you decline a proposal of marriage yesterday?"

"I did. How did you know?"

"When Captain Slater came to my office last Friday morning, soon after the *Dolphin* docked, I mentioned to him that his former chief officer had married Pamela Stacewood. You should have seen his face light up."

Feeling distressed, I said nothing.

"Then last night," Gerald went on, "I dropped into the Hornpipe." The Hornpipe, the most respectable of the waterfront taverns, was patronized by some of the town's businessmen as well as whaleship officers. "Young Slater was there, staring into a glass of rum as if he wished it were hemlock."

"I'm sorry."

I halfway expected Gerald to exhort me, as Torrance had done, to appreciate Steven Slater's qualities. Instead he said, "Well, he'll get over it in time. But I don't wonder that he's kept trying." He laughed. "In fact, if I didn't realize that the last thing in the world you want is another elderly husband, I'd try courting you myself."

"Elderly!" I said in genuine astonishment. "Why, when Torrance died you couldn't have been much more than half his age."

"True. But I'm still old compared to—" He broke off. I was sure he had been about to say that he was old compared to Brian Ravencroft. After a moment he added, "Compared to you."

I smiled. "If I refused you—and I would do just that— it would not be because of your state of decrepitude." After a moment I added, "Anyway, it's hard to picture you suffering from unrequited passion."

Again he laughed. "That's true. One way or another I manage to find a certain amount of female companionship."

He certainly did. For years he had been a gallant figure at balls and parties throughout eastern Long Island. And there were stories that during his frequent trips to New York he had been seen squiring attractive ladies of dubious repute in Manhattan theaters and restaurants.

He said, "But how about you? Will you be content to spend the rest of your life as Torrance Ravencroft's widow?"

It was the sort of question that often caused me to

stare at my bedroom ceiling when I awoke in the dawn light. "I don't know," I said curtly.

He glanced at me sideways. "All right, Fiona. I won't pry."

A few minutes later we turned down a side road, little more than a rutted lane, through the thick woodland. Ahead I could see the blue waters of the cove, almost millpond smooth on this windless afternoon. Gerald got out, tethered the white horse to a maple sapling, and helped me to the ground. We crossed a little sandy beach to where a half-rotted wharf, bleached to a satiny gray by years of sun, stretched out into the water. Beside the wharf lay the *Sprite*, its mast bare and its white hull gleaming. Hand under my elbow, Gerald guided me along the wharf and onto the gently moving deck.

With a key he opened the padlock on the companionway door and then swung the door back so that I could look down the short ladder into the small cabin with its canvas chairs and its narrow settee upholstered in brown leather. He did not suggest that we go down into the cabin for a closer look, and if he had suggested it I would have rejected the idea. There were houses on the North Haven side of the cove. Someone standing at a window, particularly someone with a telescope, could have seen us descending into the cabin. And although I was resigned to being an object of gossip, I saw no reason to court additional and unmerited notoriety.

He closed the companionway door and said, "I thought that next week I would get a small party together. We could sail over to Shelter Island for a picnic. Would you like that?"

"Very much."

We walked back to the carriage. Through lengthening shadows we drove back to my house, and to the watercress sandwiches and little cakes Dilsey had prepared for tea.

All that summer the question Gerald had asked, "Will you be content to spend the rest of your life as Torrance Ravencroft's widow," echoed through my mind. I knew there was no practical reason why I should remain in Sag Harbor. I could sell my house, leave my business affairs in Gerald's hands, and live in New York, or join my mother in Scotland, or just travel for a while. Perhaps I would meet some man who would enable me to forget Brian. But as if under some strange spell I remained in the village and in that house, filled as it was with memories of the Ravencrofts and of my own isolated childhood. And whenever I went out I was apt to catch a glimpse of Brian, and thus be reminded afresh of the happiness he and I might have been enjoying now, despite all the past bitterness between ourselves and between our elders.

One thing that I found good about that summer was the behavior of Steven Slater, who had remained behind when, in mid-July, the *Dolphin* had sailed under another captain for the South Atlantic whaling grounds. It was obvious that Steven was recovering from the disappointment I had dealt him. Oh, I knew from his manner whenever we met that he still felt attracted to me. But at parties to which he was invited—and he seemed to be asked to nearly all of them—he was attentive to both attractive young matrons like Pamela Stacewood Ravencroft and to unmarried women like Brian's sister Dora.

On the surface, my own life continued pleasantly enough. I went on sailing parties, one of them by moonlight, on Gerald Winship's sailboat, and to parties and balls. Even so, I was by choice alone most of the time, reading or doing the embroidery I had been taught at Miss Frawley's, or taking long rides on the bay mare through the woodlands and along the beaches.

It was on one such ride, on a hot afternoon in late August, that I learned that Pamela Ravencroft had a lover.

I had not ridden to Redwood that day but in the opposite direction to Russel's Neck, a point of heavily wooded high ground overlooking the bay. There were no habitations at all on Russel's Neck, only the ruins of an old stone fort, which the British had built when they occupied eastern Long Island during the Revolution. Three of the walls and part of the timbered roof remained, but the fourth wall, which must have held gunports so that the British cannoneers could sight out over the bay, had disappeared long ago, and so had the cannons themselves. I loved going there and spreading a blanket from my saddlebag on the layers of dead leaves, the accumulation of scores of past autumns, inside those three sheltering walls. Some days I read whatever book I had brought with me. Other times I would just look out over the water and think about the Englishmen who had manned this fort almost three-quarters of a century ago and try to imagine what they must have thought of this beautiful but wild Long Island with its painted savages and its rebellious white settlers who, although Englishmen like themselves, insisted that they were Americans.

As I approached the fort on this particular afternoon I now and then caught glimpses through the trees of its rough gray stones. When I was not more than sixty feet away from it I reined in, feeling a resentful surprise. Always before I had encountered no one at the fort or in the woods around it. But now others were using my hideaway. I could not see them but I could see their horses, a dapple gray and a sleek black mare with two white forefeet and a white forehead blaze. A pair of man's riding gloves had been thrust beneath the pommel of the dappled gray's saddle.

Someone I knew, some woman, owned the black mare. Suddenly I realized who it was. Several times I had seen Pamela, lovely in a dark-blue riding habit, perched on the mare's sidesaddle. As if to confirm my recognition, Pamela's silvery laugh came from inside those stone walls, followed by the murmur of a man's voice.

I looked at the other horse, the dapple gray. No one I knew owned such a horse, nor did it look like any of the Sag Harbor Livery Stable hacks—horses rented to out-of-town visitors or to local poeple who did not keep saddle horses of their own. Perhaps the man was from somewhere else in the Hamptons, or had even come across on the ferry from Long Island's North Fork. Or, if he was a Sag Harbor man, perhaps he had taken the precaution of renting a horse in some other village.

Had Pamela and this man, whoever he was, ridden together to this isolated spot? I was sure that instead they had met here by prearrangement. Pamela had probably known of this fort's existence since childhood, just as I had. Perhaps the man had known of it too. It depended upon whether or not he was a local man.

I turned Satin's head. Hooves noiseless over the thick leaf mold, she carried me back the way I had come.

The discovery that Pamela had a lover—exquisite Pamela, always so demure during our teens—had been a shock to me. But I found it impossible not to sympathize with her behavior. How wretched she must have been this past year, married to a man who loved another woman, and who had taken as his mistress still another.

Who was he, I wondered, that man with Pamela up at the old fort? A married man or a single one? Someone I had never met, or someone I had known several years, or even most of my life? Whoever he was, I did not wonder that Pamela had turned to him for at least a little happiness.

Chapter 16

∽∾∽∾∽∾∽∾∽∾∽∾∽∾∽∾∽∾∽∾∽∾∽∾∽∾∽∾

The summer continued to pass pleasantly enough, although I was never free of that sense of inner emptiness. I went to parties, sometimes alone, sometimes escorted by Gerald Winship or some other eligible man. I continued to ride almost every day, although I avoided the vicinity of the old fort.

September came, so humid that Dilsey and I found mildew under the carpets, and then a glorious October, with clear, warm days and cool nights. After the first frost, oaks and maples and beeches turned all colors, from pale yellow touched with pink to scarlet and orange and purple. When I rode through the woodland, sunlight filtering through those brilliant leaves made me feel I moved along the aisles of some vast cathedral, with light slanting through windows of stained glass.

It was on such a beautiful day that Pamela Stacewood Ravencroft died.

I had returned not long before from a ride that had taken me across the bridge to North Haven and past the lane to Josie Carpenter's old house, now occupied by Connecticut people I scarcely knew. Home again in my own parlor, I sat turning the pages of *Harper's Weekly* while I waited for tea.

The clop of hooves outside made me turn and look through the window. I saw Pamela dismount from her black mare, tether the reins to the hitching post in front of her parents' house across the street, and then go up the walk. I felt mild surprise. Her parents were not at home. Two days before they had left for New York, where Mr. Stacewood was to attend a bankers' convention. Surely Pamela knew that.

I saw the front door open, saw Pamela speak to a maid. Then she turned and came down the walk. Even from a distance I could see that there was something wrong with her. Her face was pale under her dark-blue velvet riding hat, and her walk was unsteady. When she reached the mare she started to step onto the stone mounting block beside the hitching post. Then, as if feeling too weak to get into the saddle, she stood leaning against the mare's sleek neck. I laid my magazine aside, left the house, and crossed the street.

"Pamela."

The lovely face she turned to me was pale indeed. I saw a brief flare of hostility in her blue eyes. Then she said in a dull voice, "They aren't here."

"Your parents? No, they went to New York. Didn't you know?"

"Yes, but I forgot."

After a moment, I asked, "Did you need to see them about something?"

"Yes. No. I mean, I couldn't tell *them*. But I thought it might be a comfort, just being with—"

Her voice trailed off. I said, "You'd better come into my house, Pamela. Perhaps a cup of tea will make you feel better."

For a moment I thought she was going to refuse. Then she nodded.

As soon as she was seated in my parlor, in one corner of a Louis Sixteenth sofa that Torrance had bought from a New York importing firm, I rang for Dilsey. When she appeared in the doorway, I said, "Mrs. Ravencroft will be staying for tea." I turned to Pamela. "Or perhaps it would be better for you to have coffee."

"Yes, coffee, please."

I turned to Dilsey. "We'll have a pot of coffee as well as a pot of tea."

Whenever others were around, Dilsey's manner was always very correct. Although I had seen surprise in her face at sight of Brian's wife, all she was "Yessum," and then turned away. I closed the double door and then turned back to my guest. She had taken off her velvet hat and placed it beside her on the sofa. The chignon into which her pale hair was gathered looked almost too heavy for her slender neck to support it.

I sat down near her in an armchair and asked, "What is it, Pamela?"

She stared at me for a moment and then gave a wild little laugh. "I'd never have believed that you'd be the one I'd choose to talk to. But in a way it makes sense, doesn't it? You were down there on that island all that time—I mean, you're a long way from being the proper type, aren't you?"

Reminding myself that she obviously was distraught, I managed to bite back an indignant retort. After a moment I said, "What is it you want to tell me?"

She was shivering now. "I'm going to have a baby."

My first thought was, Brian's baby. For a moment anguished jealousy closed my throat. Then I said, "When?"

"Sometime in March, I think."

With an effort I said, "I congratulate you."

She stared at me for a moment and then again gave a wild little laugh. "Of course! You think the baby is Brian's. But it isn't. It couldn't be."

I said, after a long moment, "Does Brian know?"

"Maybe he suspects that I have a lover. I think he does. But of course I haven't told him about the baby. And when and if he does find out, he will know it is not his."

Now she was not my old enemy and rival. She was just another woman, a woman caught in a trap. I said, "What are you going to do?"

"I'm going to make him take me away!"

"The child's father?"

She nodded. "He's got to."

"He doesn't want to?"

"No. But I've been telling him for weeks that he must. And yesterday I—I threatened him."

"Threatened him?"

Her eyes had narrowed. She did not look beautiful now, or even pretty. "Yes. I know something about him. I've known it a long time. And if he doesn't take me away from here, I'll tell it. I told him I would."

"What did he say?"

"Yesterday? He said he wanted to think it over. And

when I met him today he said we would go away together next week. But I don't trust him!" she burst out. "I think he'll go back on his word."

"Surely not. After all, if you know something about him that he doesn't want others to know—"

"What good would it do to tell it?" Her voice was dull once more. "It would bring me revenge. But it wouldn't change the—the fact of the baby."

Silence settled down. I wondered where they had met, yesterday and today. Up at the old fort? Probably. I thought of the summer afternoon up there when I had heard Pamela's musical, provocative laugh, and the ardent murmur of a man's answering voice. Then I thought of them as they must have been today, with their lightheartedness and laughter as dead as the leaves that had accumulated for decades inside those walls. Today he had not been a lover but just a man, sullenly giving the promise she had forced out of him, while she listened, narrow-eyed and disbelieving.

I heard a knock at the parlor door and called, "Come in." Dilsey wheeled in the cart, with its silver pots of tea and coffee and its plates of thin little sandwiches and slices of cake.

She said, "Will that be all, ma'am?"

"Yes. Thank you, Dilsey."

Without my asking her to, Dilsey closed the parlor doors behind her. I poured coffee into Pamela's cup, and tea into my own. Perhaps the formality of the tea ritual had made her realize just how unorthodox her behavior had been. Anyway, as she sipped from her coffee cup she began to chatter about how brilliant the fall colors were this year. I replied in kind, not wanting to force her back to a discussion of her appalling situation until she was ready for it.

Suddenly she drew in her breath sharply. I asked, "What is it?"

"A pain. A bad one, just here under my ribs."

I refilled her coffee cup. "Drink this. And try to relax."

She did try. She drank the coffee and drew deep breaths. But her pallor had a greenish tinge now, and perspiration gleamed on her forehead. She picked up one of the tiny sandwiches, then dropped it onto the carpet, and set her cup and saucer down with a clatter on the tea cart.

"I'd better—fresh air—"

Hand on the arm of the settee, she hoisted herself to her feet. I too stood up. She took a few steps forward, body bent, one forearm pressed against her stomach, and then collapsed onto the carpet. Brownish liquid gushed from her mouth.

I ran to the fireplace, grasped the bell rope, and rang for Dilsey. Then I moved to a side window, threw the sash high, and leaned out until I could see Joseph Todd, raking leaves from the south lawn. "Run and fetch Dr. Dillworth!" I cried. "Tell him Miss Stacewood—I mean, Mrs. Ravencroft—is very ill. Hurry!"

I turned back into the room. Pamela, still on the floor, was groaning now. Tremors shook her body. Not knowing what else to do, I took a pillow from one of the sofas and slipped it under the small, pale-blond head.

I became aware that Dilsey stood beside me. When I looked up, I saw that her eyes were wide in her brown face. But all she said was, "You send for the doctor?"

"Yes." Pray God he was at his house, only a few doors away. If he was, he could be here within minutes.

"You want me to take the cart out?"

"Yes." I said distractedly, "you might as well."

Within two minutes after she had wheeled the tea cart away, Dr. Dillworth arrived. Without the formality of knocking, he came into the house, followed by Joseph Todd. As he paused in the parlor doorway, his round face appalled, I suddenly remembered that he was more than the Stacewoods' family doctor. He was a relative, a first cousin of Pamela's mother.

He hurried across the room, knelt on the rug, and lifted one of Pamela's eyelids. Then he looked up at me. "I'll take her down to my examining room." He turned to Joseph Todd. "Here, give me a hand. You lift her under the knees, I'll take her shoulders."

Those long shudders were still rippling down Pamela's slender body. Dazedly I watched the two men lift her and carry her from the room. I heard Dilsey open the door for them. Then she came back into the parlor. "Don't stand there, child," she said. "Go up to your room or someplace and let me clean up in here."

I went, not to my room, but across the hall to the library, where I sat with a book opened but unread in my lap. Gradually the light faded. I had just lit the lamp when Dilsey came in to ask when I wanted dinner served. "You have your own meal," I told her. "I'm not hungry."

It was past eight when I heard the knocker strike, and then Dilsey's voice greeting Dr. Dillworth. As soon as he appeared in the library doorway, looking tired and old, I knew that Pamela was dead. Nevertheless, after he had sat down in an armchair, I asked him how she was.

"She died a little over an hour ago." He sighed heavily. "It's so terrible, a young and beautiful woman like that. And she was going to have a child."

"Yes, I know. She told me that this afternoon." I saw his gaze sharpen. "How did she—what was it she died of?"

After a moment, he said, "I'll tell you. But first I want you to tell me everything that happened here this afternoon." He must have seen resistance in my face, because he said, "Believe me, Fiona, this is no time for qualms about betraying confidences. And please remember too that Pamela and I were not only patient and doctor, but members of the same family. I have every right to know what she said to you."

I told him then. I told him of how Pamela had spoken of the child who was not her husband's, and of the lover she feared would not keep his promise to take her away with him. Before I had finished, Dr. Dillworth had sunk his head in his hands.

Finally he looked up at me. "You have no idea who this man is?"

"None. I didn't ask, of course. Perhaps she would have told me later, but she didn't have a chance to. Now please, Dr. Dillworth, tell me what Pamela died of."

He was silent for several seconds and then said rapidly, "She died of arsenic poisoning. I don't believe it was suicide. I think it was an accident. Lately, in her agitation over this love affair, she must have been taking too much."

I said, utterly bewildered, "Too much? What are you talking about?"

"Pamela was one of several young women in town

who have been buying arsenic from the local pharmacist and taking it in small doses for their complexions. As you doubtless know, it's supposed to refine the pores, and make the skin soft, and all that nonsense. I've warned Pamela and several of my other patients about the long-range effects, but I might as well have saved my breath.

"Now I suppose there will have to be an inquest," he went on, "since she did die of poisoning. But listen to me, Fiona, I want you to testify *only* that you brought Pamela into your house because she did not seem well, and that soon she became very ill indeed, and so you sent your servant to fetch me. Say *nothing* about the baby, or about this other man. Do you understand?"

"No, Dr. Dillworth, I do not understand! You are asking me to suppress evidence, evidence of a possible murder! What if, when she met that man today, they shared a lunch of some sort, or a bottle of wine? What if he managed to poison her that way?"

As he looked at me, lips compressed, I went on, "After all, she had become a nuisance to him. Worse than that, a danger. She was threatening to tell everyone something unsavory about him. He might have had good reason to—to want her dead."

Dr. Dillworth said, eyeing me narrowly, "And so might her husband. Did you think of that, Fiona? No, I can see you didn't. Even an unfaithful husband doesn't relish the thought of others knowing he is a cuckold. And if he knew she was about to run off with the other man—"

Stiff and silent with shock, I looked back at him. He said, "Don't you see? Nothing you can say would restore Pamela's life. But you can say things that would blacken her name and bring added grief to her family. Why do it?"

I cried, "But if this man did murder her? Don't you want him punished?"

"If I were sure that he had murdered her, and sure that we could see to it that he was punished—yes! But we don't even know who he is, and might not be able to find out, let alone prove that he killed her. All we can be sure of is that, if you tell your story, everyone will know Pamela Ravencroft was an adulterous wife and about to become the mother of a bastard child.

"And then there's Brian," he went on inexorably.

"No matter what the verdict of the coroner's jury, if you tell your story there will always be those who will suspect him of killing her."

When I didn't answer, he said, "One more point, Fiona. You say that she was already looking unwell before you brought her into your house. Nevertheless, it was in your house that she became violently ill. In view of the talk about you and Brian, what do you think people may make of that?"

So he'd heard talk about Brian and me. Well, I thought numbly, perhaps everybody had by this time. And he was right that I might be suspected of poisoning her, especially since people would be reminded of the suspicion that had swirled around me after Torrance died.

Dr. Dillworth's round old face had taken on a pleading look. "Fiona, please do as I say. Do it for your own sake, and for the sake of Pamela's memory, and for Brian's sake. I wouldn't ask you to do this if I weren't honestly convinced that her death was an accident. Distraught as she must have been of late, she took more arsenic than she intended to, perhaps not just once, but several times. And today the cumulative effect killed her. If I tell a coroner's jury that, they will believe me, especially since the pharmacist has the record of her purchases of arsenic in his poison book.

"Now I know there's a chance that I am wrong," he went on. "I know there's a chance that someone who knew she had been taking arsenic managed to give her a large dose of it without her knowing it. But it seems to me that is only a small chance. Whereas, if you repeat the things that poor girl told you, it is a certainty that her memory will be blackened forever."

After a moment, he added, "Well, Fiona?"

"I don't know! I just don't know!"

He got to his feet. "All right. You think about it, hard. I'll be back later this evening to learn what you've decided."

Chapter 17

I n the end, of course, I did as Dr. Dillworth had advised. With a sense that time had turned backward almost two years, I sat at the same table, in that same upstairs hall where, on a January morning, I had testified at the inquest into Torrance's death. In a few sentences I told them the story Dr. Dillworth and I had agreed upon. That testimony, plus the doctor's own testimony and that of the pharmacist, was enough to bring a prompt verdict of accidental death.

Out on the sidewalk, I lingered in the chill—it was the first really cool day we'd had that fall—to exchange a few words with the Grants and with Mrs. Markley and several others. Then I turned away to walk the few hundred yards to my house.

Seconds later I saw Brian. He had just untethered his roan gelding from a hitching post at the curb and swung into the saddle. When I had testified at the inquest I had avoided looking at him, even though I was acutely aware of his presence in the fourth row. I knew that, because of all those rumors about Brian and me, the townspeople would be alert to see if any looks of unseemly warmth passed between us. Aware that the group in front of the constable's office might still be watching, I did not slacken my pace. I nodded to him, and then walked on.

But in the instant or so we had looked at each other, I had received a shock. His eyes had been guarded, remote. But behind the guardedness I had glimpsed something. Was it guilt? Suspicion? I could not be sure, but I had a stricken feeling that it was one or the other.

Distraught as I had been for the sixty hours or so since Pamela's death, I nevertheless had been visited by thoughts concerning Brian and myself. We were both free now. After an interval, surely we could have the happiness that, if it had not been for my folly, would have been ours this past year and a half.

But now, remembering that ambivalent look in his eyes—and remembering my own involuntary thought, "Is it guilt?"—I felt a cold premonition. Pamela no longer stood between us, but her death might prove an even greater barrier. In spite of Dr. Dillworth's theory, in spite of the jury's verdict, I might always wonder if there was a chance that Brian had used arsenic to dispose of an unloved and unfaithful wife. And he, if innocent, might always wonder if I had put something in the coffee I had poured for Pamela that afternoon.

Feeling tired and chilled and hopeless, I climbed the steps to the front door. Dilsey, who had stayed away from the inquest because she had a bad cold, opened the door for me. I said, "The jury said it was an accident." Then I saw that her eyes were bloodshot. "You're feeling worse, aren't you?"

"I can manage," she said, and went into a paroxysm of coughing.

"Oh, yes!" I said. "You're going to manage yourself right into pneumonia. Now go to bed, Dilsey, and stay there until you're over this."

"You going to carry my meals clear up from the kitchen to the top floor? Don't talk foolish."

"You won't be on the top floor. There's a couch in the sewing room. We'll make it up with sheets and blankets."

She continued to protest, but so feebly that I realized she really was quite ill. Worried as I was about her, I was at the same time grateful that I had something to distract me from the thought of the look in Brian's eyes as he sat in the bay gelding's saddle. For the next week I cooked light but nourishing meals for her, carried them to the sewing room, and saw to it that she took the medicine Dr. Dillworth prescribed for her.

I did not go to Pamela's funeral. Brian, of course, would be there. I could not bear the thought of sitting in the same church with him during the eulogy for his beautiful and unloved wife. Even less could I bear the thought that our eyes might meet, and that again I would see that enigmatic remoteness in his gaze.

Late in the afternoon, the day of the funeral, I was aware of activity across the street. The Stacewoods, shattered by the death of their only child, had dismissed their servants and were going to Virginia, where Mr. Stacewood had relatives, for an indefinite stay.

On the fifth day of Dilsey's illness, a day so dark with gray-black clouds that I had to start lighting lamps at three in the afternoon, I carried a small lamp down to the kitchen and set it on a table. Then I lighted the big lamp, the one that threw enough light to illuminate the whole kitchen. After a moment it sputtered and went out, and I realized I had neglected to fill it with oil. Well, I wouldn't stop to attend to that now. There was a smaller lamp on a low shelf across the room. Its light, together with that of the lamp I had brought down from the floor above, would be sufficient for me while I made tea and dished up the broth I had been simmering all day. I crossed the room, lit the second lamp, and started carrying it toward the table.

From the corner of my eye I saw the flash of a tiny red light over there on the stairs. I halted, turned my head. Nothing. I took a step backward. There it was again, a pinpoint of red light at one edge of the staircase. It appeared to be in the angle between the fourth step and the riser of the step above it. Carrying the lamp, I mounted the stairs. Halfway up I halted and held the lamp close to the spot where I had seen that flash of red. There was no flash now, but I could see a small crack in the stone. I set the lamp down on the step, took a wire hairpin from my hair, and straightened it. Carefully I dug into the crack. Something that looked like a red pebble popped out onto the step.

I picked it up and held it close to the lamp. It was a small ruby, backed with gold and surrounded by seed pearls. A setting from a ring? Undoubtedly.

How long had it been there, invisible except to someone carrying a lamp across the room at a certain angle, with the lamp held at a certain height? Years? Decades? Scores of years?

And to what woman had the ring belonged? Certainly not to me, nor my mother, nor Dilsey. I had never seen Mrs. Todd or her daughters wear such a ring, nor Mary nor

Ellen, those two maids who took their meals in this room during my childhood. In fact, it seemed unlikely that any domestic who ever toiled in this house would have possessed a ruby, even a small one.

Who had owned it, then? Aurelia Ravencroft or her daughter Dora? Dora's grandmother, the wife of the Revolutionary privateer?

But it need not have been the property of anyone who had ever lived here. It might well have belonged to one of the many hundreds of women guests who must have been entertained in this house during its almost three-quarters of a century of existence. But whoever it had belonged to, I felt fairly sure of how it had ended up here on the kitchen stairs. A broom wielded by some housemaid had, without her knowing it, propelled the tiny object onto the steps, either through the door to the kitchen stairs, if it had been open, or under it, if it had been closed. Somehow it had taken a bounce and lodged itself in that small crack, to remain hidden there until a ray of light from the lamp I carried found it.

I dropped the little gem into the pocket of the blue apron I wore, one of Dilsey's. Later I would take the ruby up to my room and drop it into my jewel box. I realized it was too small to be of much value. But it was pretty, and I was intrigued by the thought of its lying hidden for many years. The next time I met Aurelia Ravencroft or Dora, I would ask if either of them had ever owned such a ring.

The weather turned warmer the next day. Dilsey seemed much improved. When I proposed that we take the stage to New York the next Friday to do some shopping, she promptly agreed.

We stayed in a fine new hotel on Broadway, one that had an entire floor reserved for the servants of its guests. In the daytime we shopped along Broadway and in Union Square, which was rapidly turning from a residential neighborhood into a fashionable commercial and theatrical district. I bought two ready-made dresses for the holiday festivities ahead, and from a modiste ordered a white woolen evening coat and matching hood, both trimmed with white fur. In a department store I bought many yards of linen and muslin, together with several dress patterns from France, so that Dilsey could sew some spring and summer daytime dresses for me.

After three days in New York, we took the stage home. The excursion had done little to lift my spirits. Despite my new gowns, and despite Dilsey's urgings that I go out, I found myself declining party invitations. The reason, of course, was that I feared to come face-to-face with Brian, feared to see in his eyes that withdrawn, enigmatic expression that had been there the day of the inquest.

Late in the afternoon, on a Thursday, Dilsey's day off, my evening cloak and hood and the lightweight fabrics I had ordered arrived. I asked the driver to carry both boxes back to the sewing room. When he had gone, I opened the longer box and saw, as I had expected, that it contained the cloak and hood. Because Dilsey, not trusting any workmanship but her own, always went over such newly arrived garments for faulty seams or loose buttons, I took a hanger, hung the cloak from a coat tree in a corner of the room, and placed the hood on the tree's upright center pole. The box containing the dress materials I set on the couch.

After that, I went down to the kitchen to cook my dinner. Dilsey, I knew, would not be home for several hours. She always spent Thursdays with cousins of hers, one of several families of mixed white and African blood who had farms about three miles away along Old Sagg Road. She always stayed at their house for dinner, and then was driven home by some member of the family.

I was in the library reading when, around eight o'clock, I heard a wagon stop out front. An interval later I heard the back door open. Just as Dilsey's sense of fitness caused her to sleep on the third floor, it demanded that she come in the back door—and never mind that, once she was inside the house, she often tried to order me about as if I were still six years old.

I stepped out into the hall in time to see her hanging her cloak and bonnet on a wall hook near the foot of the rear stairs. "The dress material came today," I said.

"Did they send the patterns, too?"

"I don't know. I didn't open the box."

I turned back into the room and picked up my book from the library table. But before I could sit down again

Dilsey screamed. The sound held such terror that I felt cold waves of fear rippling down my own body. I dropped the book and rushed out into the hall. Dilsey was leaning against the wall about twenty feet away. I hurried to her.

"What is it, what is it?"

Her eyes looked enormous. "I saw her."

"Her?"

"Miss Pamela, there in the sewing room."

"Miss—Dilsey, for heaven's sake!"

I moved swiftly past her to the doorway of the sewing room and looked inside. Light from the hallway penetrated only a little way into the room. In the dimness of the far corner, that evening cloak and hood on the coat tree might indeed have suggested a white-gowned woman.

I walked back to Dilsey. "It's my new evening cloak and hood. Don't you remember? You were with me when I ordered them."

Her face went slack with relief. "I thought she'd— she'd come back to haunt me." As she spoke the word, it sounded more like "hant."

"Oh, Dilsey! Now why should that poor woman haunt you?"

She looked at me for a long moment. Then she said, in a dull voice, "Because I killed her."

For several seconds my mind seemed not to function at all. Then I thought numbly, "So there was something in Pamela's coffee that day." Dilsey had brewed that coffee. And there was rat poison down in the kitchen.

I whispered, "Oh, Dilsey. Oh, my poor Dilsey. Why?"

"The same reason I killed the old man. I wanted you to be happy. I wanted you to have the man you wanted, the one you should have had. But first the old man was in the way, and then she was—"

Her voice trailed off. I had a sickening vision of her holding something over Torrance's face—a pillow, per- haps?—as she wheeled him to those stone stairs and then pushed him down into the blackness. Or had she, before she wheeled him from his room, struck him with something to render him unconscious? She would know that after such a plunge one more bruise would not matter.

She went on, in that dull voice, "But none of it's done

any good. I been facing up to that, these last few days. You won't even go out where you might see him. And after a while he'll marry someone else, and a few years after that you'll marry someone you don't really want, or maybe you won't marry anyone at all, just go on living here until you're all dried up and finished."

I said, in anguish, "Oh, Dilsey!"

What should I do? Tell the constable? No! Dilsey was going to need legal help, right from the start. The first person to consult was Gerald Winship. "Come." I put my arm around her shoulders and led her back to the library. "Now sit here," I said, "and wait for me."

I had expected her to ask questions, but evidently her confession had left her apathetic. She sank into a chair and looked up at me with hopeless eyes. "Wait," I said again. I went to the front door and left the house.

The night was calm and fairly warm, but evidently strong wind currents moved in the upper air, because the almost-full moon appeared to sail rapidly among ragged clouds, casting alternate light and shadow on the sidewalk. I hurried along Madison Street and then turned onto Latham Street. Gerald lived only a few doors from the corner. As I neared his house I saw him moving down the walk toward his light carriage at the curb.

"Gerald!"

He turned. I saw a gleam of white shirtfront beneath his evening coat, with its ruffled shoulder cape. "Fiona! What is it?"

"It's Dilsey. Gerald, we've got to talk to you. I can see you're going to a party—"

"No, I'm not." Hand under my elbow, he led me toward the carriage. "I'm going to your house to see what the trouble is."

During the short ride I told him what Dilsey had confessed to me. When I had finished he said quietly, "My God."

I said, from the depths of my misery, "And for me, the most horrible part is that she did it for my sake. Oh, Gerald. I know that she committed two terrible acts. But if there is any way that she won't be condemned to—to—"

"I'll do the best I can for her," he said in that same quiet voice.

Dilsey must have heard the carriage stop outside because she had the door open before we reached the top step. We moved into the hall. She closed the door and then stood facing us, statue still.

Gerald said, "Shall we go into the library, Dilsey, so that you can tell us all about it?"

"Better that I show you," she said, and turned toward the stairs.

"Dilsey," I cried, "what are you doing?"

Already partway up the first flight, she repeated over her shoulder, "Better I show you," and kept on walking.

Gerald and I followed her up to the second floor, the third. A lamp burned on a table outside her room. She opened the door, picked up the lamp, and stood aside for us to enter. Then she herself came into the room. Lamplight gleamed on the four-poster mahogany bed, and on the matching wardrobe and chest of drawers. Even though she had insisted upon occupying a room on the servants' floor, she'd had Joseph Todd carry up furniture she had selected from among the finest in the second-floor bedrooms. She set the lamp down on the bureau, lit a larger lamp, with a globe ornamented with painted red roses, which stood on the bedside table, and carried the first lamp back into the hall. When she returned to the room she opened a middle drawer of her bureau, took something out of it, and laid it on the bed.

I stared at it in utter bewilderment. A pink ribbon had been drawn around the wrist of a white kid glove of mine, one that I had discarded more than two years before because it had two split finger seams. Attached to the ribbon was a small bag made of white muslin strewn with tiny violets. That, I knew, was part of a summer frock I had ceased to wear even before I married Torrance.

I said, "Dilsey, what is that?"

She said, gaze fixed on the white glove and the little bag attached to it, "A juju I made."

A juju. A charm. No doubt the little bag contained a lock of my hair, as well as a powder made up of dried plant leaves and other magical ingredients.

"But why, Dilsey? What is it for?"

"To bring you what you wanted," she said in that dull

voice. "And the juju tried. First it killed that old man so you'd be free, and then it killed *her*."

"Dilsey!" In my relief I felt a hysterical impulse toward laughter. "My husband's neck was broken in a fall, an accidental fall!"

She nodded. "That's what I been telling you. The juju made it happen."

"Oh, Dilsey, Dilsey!" I was still struggling with that wild urge to laugh. "And what about your—your other victim? Did you put poison in her coffee?"

"No, I didn't have to."

"But Dilsey! Dr. Dillworth said she died of arsenic poisoning."

"Doctors got to say something," she said, quietly stubborn. "But it was the juju that gave her the pain, and the pain was so bad it killed her." Her voice quickened and became almost shrill. "I was sorry that the old man died. I even tried to believe it was just what you said, an accident. But when she died too I had to see it was the juju. The juju did what it had to do to try to make things come out right for you."

Helplessly I looked at her, this woman I had known and loved for nearly all my life. Although illiterate, Dilsey had a good mind. But like some otherwise intelligent people of all races and all classes, she had an ineradicable streak of superstition.

"Dilsey, we'll talk about this tomorrow."

She covered her face with her hands. A shudder went down her body. "Talking's no use. I guess I knew all along the juju would kill them. And now they're dead and it was all for nothing."

I put my arm around her. "Please, Dilsey, please! There's a big difference between wanting people dead and actually killing them."

Hands still covering her face, body trembling, she shook her head. "Ain't no difference when you make juju. Juju makes them die even if you never touch them."

"Dilsey, listen to me! You'll make yourself sick again if you go on like this. Now have you still got some of that cough medicine Dr. Dillworth gave you?" He had explained to me that since the cough syrup contained opium, it would also enable her to get the sleep she needed in order to recover.

Dilsey took her hands down from her face. She said in that same miserable voice, "It's over there."

The bottle stood on the marble-topped washstand. Beside it was a half-filled water glass with a spoon in it. I measured a generous dose of the syrup into another glass and added water. I said, walking back to her with the glass in my hand, "Drink it all, Dilsey. It will make you sleep."

I waited until she had drunk it down, her face still wretched. As I took the glass from her hand, Gerald spoke for the first time since we had come into the room. "Try not to worry about this, Dilsey. Try to put it out of your mind."

I placed the empty glass on the washstand. "Good night, Dilsey."

"Good night, ma'am." Even in her misery she had recollected her self-made rule that, when others were within earshot, I was to be addressed properly. "Good night, Mr. Winship."

Gerald and I walked in silence along the dimly lit hall. But as we started to descend the two flights I said unhappily, "Can you think of any way to help her? Is she going to live out her life thinking of herself as a murderess?"

"She actually was in intent, you know."

"I don't care! It was a halfhearted intent. She even tried to avoid admitting to herself that she had the intent. And she didn't harm either of them. If only I could convince her of that!"

After several seconds he said, "Well, all you can do is to keep talking to her."

We had reached the ground-floor hall by then. I said, "Would you like a glass of sherry? Or do you want to get to your party as soon as possible?"

"It's a reception at the Carringtons over in North Haven. It won't matter what time I get there. And I'd like to have a glass of sherry with you."

In the parlor he took off his evening coat and laid it across a sofa back. I opened the liquor cabinet, placed two stemmed glasses on top of it, and filled them from the cut-glass sherry decanter.

It wasn't until I held out his glass to him that I saw

the row of jeweled studs in his shirt. Tiny rubies surrounded by seed pearls.

The glass tilted in my hand. Sherry spilled onto the Aubusson carpet. "Let me," he said. He knelt and began to sop up the wine with his handkerchief. Quickened blood drumming in my ears, I looked down at the small bald spot on the crown of his dark head.

Strange, but even then I knew what those ruby studs meant. Even then, I was seeing, in my mind's eye, an old man reach a frantic hand backward to seize the shirtfront of the man wheeling him to his death. I saw one of the tiny gems, broken off from the rest of the stud, arch down the darkened staircase. And I saw the chair and its helpless passenger take an even longer plunge—

Gerald stood up. He was smiling. I forced my lips to return his smile. Had he, I wondered frantically, guessed why I had spilled the wine?

His next words reassured me. "Perhaps I'd better pour. I'm afraid Dilsey's hysteria has upset you badly."

He took the glass from my hand and refilled it. We sat down. For interminable minutes, at least ten of them, I tried to keep my manner normal, tried to concentrate on what he was saying rather than on the hideous pictures going through my mind. He spoke of the *Sprite*, and I asked if his sailboat was still in the water, and he said yes, but he intended to get her ashore before the really cold weather started.

Then he cocked his head in a listening attitude and said, "From the sound of it, cold weather may be almost upon us."

For the first time I became aware that the wind, which I had seen driving the clouds across the moon, was disturbing the lower atmosphere now. I could hear the seethe of it through the cedar trees along the driveway, and the keening sound wind always made as it turned the north-western corner of the house.

Out in the hall the clock struck the half hour. Gerald stood up. "Well, I'd better get along to the Carringtons and let you go to bed. If, tomorrow, you think of any way in which I can help you with Dilsey, please call upon me, won't you."

"Of course." Thank God, I was thinking. I was sure

now that he, this murderer standing only two feet away from me, had no idea of what had been going through my mind.

I moved with him to the front door, said good night, listened to his footsteps go down the walk and then the sound of the carriage wheels dwindling away down the street. I locked the front door. Dimly aware that the moaning of the wind around the corner of the house had grown louder, I walked the length of the hall to the back door and locked it. Then, retracing my steps a few feet, I opened the door to the kitchen stairs and went down them. Enough light shone from above so that I could make my way across the flagstone floor to that other door, the one at the foot of the flight of stairs leading up to the rear lawn. I knew that the door must be secure, because I had locked it as soon as I had finished preparing my solitary dinner earlier that evening. Yes, it was still locked. I left the kitchen and walked back along the hall to extinguish the parlor lamps.

Then, feeling safe—at least safe enough so that I could take time to consider what to do next—I climbed the stairs.

Chapter 18

In my bedroom I undressed. In a white muslin nightgown, green flannel robe, and green corduroy slippers, I crossed to my dressing table and sat down on the bench. After I had let down my hair, I opened my jewelry box, took out the ruby and, holding it on my palm, stared down at it. Should I take it to the constable tomorrow?"

What would that accomplish? Even though I somehow was certain that Gerald had murdered Torrance, this ruby might seem no evidence at all to a third person. True, this stud matched those Gerald had worn in his shirt tonight, but that was no proof of anything. For all I knew, studs of this design might be quite common. And even if I could somehow establish that the ruby I found on the kitchen stairs had been his property, that would not prove that he had killed my husband.

Besides, I realized now, I had no way of proving that I had even found it on the kitchen stairs, rather than in the parlor or some other room where Gerald or any other visitor to this house had a right to be. And even if the constable did believe my statement as to where I had found it, he might realize, as I had, that the ruby could have been swept onto the stairs by accident.

Dimly aware of the increasing force of the wind and the rattle of windowpanes, I looked with baffled eyes at the tiny gem on my palm. Catching the light and giving it back, it seemed to pulse with some evil life of its own.

Then I looked up. And I saw him.

No, not him. His reflection in the mirror. He stood in the doorway, coat buttoned to the chin now, so that no shirtfront showed. With the pulse in the hollow of my throat leaping wildly I whirled around on the dressing-table bench. My elbow must have struck the perfume bottle and sent it, with its stopper dislodged, skittering to the dressing table's edge. Weirdly, through my fear, I was aware of liquid soaking through my robe to my gown, and the fragrance of night-blooming tropical flowers filling the room.

He moved toward me. "Don't scream, Fiona. No one's going to hear you in this wind, especially not Dilsey, with all that opium-laced medicine inside her."

I said stupidly, "So you have a key."

"No. Keys. Torrance gave them to me as soon as he bought this house from his brother."

"Gave them to you?" To my own ears my voice sounded strange, mechanical. "Why?"

"So that, whenever he was away, I could get into this house for any business papers I might need."

How strange, I thought numbly. How strange that shrewd Torrance should have trusted this man so.

"Now hand it over, Fiona." When I just went on staring at him, he said, "I know you found it. You should have seen your expression when you first saw my shirt studs tonight. You were shocked to the core.

"And I know you must still have it," he went on. "Even if, when you found it, you didn't realize it had anything to do with me, or with Torrance, you would have kept it. After all, small as it is, it's a ruby and therefore of some value. Now hand it over."

My fingers had closed automatically around the little gem on my palm. Now I clenched my hand even tighter. In my frightened, scurrying thoughts, only one thing was clear. Since he had come back here for it, it was obvious that he was afraid to leave the ruby in my possession. And that seemed to me a very good reason to hold on to it.

He took a pistol from the pocket of his coat and pointed it at my breast. "I went home for this gun, Fiona, and I'll use it if I have to. Now hand over that shirt stud."

Fascinated, I stared at the ugly mouth of that gun. My mind refused to believe that he or anyone else could possibly shoot me. But my body believed it. My body, shrinking in upon itself, seemed to know what it would be like to feel a bullet smashing through flesh and muscle and bone. Extending my hand toward him, I unclenched my fingers. He picked up the ruby with his left hand and dropped it into his coat pocket. "Now, when did you find it?"

I tore my gaze from the gun and looked up at him. His facial muscles were well controlled, but I could see a blend of fear and cold determination in his eyes. I said, "A few days ago."

"Not until then? All right. Where did you find it?"

"On the stairs leading down into the kitchen."

"You couldn't have. I came back here the night after that New Year's party three years ago, and let myself into the kitchen. I lit the lantern I'd brought with me and searched those very steps. I didn't find the stud."

A lantern. A lantern that he'd blown out when he heard me approaching the door at the top of the stairs, and that he had taken away with him while I ran to get Dilsey. So that was why, even though I had smelled only minutes before the odor of a just-extinguished wick, I had found the lamp chimney cold.

"While you were on the *Dolphin*," Gerald was saying, "I entered that kitchen twice at night and searched. Nothing. After a while I decided I must have lost it earlier in the evening, on the street or in some part of the house where it wouldn't matter. In fact, I stopped worrying about it entirely. I even had the missing ruby replaced so that I could wear the set of studs again. And then tonight—" He broke off, and then added, "So tell me where you really did find it."

"I did tell you. On the stairs." In spite of myself I was looking at the muzzle of that gun again. Surely he wouldn't—and yet he had already killed once. No, almost certainly he had killed twice. "I—I guess it had taken a funny bounce," I said. "Anyway, it was in a crack in the lower corner of a riser. I would never have seen it if the light from the lamp I was carrying hadn't struck it just right."

He gave a short laugh. "I'll be damned."

Again I forced my gaze up from the gun to his face. How strange that, in spite of the blend of fear and determination in his eyes, it still looked very much like the face of the civilized, rather amusing man I had known for several years now. Involuntarily I burst out, "Why did you kill him? Why?"

He looked at me quizzically. "You mean, you haven't figured that out? It was for the land, of course. Owning it meant I'd have a chance to become at least moderately rich, and those chances aren't too plentiful when you're almost forty. But Torrance, the stubborn old bastard, wouldn't sell to me."

I asked dazedly, "What land?"

"Why, the land adjoining my former property on the Bridgehampton Turnpike."

The land that I, as Torrance's widow and sole heir, had sold to him. And the man who'd murdered my husband to get it hadn't even had to ask me for it, I thought bleakly. I'd offered it to him.

Gerald said, "All right, Fiona. Stand up. You're coming with me."

I stared up at him, paralyzed. After a moment I managed to say, "Where?"

"Never mind where. Just come on."

I knew then that he meant to kill me. Probably he had meant to ever since, down in the parlor, he had read the knowledge of his crime in my face. Oh, he wouldn't do it here. The shot might be heard. Not by the Stacewoods, since they were away, and not by Dilsey, deep in opium-induced slumber. But some passerby in the street might hear, despite the soughing of the wind through the trees. No, he meant to use the gun somewhere else.

Then the thing to do, I told myself desperately, was to stay here as long as possible, in the hope that I could think of some way to save myself. I must keep talking, keep asking questions, keep him answering me.

"Gerald! There's no need to—to kill me. I won't tell anyone. Why should I? It won't bring Torrance back."

"Fiona, I'm sorry." He actually did sound sorry. "But you can't expect me to believe ridiculous statements like that. Now stand up."

My hands tightened around the edges of the dressing-table bench. I said, "You killed Pamela, didn't you?"

That jolted him. I saw the shock of it leap into his eyes. He regarded me silently for a few seconds, while the shocked look faded. Then he asked, in a voice that sounded carefully controlled, "What do you know about it? What do you know about Pamela's death that you didn't tell at the inquest?"

"I know what she told me the day she died, all those things that Dr. Dillworth persuaded me not to tell. She told me she had a lover, and she'd been trying to get him to take her away with him. In fact, she'd been threatening to tell something she knew about him."

"You mean she named me?" His voice was sharp. "You're lying. If she had, you'd have told Constable Simon about it after she died, and Dr. Dillworth, too, and, at the very least, I would have been questioned about her death."

"But she didn't name you."

Too late, I realized my appalling blunder. Why hadn't I thought to say, "But I did tell Dr. Dillworth that you were Pamela's lover and that I thought you might have killed her. And if anything happens to me now, you'll be suspected."

Well, I reflected despairingly, even if I had been quick-witted enough to say that, he probably wouldn't have believed me.

"Just what did she tell you, Fiona?"

At least he was still asking questions. At least I was still here in this lamplit room. "She said that her lover had finally agreed to take her away, but she still didn't trust him."

After a moment, he said grimly, "That's right. She'd blackmailed me into agreeing. You see, she was still awake that New Year's Eve, three years ago, when I came back to this house in the early morning hours."

He meant, I thought numbly, when he had come back to kill Torrance.

"What was more," he added, "her bedroom in her parents' house overlooked the street."

"And she saw you?"

He regarded me silently for a long moment, his lips curving into a wry little smile. Then he said, "I know that you're playing for time, Fiona. But that's all right. There's plenty of time. And I find I want you to know just how it was."

He paused, and then went on, "Yes, Pamela saw me. I'd come back here on the piebald saddle horse I rode back in the days when I was a poor man. She saw me tether the horse a few doors from here and then walk back along the driveway beside this house. Later, she saw me leave. The skies had cleared by then and there was enough light from the half-moon for her to recognize me, and the piebald, too."

And she had never told about Gerald Winship's visit at that predawn hour, when Torrance had died. Along with everyone else who had been able to crowd into the hall, she had sat there at the inquest—an inquest that might have resulted in a murder charge against me—and never said a word.

As if he had read my thoughts, Gerald said, "Pamela hated you, you know. When she heard Torrance was dead, she hoped you'd be convicted of causing his death, or at least be so strongly suspected of it that Brian Ravencroft would turn completely away from you. That way, she'd have had a clear field with him." He gave a short laugh. "Well, she got him, and within less than a year she'd turned to me."

He looked down at me. "I guess you wonder about that. How she could have, I mean, when she knew what I had done."

I repressed a shudder. "Yes, I wonder."

"I told her it had been an accident. I told her that the door to the kitchen stairs had been standing open when I came back that early morning to argue with him again about selling me the land. I told her that, as I started to leave, he followed me in his chair from his room out into the hall, still taunting me, and I gave him an angry shove, and, somehow, his chair tumbled down those stairs."

"But it wasn't like that."

"No, it wasn't."

"And yet she believed you."

"She seemed to. Probably it was because she wanted to believe it. She was badly in need of a lover. But she also knew that, at any time she chose, she could have me arrested on suspicion of murdering Torrance. And when she became desperate enough, she threatened to do just that."

"So you poisoned her. How?"

"We met that day, at the spot where we usually did, and shared a bottle of wine. It's not hard to slip something into a person's glass. I'd chosen arsenic because I knew she had been buying it and taking it. She'd told me so. But the arsenic I gave her did not come from the pharmacist in Sag Harbor. I bought it in New York, and under another name."

In some part of my consciousness not wholly absorbed by my own peril, I thought of that glorious October day and the two of them up at the ruined fort. I thought of Pamela sipping the deadly wine, and hoping against hope that he would keep his promise to her. Then, already feeling the effects of the poison, already doubting that he meant to keep his word, she had ridden to her parents' house—

Gerald said, "I'm not a monster, Fiona. Somehow it's important to me that you realize that. I needed the land desperately—or rather, the money for which I knew I could sell it. Torrance didn't need it at all. As for Pamela—well, what would my life have been with her, a woman who'd threatened me with a murder charge? And, whether or not Brian ever divorced her, leaving her free to marry me, I'd have been tied to her for as long as she chose to hold me. I've *had* to do what I've done, Fiona."

"And—and now? What about me, Gerald? You've always liked me, perhaps quite a lot. You still do. You say that it's important to you for me to realize that you are not a monster. You wouldn't care what I thought if I meant nothing to you. And so you can't, you just can't—"

My voice trailed off. He made no reply to what I'd said, except for the answer I could read in his eyes. As with the other two, he was going to do what he had to do.

With the gun still pointed at me, he moved a few feet to his right. Still watching me, he reached out with his free hand and ripped loose first one, and then the other, of the heavy silk cords that held a pair of window draperies apart. With the cords dangling from his hand, he came back to stand in front of me. He said, "We're leaving now."

I had kept him talking—or perhaps he had chosen to keep talking—and what good had it done? No inspiration had come to me. All that was left to do now was to attempt a desperate dash to one of the front windows, to throw the sash high, and to scream as loudly as I could into the windy night.

I had not moved and yet, in some way, I must have communicated my intention to him. He said, "Believe me,

Fiona. I don't want to shoot you, but I will if I have to, right here and now. And if Dilsey wakes up and sees me before I can get out of this house, I'll kill her, too. What other choice have I got?"

I heard a click, and knew that he had cocked the gun. I got to my feet. "Go ahead of me," he said. "Go down the back staircase."

I said, dry mouthed, "I'm not even dressed."

"That won't matter. Go on."

The very lamplight had an unreal quality now. Aware that he followed close behind me, I walked out of the bed-room and turned to my right toward the back stairs. Light from the wall lamps in the hall below shone up the stairwell. The sense that I moved through a dream grew stronger. Perhaps, I thought, my mind was trying to protect me from the knowledge that this probably was the last time my fingers would touch this or any other bannister, the last time my slippered feet would touch this brown stair carpet, and my eyes record the fact that there were badly worn spots on some of the treads.

We had reached the ground-floor hall. "Now go to the back door," Gerald said, "I left it unlocked."

Turning to my right, I obeyed. The doorknob was cold against my palm. As I stepped out into the night, the wind tore at me, blowing my unbound hair across my face, flattening my robe and nightgown against my body. Then I felt pain at the back of my head, and saw a blinding light. After that, for an unmeasured interval, there was only blankness.

Chapter 19

Somehow, lying on my stomach, I had gotten the bed-clothes over my head, and now I was smothering. I started to reach up to draw the sheet and blankets away from my face and found that I could not. My wrists were fastened together. At almost the same instant I realized that I could not move my legs, either, and that a cloth gag held my tongue down and bit into the corners of my mouth. And the bed was in motion. With bewilderment adding to my terror, I strained at whatever it was that bound my wrists and my ankles and tried to roll over onto my side. The only result was a heightening of that sense that I was about to suffocate.

I forced myself to lie still. Unless I truly wanted to smother, I must not thrash about in that panicky fashion. Instead I must try to guess where I was, and how I got here.

With Gerald Winship following, I had gone down the stairs to the back door, stepped out into the night—

Now I knew what had happened. Earlier he had driven his carriage, the noise of its wheels lost in the wind, up the driveway, and left it beside the rear lawn. After knocking me unconscious, undoubtedly with the gun butt, he had placed me on the carpeted floor between the carriage's seats, gagged me with a handkerchief or some other length of cloth, and bound my wrists and ankles with drapery cord. And then he had covered me with a woolen lap robe. I could feel its roughness against my bare ankles.

Where was he taking me? Struggling to keep my panic in check, I lay motionless and listened to the clop of hooves, the faint creak of wheels, and the soughing of the wind.

With a hollow sound, the hooves clopped briefly over

a bridge. Not the North Haven bridge. One much shorter than that. Suddenly I knew. We had just crossed a bridge that spanned a marshy spot in the low-lying Redwood area.

He was taking me to that old wharf where his small pleasure boat was anchored.

So that was how it would be. In the boat he would take me to the deepest part of the cove. He would weight my body with something, probably the *Sprite*'s anchor. And I would disappear. There would be nothing anywhere—no bloodstains, no signs of struggle—to indicate what had happened to me.

Would I be dead when I went into the black, cold water? Would he be at least that merciful? Or would he fear that the sound of the shot might be heard by someone?

Deep inside myself I was screaming. Strange to scream and scream and make no sound.

But there was an additional sound now. Approaching hooves, moving at a faster clip than those of the horse that drew this carriage. Through the terrified pounding of my heart I heard a man's voice call out, "Hello, Winship." The carriage stopped moving.

"Where are you off to, at this time of night?" the man asked, and this time, with a wild leap of hope, I recognized the voice. Brian's. Brian, on his way back from a visit to Addie Crane. I could almost see him there in the moonlight, astride the big roan horse.

Gerald Winship said, "I thought I'd take a look at my boat."

"She's still in the water?" Something strange in Brian's voice now. Not the suspicion I had desperately hoped to hear, but a cold hostility.

If only I had shoes on my feet, rather than soft slippers. Then I could drum my toes against the carriage floor—

"Yes, I know it was careless of me not to bring her ashore before this. But at least I can make sure tonight that those rope fenders are in place, so that she won't pound against the wharf in this wind."

I lifted my head as high as I could and brought it down against the carpeted carriage floor. A flash of pain reminded me that my skull had already suffered damage that night.

Brian said, in that same hard voice, "Well, good luck," and I knew with despair that the muffled thump my head had made had been lost in the seething of the wind through the trees and the jingling bridle of Brian's restless mount.

"Thanks," Gerald said. "Good night."

The carriage started up. The sound of Brian's trotting horse dwindled rapidly away. The fury and despair that filled me was all the more agonizing because briefly I had known hope. For a few moments I had thought that perhaps I was going to live. And now I knew how fervently I wanted to live, on any terms at all, even if I never found happiness again, even if I lived alone in that Madison Street house until I was an old, old woman.

The carriage stopped. I pictured Gerald getting out, tethering the horse to a tree. The blanket that covered me was flung aside. With his hands under my armpits, he drew me out of the carriage until the toes of my bound feet struck the ground. I caught a glimpse of his face in the moonlight, expressionless as a dark mask, before he bent and hoisted me over one shoulder. Wind whipped my hair across my face as he carried me along the dock. He paused, and then leaped to the small boat's moving deck.

I heard him fumbling with his free hand at the padlock on the companionway door. Finally the door creaked open. He carried me down the short ladder into the blackness of the cabin and lowered me, face upward this time, onto the leather settee. I heard the scratch of a match and saw the glow of the bulkhead lamp in its gimbals. Feeling strangely listless, almost as if I had already died, I watched him leave the cabin.

His footsteps moved along the deck overhead. I heard the sound of wind-whipped canvas, and knew that he was hoisting sail. Only minutes left now. Once the sail was up, he would unmoor the boat, maneuver it away from the wharf—

"Hey, Winship!"

His voice, which seemed to come from somewhere along the wharf, made my heartbeats surge with half-incredulous hope. Stretched out in the rocking cabin I heard, or thought I heard, the low cursing of the man on deck. Then he called, "Yes, what is it?"

For a few seconds I heard nothing but the slap of small waves against the hull, and the rattle of half-hoisted sail, and the wild pounding of my heart. Then Brian said, from somewhere very close now, "Good Lord, man! You're not planning to take her out at night in this wind, are you?"

Gerald's voice sounded as if he were forcing it past rage-tightened throat muscles. "Just across the cove. There's a very sheltered inlet over there."

"Much safer to leave her right here and put an extra line onto her to snub her close to the wharf. I'll give you a hand. That's why I came back."

"Thanks, but there's no need. I can handle it myself."

I heard a thumping sound, and knew that Brian had jumped from the wharf to the deck. "Oh, come on, man! No point in your risking your—"

"Mind your own damned business!" Gerald's voice had been taut, almost hysterical.

After a moment Brian said, "Tell me, Winship, how is Fiona?"

"How should I know? Now get off my—"

"You were with her tonight."

"Fiona? You're crazy. I haven't seen her for days."

"Oh yes you have. It's no good, Winship. You see, I smelled the perfume."

"Perfume! What kind of crazy—"

"Perfume I gave her. When you and I stopped and talked back there on the road I smelled it. At first I thought it must be on your clothing. I thought—well, never mind what I thought. But it was all I could do to keep from hauling you off that seat and knocking you down. After I rode on, though, I realized I'd been wrong. The smell of perfume had been too strong. Even there in the open air, and with a wind blowing, there had been almost a reek of it."

He paused, and then said. "I don't know why Fiona should have drenched herself with perfume, but I think she must have. And I think she was lying on the floor in the back of your carriage. She's not there now. I looked. So where is she, Winship? Down in the cabin?"

Gerald's voice was so thick I would not have recognized it. "All right. I asked you to leave. But you wouldn't."

A fraction of an instant before I heard the shot I thought, "The gun!"

In these last few minutes I had forgotten that Gerald was armed. That was why I had been able to feel that wild surge of hope.

The hope was gone now because Brian was dead, lying up there on the rocking deck in the moonlight. If that first shot had not killed him Gerald would have fired a second, and he had not.

Well, soon I would be dead, too. It was bitter, inexpressibly bitter, that we two, who had persisted in throwing away our chances for happiness together, should now be united in death.

I saw a man's feet and legs on the ladder, and the gun dangling from his right hand. Then, as he ducked under the low overhead, I saw the rest of him.

With unbelieving joy I watched him move to the settee, kneel beside me, and place the gun on the seat of a canvas chair. He untied the knot at the back of my neck. As he took the gag from my mouth I saw that it was a man's white silk scarf.

Brian asked, "Can you roll over on your side?"

I did. Voice muffled against the back of the settee, I said, "Oh, my darling! I thought he'd killed you!"

He answered, fingers busy with the cord binding my wrists, "He tried to. But I saw his hand go into his pocket and come out with the gun. Before he could aim it I hit him, and the bullet went into the deck. I knew he was unconscious, but just the same I gave him a tap with the gun butt to make sure he stayed that way."

He untied my ankles and then, hand on my shoulder, turned me so that I lay on my back. "Stay here." He got to his feet and picked up the gun from the chair. With the two lengths of drapery cord dangling from his other hand, he left the cabin.

I sat up and stared at the perfume stain on my robe. I touched it. It was still faintly damp. From up on deck came the muffled sound of movement. Then Brian was back in the cabin. "Can you walk?"

"I think so."

I followed him up to the deck. Gerald lay, facedown and motionless, in the bow. The moonlight was bright enough so that I could see the cords binding his wrists and ankles.

Brian said, "Go up to the carriage and wait for me."

"What are you—"

"Even though he's tied up, I'll feel safer if he's also down in the cabin, with the companionway door locked from the outside. That way he'll be sure to be here still when I come back with the constable."

"Brian, he—he pushed Torrance down those stairs. And he killed Pamela, too."

Brian looked at me silently for several seconds, his face somber. Then he said, "You can tell me about that while I'm driving you home. Now go up to the carriage, dearest. There's a blanket on the back seat. I saw it there a few minutes ago. Wrap yourself up in it. You must be freezing."

For the first time, I realized that in my thin garments I was very cold indeed. Brian helped me onto the dock. Half running, I moved through the wind-whipped night toward the grove of trees where the carriage stood.

Chapter 20

For a few moments after waking I lay with eyes closed, wondering why my muscles ached and why I had a dull pain in my head. Then my eyes flew open, as memory of the night before rushed back to me—all of it, including the carriage ride back to town, with me shivering, despite the blanket and despite Brian's arm around me, and with my voice going on and on.

I recalled that I not only had told him what I had learned of Torrance's death. In spite of a reluctance to talk to him in detail of his dead wife, I told of Pamela's meetings with her lover, including that last, fatal one.

Brian had said, his voice sober, "I don't blame Pamela for turning to another man. And it's not just because she's dead that I am saying that. It was unfair of me to marry her, no matter how much she herself wanted the marriage."

After a moment I burst out, "That day, when I saw you right after the inquest. You looked—so strange, almost as if you suspected me."

"Suspected you of Pamela's—God, no, Fiona! It was the other way around. I knew what a lot of people might be thinking about me, especially since everyone knew how badly Pamela and I had been getting along. I was afraid you might be suspecting the same thing." His arm tightened around my shoulders. "Now rest, darling. You'd better have Dr. Dillworth look at that bump on your head tomorrow. In the meantime, try to relax as much as you can."

When we had reached the house and driven back along the drive, we found that Gerald had left the back door unlocked. We climbed through the silent house to the door of my room.

"Please, Fiona. Let me wake Dilsey, so that she can help you get to bed."

"You'd find it hard to wake her. Besides, I won't need any help. Go now, Brian. Get Constable Simon and take him back to that boat."

I went into my bedroom. I stripped off the perfume-soaked robe and nightgown and put on another gown I had taken from a bureau drawer. Then I fell into bed.

Now, looking around me, I realized that the day must be overcast, for the room was filled with a gray light. What time was it? I looked at my bedside clock, saw that it pointed to half past two, and then remembered that I had forgotten to wind it the night before.

A light tap at the door. I called, "Dilsey?"

She came into the room with a strange, shaken look on her face. I said, "Dilsey, I—"

"You don't have to tell me about what happened here last night. Constable Simon told me. He came here while I was still fixing breakfast."

"When did he leave?"

"Didn't. He's still down there. He wants to see you, but I told him I was going to give you your breakfast first. Told him I wanted you to stay in bed, too."

That I was quite willing to do.

She said, "Looks as if I was wrong about the juju. I guess it didn't have a thing to do with what happened to old Mr. Ravencroft and Miss Pamela."

"No, Dilsey, it didn't."

"I'm glad. I did a wicked thing in my heart. I'm glad it was just in my heart." But I could see that that was only partly true. She was disconcerted, too, to learn that her magic did not possess the power she had thought it did.

"What time is it?" I asked.

"Almost nine-thirty. I'll bring your breakfast now."

It was near ten-thirty when Constable Simon drew a chair up beside my bed. "How do you feel?"

"Not too bad. Constable, where is he?"

"Gerald Winship? In the lockup."

"Did he tell you about what he'd done?"

"Sure did." I could see that the constable was very pleased with himself. "I told him we had him dead to rights, and he might as well make it easy on himself and all the rest of us by making a complete confession."

"Then he told you that he'd killed my husband because Torrance wouldn't sell him some land?" The constable nodded. "I still don't understand everything about that. He told me that even before he bought it from me he knew that he could resell it."

Again the constable nodded. "He'd heard a New York syndicate wanted to buy acreage out here in the hope that soon a railroad would want it as a terminal site."

"But he didn't tell the syndicate where the land was?"

"No, nor that Torrance Ravencroft owned it."

"Then he found Torrance wouldn't sell to him."

"That's right. The syndicate had told him that if he couldn't deliver the land within a few months they'd buy another property. Winship argued with your husband about that at that New Year's party three years ago."

I nodded. "In the library. I overheard them quarreling."

"Winship felt there was only one way left—kill Torrance and then buy the land from you. He came back here an hour or so before dawn and used his own key to get into the house. Torrance was still awake, sitting in that chair of his with the wheels. Winship hit him over the head with the fireplace poker. Didn't knock him out entirely, though, because the old man came to, just as Winship was about to push him down the stairs, and reached back and grabbed Winship's shirtfront."

The constable paused and then asked, "Do you feel strong enough to give me a statement about all that happened between you and Winship last night?"

"Of course," I said. He took a notebook from his pocket.

The constable left about half an hour later. Almost immediately, Dilsey appeared in the bedroom doorway. "He's here."

From the blend of eagerness and anxiety in her face, I knew that she must mean Brian. "Send him up," I said.

When he came in, he sat down in the chair the constable had vacated. "How are you, my darling?"

"I'll live."

"I should hope so." He leaned over and kissed me, his lips lingering warm on my mouth. When he straightened up, he said, "The question is, where? I doubt that either of us feel we should live in this house."

I smiled at him. Things were not simple here, as they had seemed to be for a few intoxicating hours that night on Oluca. Here we were faced with questions, such as whether he would continue working with his father on the packet-ship enterprise, or whether he—and I—would take the *Silver Dolphin* to sea again.

But the question he had just asked was easily answered. I did not want us to start our lives together in a house associated with so much tragedy, from my father's to Pamela Stacewood Ravencroft's. "Let's find another house," I said.

"Good." He leaned over and kissed me. "I'll be back this afternoon. Probably you'll have seen Dr. Dillworth by then. I want to know what he says."

Not much more than a minute after he had left me, Dilsey hurried into the room. "He's gone!" she said, alarm and accusation in her eyes. "Why did he leave so soon? What did you say to him?"

I laughed. "Don't worry, Dilsey. It was not like that, not this time. He'll be back, he'll be back."

ABOUT THE AUTHOR

VELDA JOHNSTON was raised and educated in California and now lives in New York. She and her husband divide their time between an apartment in Manhattan and a nineteenth-century house in Sag Harbor, Long Island. She is the author of many novels, including, *The Late Mrs. Fonsell*, *The Phantom Cottage*, *The Silver Dolphin*, *I Came to a Castle*, *Masquerade in Venice* and *The People from the Sea*.